The Greenies

The Greenies

Myra Paperny

Harper*Trophy***Canada**™
An imprint of HarperCollins*PublishersLtd*

Published by Harper*Trophy*Canada™,
an imprint of HarperCollins Publishers Ltd

First edition

HarperCollins books may be purchased for
educational, business, or sales promotional use
through our Special Markets Department.

HarperCollins Publishers Ltd
2 Bloor Street East, 20th Floor
Toronto, Ontario, Canada
M4W 1A8

www.harpercollins.ca

Library and Archives Canada Cataloguing in
Publication

Paperny, Myra
The Greenies / Myra Paperny. – 1st ed.

ISBN-13: 978-0-00-639355-9
ISBN-10: 0-00-639355-1

1. Jewish orphans – Canada – Juvenile fiction.
2. Canada – Emigration and immigration –
Juvenile fiction.   3. Holocaust survivors –
Juvenile fiction.   I. Title.

PS8581.A665G74 2005   jC813'.54
C2004-905818-5

HC 9 8 7 6 5 4 3

Printed and bound in the United States
Set in FF Scala

This book is dedicated to my grandchildren: Michael, Anna, Samara, Daniel, Juliet, Shoshanna, Leo, Yaelle and Alex.

May they always remember the six million who perished.

Chapter One

Danny

Danny sat silently in the crowded room, waiting for the doctor's report. Would he receive that magic slip of paper granting him a brand-new life, or would the doctor condemn him to live forever in limbo?

Most of the patients waiting to see the doctor appeared to be refugees like him; perhaps they, too, hoped to pass the battery of medical tests that would eventually allow them to escape Europe and emigrate to other countries. Whether they were adults or children, their threadbare clothing was a giveaway. He gnawed on the cuticle of his right pinkie and listened to two boys sitting directly across from him.

"Remember, Max," one of them was saying, "you have never had a headache in your entire life—absolutely and positively never—or this Dr. Sylvain will say you have a brain tumour and you'll never reach the Promised Land. Do you understand, Max?"

Danny leaned forward to hear a bit better, keeping a tattered magazine in front of his face. The boys paid no attention to him, or to the twelve other patients wedged in the chairs around them.

The boy called Max nodded his understanding and tried to say something. The speaker, who looked older, immediately raised his open palm demanding silence, then continued to lecture Max on appropriate behaviour in the examination room.

Danny wanted to warn the older boy that if he kept haranguing his friend, the kid would probably crack up before he even saw the doctor. As it was, Max was already looking agitated, rubbing his hands back and forth on the knees of his pants. Danny took another hunk out of his cuticle, this time to prevent himself from offering any advice. *Don't get involved,* he cautioned himself. *This is none of your business and you already have enough problems of your own.*

It was Danny's fourth visit to the doctor from the Oeuvre de Secours aux Enfants, the rescue society for orphaned children in France. There had been problems on each of his earlier visits—the results of certain screening tests hadn't satisfied the authorities, and the doctors always insisted that his blood pressure was too low for him to qualify for a visa. Each time he sat here, at the Paris office, he felt an increasing sense of despair that matched the throbbing inside his head. And he knew that every orphaned refugee in this waiting room had the same apprehension and impossible dream. Each one prayed for a positive decision from the various authorities—the social workers, doctors, nurses and volunteers who interviewed them—that final stamp of approval that would ensure them entry visas for this North American country called Canada

Dr. Sylvain would make that final decision. He had the power to decide whether the children were healthy enough—in both mind and body—to be included in the miraculous quota: the one thousand Jewish war orphans chosen to enter Canada. Without the physician's okay, Max, and all the orphans, could languish in refugee camps for many more months, or possibly years.

Like the others, Danny had been drifting from one temporary camp to another ever since the Allied troops had set them free at the end of the war. He could barely remember how long it had been since liberation. How many years had he been waiting for someone—any-one—to claim him? He had been released from the Buchenwald con-centration camp in Germany on April 11, 1945. Today was July 17, 1947. More than two years had passed since the children were freed from the camps, and from hiding places in forests, basements, barns, convents and cupboards. In Danny's case, all the adult mem-bers of his family were dead. Nobody was searching for him.

His first residence after the war had been in the small village of Ecouis. This was followed by a transfer to the huge mansion of Vaucelles in Taverny. And eventually a group, including Danny, was moved to a refugee home in Le Vesinet, near Paris, where he also attended regular school. He always carried a provisional ID card, declaring him a *résident temporaire*, temporary resident of France. It meant exactly what it said: he was not welcome to stay.

During a concert at the school Danny had met a wonderful French family, the Balsams. They had invited him, as their guest, to several concerts and plays and eventually treated him like another son. They had wanted to adopt Danny, but that would have meant his taking their family name, and Danny could not give up his own surname, Goffman—no, he owed that much to the memory of his lost family. Had he made a mistake? He shook his head trying to stifle such disturbing thoughts. *Patience*, he chided himself, looking at the clock again. He barely glanced at the adult refugees who also fidgeted in the hard chairs in this waiting room.

"This doctor is a real tough one." The older boy was still warning Max. "Operates strictly by the rules. Flat feet, you're out. A suspicious cough means tuberculosis to these guys, so choke back any coughs or sneezes. And don't even think of squinting, kiddo, or frowning either. Glaucoma, you've heard of that eye disease? No? Well, it's time you learned. Your life is kaput, finished, if the doctor suspects there's the slightest chance that you have eye trouble. Why, just last week I heard the authorities failed this perfectly healthy boy because he had trouble with the reading test."

"No kidding." Max shook his head in disbelief and drew a ratty hanky from his pocket.

"I kid you not. Six years in a concentration camp. Where could the poor fellow have learned to read fluently? Did those officials actually believe the German commandant was going to teach a little Jew-boy his ABCs in a death camp? They decided that kid was either illiterate or blind. End of story. What ignorant people. They are the toughest."

"It's okay, I know lots of languages. The prisoners in our camp— the ones in my section—came from all over Europe. We had to communicate in many languages."

To make his point, Max grabbed a magazine from a table and read aloud, haltingly, in German.

"See?"

"Take it easy, kid. You don't have to prove nothing to me. I am simply warning you for your own good."

Danny absently flipped the pages of his book. Although he knew the big guy was scaring the living daylights out of this Max kid, he also knew the older boy was right. It was nearly impossible to get a clean bill of health. All the boys from the orphanage knew you had to be 100 percent healthy. Wearing glasses was enough to disqualify you. Each refugee child struggled through treacherous mountains of red tape to prove that he or she was eligible—or acceptable—for emigration to Canada.

Danny's own case was still not settled after a year. The Canadian authorities had insisted that the people from the Canadian Jewish

Congress and the United Nations Relief and Rehabilitation Association uncover every tiny detail from his past (at least the facts he was willing to discuss with them). In duplicate, no less. Psychological as well as physical. They had plied Danny with questions and more questions. Like that loaded inquiry from one social worker: "After all those things that happened to you while you were in the concentration camp, do you think you could adjust to living with a family in—a *normal* life?" After what he'd lived through, Danny couldn't begin to imagine what she called a *normal* life.

He'd listened as they spoke aloud about his case, not realizing that he understood enough languages to translate their words. "Many of these children from Buchenwald seem incurable. Perhaps this one is too ruined by his wartime experiences to be saved?"

What kind of question was that? It reminded him of another time when he had been eavesdropping on a social worker's conversation through the open door of an examination room. That lady had told her colleague that Danny might prove too traumatized to rescue. It made him sound like a wild animal pacing up and down in a cage waiting to snap off somebody's head.

Obviously the surviving children had suffered what the authorities cautiously labelled "significant impairment." The words felt gritty in his mouth, like something disgusting that he needed to spit out. So maybe he wasn't particularly friendly to outsiders. In the concentration camps, nobody wrapped you in layers of gauze. Either you toughened up fast or you were finished.

He'd started life as a softie. As the youngest of four brothers, he'd received more than his share of pampering. His mother had always managed to save an extra helping of dessert for him, while his big brothers often allowed him to tag along like a puppy when they joined their friends. The family lived in Brest-Litovsk, a city on the Polish side of the Polish-Russian border. Although of Lithuanian background, his parents spoke Polish, Yiddish and Russian.

"Comfortable," that's what the social worker had labelled his family. As if that had made any difference to the Nazis.

It seemed so long ago, like some incredible dream. He still remembered his Papa taking him to synagogue and cocooning him in his prayer shawl . . . so snug and safe. Mama had always saved the chicken legs for him when they returned home. After dinner, Papa read them stories by Shalom Aleichem. Danny saved those memories for especially black days, savouring this loving chapter from a past that was nothing like the world he now occupied.

The Germans invaded Brest-Litovsk on September 15, 1939, two days after Danny's ninth birthday. They immediately kidnapped his oldest brother, Zarish, for forced labour. A week later, the Russians took control of the city after Hitler and Stalin signed an agreement dividing Poland, with the eastern section ending in Soviet hands.

By June 1941 the situation had seesawed once again and the Germans were at war with the Soviets, but it was too late for his oldest brother, who had already disappeared from their city. The Germans re-entered Brest and the murdering and looting began.

Danny and his mother, like the majority of the Jewish citizens, were forcibly segregated in a ghetto, while his two remaining brothers and father remained as workers outside, on the Aryan side of the city. Then his mother died. Typhoid fever. All so fast. His brothers smuggled him out of the ghetto before the Germans destroyed the community and shipped the survivors off to concentration camps. The three boys and their father worked together in a munitions factory until Danny took sick with a high fever. The hospital staff separated him from his father at the entrance to the makeshift hospital. When they finally declared him free to return to his family he found their rooms deserted. The neighbours could only talk about a recent roundup, and Danny, who was still weak, could only hope one of his brothers might return shortly to take him away to wherever they now lived. They never did.

"No!"

Danny jumped and looked around the waiting room. Had he accidentally spoken aloud? Nope, the other patients continued their private conversations or dozed away behind crackling newspapers. Suddenly that dreadful swishing sound filled his head, as if someone had unexpectedly dunked him under water. It was one of those things he couldn't account for, a feeling that sometimes overcame him when he was anxious. It hadn't happened in a long time. He coughed and somehow managed to struggle back to the surface. He studied the room reluctantly, fearing that the others had noticed his strange behaviour. Fortunately nobody paid any attention to him, and he focused intently on the strangers surrounding him to prevent it from happening again.

After liberation, during their processing, the United Nations workers had documented the orphans' case histories and eventually issued identity certificates. None of the surviving children even had birth certificates. They owned zilch. Even Danny's trousers were hand-me-downs. Immediately after their liberation, he and his buddies had exchanged their rags for new clothing. What an irony that the first new garments given to them since their childhood had been fashioned from the uniforms of the Hitler Youth members. At least they were warm. Sometimes the children could recall only the flimsiest bits of information about their lives before the war. Danny could remember everything. He had thought of his family every single day of his captivity.

The next step had been proving his full orphan status—that he had no surviving parents. After that problem had been cleared away, the authorities had eventually concluded that Danny was not a whacko, despite his wartime experiences. Now the final hurdle in qualifying for Canadian immigration was a battery of physical examinations, X-rays and blood tests. They seemed endless.

Of course only a dummy would mention typhoid or pneumonia

or other illnesses contracted while in camp. That would mean a further barrage of tests, questionnaires and towers of additional paperwork.

From his experience over the past months, Danny knew these examiners didn't even trust their own test results. In one instance, he'd been required to repeat an X-ray test because it was on paper not film. No matter how much information they added to his bulging file, it never seemed to satisfy the authorities. So here he sat in the doctor's waiting room more than a year after he had begun the whole process. He remained in no-man's-land because his blood count was considered a bit off and his blood pressure slightly depressed. Perhaps, he mused, a transfusion of somebody else's blood might create a healthier, better-behaved person—the ideal child immigrant.

There were now no more hurdles left to jump or tests to repeat. *Please, please make the tests come out right this time, or I am kaput—ruined,* he silently begged. Then he noticed that the older boy was looking at him expectantly.

"Excuse me?"

"I asked which camps were you in." The boy spoke in Yiddish, and then, as he repeated his question in French, a nurse appeared.

"Max Katz? Which of you is Max?" The nurse asked the question slowly and deliberately, as though she imagined they were all too stupid to recognize their own names. Nobody replied so she called the name a second time.

The older boy jerked Max from his seat and pushed him toward the nurse. "He is a very shy person, that's why he didn't speak out immediately," he explained in French, smacking the smaller child on his back. "Do exactly what the lady tells you, Max, and you'll be fine. Call me if he doesn't understand anything, miss." He had automatically switched back to Yiddish.

When the door to the inner offices closed behind the nurse, he turned back to Danny. "My name is Kurt Goldstein. I was in Auschwitz—actually Birkenau, the work camp."

"Danny Goffman. Buchenwald."

"Wow, you're one of them? I heard it was a miracle you guys survived that hell-hole." Kurt whistled through his teeth and gave Danny an admiring glance. "That was one of the worst death camps. Unbelievable that any children survived that place. They call you guys 'the wild ones,' don't they?"

"Yeah, we were pretty angry. Our French rescuers called us *'les enfants terribles.'* But we survived, and that's all that matters, isn't it? The Allied army was surprised to find hundreds of Jewish boys in the camp." Danny shrugged.

Immediately after their rescue, the Buchenwald boys had been rebellious outlaws, resisting all authority. The first time the boys were served a lettuce salad for lunch, they threw their plates on the floor and demanded proper food. They pounded the tables with their fists. Danny remembered screaming: "We aren't rabbits. We are human beings and we deserve to eat like human beings!"

"Stubborn" was the word one of the staff members had chosen to describe them. "Cocky and nasty," said another. "Hopeless," said a third person. The boys had checked out the words in a dictionary and delighted in the descriptions. Danny shrugged a couple more times as if struggling to shake away the memories.

The fair-headed Kurt laughed as he pulled a crumpled pack of cigarettes from his pocket and offered one to Danny.

Danny shook his head. "No thanks, too expensive a habit. You might want to butt out. They could decide you're too old to qualify if they catch you smoking."

Kurt laughed as he fanned smoke away from his face. "What a ridiculous idea."

Then he brushed back the thick mass of hair from his high forehead. "Let me tell you a story. Our *Lagefuhrer*—the German in charge of my first work camp—gave us the straight goods right away. I took his advice to heart.

"'Forget your name,' he said, 'forget your family. This is your place. Your number is your name. This is where you will work, and when you die you will go up in smoke.' Then he stamped his shiny boot in the dirt like he was stamping out each one of us. I got the picture fast. Maybe that's why I'm still alive. I'm a very careful person.

"A guy I met while hopping a ride on a freight train told me about this opportunity to go to Canada—that they were letting in one thousand Jewish orphans. I jumped at it. Don't know anything about Canada except that it borders America. Everybody loves America, right? So Canada must be an okay place too. The Canadian Jewish Congress and the relief organization moved the orphans who applied for Canada to a special home. It had a lake where we could swim.

"But now, the Canadian government has changed the rules." Here, Kurt's voice dropped to a whisper. "If you reach eighteen years before they complete your papers, you're out of luck. I heard it was originally sixteen, but no longer. So I've changed my age to seventeen. Who's got papers to disprove it? I've been changing my age back and forth for a long time already—in the camps it was always safer to appear older. This time I chose ten as my magic number. The tenth day of the tenth month. So I was born on October 10, 1930. Right?"

"Easy dates to remember so you won't foul up," Danny said approvingly.

"Attaboy, you got it." Kurt pointed a finger at him. "I'm sticking to that, although I was actually born in 1927. What about you?"

"Born in Poland in 1930. Work camps and then the long march to Buchenwald. I've been living in France since our release and trying for the Canadian list for over a year."

"Spot on your lungs from TB?"

"Nope, low blood pressure. Waiting for the results from my last test. If I don't get into this Canadian group I'll sign on for Argentina, or maybe try Palestine again, but with the British naval blockade preventing ships carrying Jewish immigrants from landing there . . ."

Silence. Who was he kidding? He knew this was the end of the line. If Canada wouldn't take him, it was hopeless. He hated Europe now, but there were few options for survivors. Not many countries were willing to change their restrictive immigration policies. He might spend years wandering, homeless, from one camp to another, forever a displaced person. Trapped. No chance of more schooling or learning a trade. What would become of him then?

"No point in returning to my hometown again," Kurt said. "I hopped a few trains and just plain walked to the Czech border. The people in my town still hate us Jews, even though there are practically none of us left to hate. And those of us who foolishly returned? They chased us away a second time."

"I know exactly what you mean." A boy with short ginger hair and a strong overbite took Max's vacated seat. "Couldn't help overhearing your conversation." He introduced himself as Berish Tannenbaum. "When I finally steeled myself to knock on our neighbour's door, back home in Budapest, they pretended I was a stranger. I thought they might have some news about my family. Maybe some of my relatives had returned? My entire family lived in Budapest. But our former neighbours wouldn't allow me past their front door. I stood there, staring down at our family's Persian rug. Sometimes Mom made us kids sit on that carpet when we had lots of company, so I could trace that pattern of burgundy and green swirls in my sleep. Obviously they'd taken the carpet from our living room and put it in their own home. No mistaking it.

"Just as I pointed to the rug, they slammed the door shut in my face. That ended any foolish dreams I had of remaining in my native land. They hated me, and every Jew like me."

The nurse reappeared before Danny or Kurt could reply. This

time she was accompanied by Danny's caseworker, Miss Kramer. Danny attempted to read Miss Kramer's moon-shaped face but she looked blankly back at him. She'd probably learned to shut down any emotion, Danny thought. He wrapped his fingers tightly around the metal arms of the chair to steady his hands.

"Danny Goffman?" the nurse bellowed from behind Miss Kramer. "It's up."

So, it's all over, he told himself. *Finished. Bye-bye dreams.* Danny stood up too quickly and sensed he might topple over. It had been a mistake, skipping breakfast, but that morning he'd been unable to swallow a bite. *Zei a mensch,* be a strong person. It was one of his father's last instructions. He must remain calm. He shrugged as if he didn't care, then ambled reluctantly toward the desk.

"Danny," Miss Kramer exclaimed, "it's up! Don't you understand? Your blood pressure is up within normal bounds. You've done it. Congratulations. You've been accepted into Canada!" She grabbed his arm and gave him a big hug.

Danny stood awkwardly, his arms pasted to his side. It was the first time in years he'd let anyone touch him like that.

Miss Kramer let go and Danny remained rooted to the spot. It was impossible to believe this was finally happening to him. He wanted to tear the acceptance paper out of her hand and hold it close to his chest before it vanished. Instead he clenched his fists and willed them to remain against his thighs. He was speechless but managed a lopsided grin.

"*Mazel tov.* Congratulations." Kurt strangled on the words. Danny realized the other boy was trying to swallow a trickle of smoke from his cigarette as he stepped forward to grasp Danny's hand.

"Yeah, good luck, kid," Berish added. "Meet you in Mount Real or Whiny Pig."

As Miss Kramer grasped Danny's elbow, leading him to the door, Danny suddenly swivelled round and bent over Kurt's ear.

"Just one piece of advice," he whispered. "Go shave before your next examination. You've got an awfully heavy beard for such a young boy. I'd suggest you get in the habit of shaving twice a day until you arrive in North America. See you in Canada."

Kurt gave him a thumbs-up signal as he ground out the cigarette under his chair. "Cheerio, Canuck," he chortled.

Chapter Two

Lilli

Lilli scrambled up the gangplank of the RMS *Aquitania*, carrying her battered suitcase. A girl walking behind her tripped and knocked Lilli to her knees.

"Sorry," the girl mumbled as she helped Lilli pick up her suitcase, "but, you see, I'm an *orphan*." Then her green eyes twinkled at her little joke.

"And you think that is a reasonable excuse for knocking me down?" Lilli placed her hands on her hips and glared at the younger girl, Sylvie. They had been billeted at the same English dorm the previous night and she'd already become Lilli's permanent shadow.

A tall, gangly boy climbed past them, mumbling, "Aren't we all orphans?"

"No, we're not," a stooped boy piped up when they reached the deck of the ship. "My mama and papa are going to take me away just as soon as they catch up with us. Any time now." He turned briefly to face Lilli, his long, square chin poking in her face as though he dared her to disagree with him.

Lilli turned to look at him and glanced briefly at his name tag: Max Katz. The boy was obviously an orphan like the rest of their group; if his parents had been alive, the authorities wouldn't have shipped him off to Canada. Poor, deluded boy. By now tons of letters requesting any information about surviving family members had been sent through the Red Cross and the Joint Distribution Committee—the Jewish organization appointed to feed, house, clothe and identify all survivors. Lilli had checked out each week's posted lists of survivors and eventually figured out the truth for herself.

The search was over. She didn't have to be a genius to understand what had happened. Lilli no longer had any family except for her older sister, Feyla, who had remained with her throughout the war. No parents or sisters or brothers or uncles or aunts or distant cousins. Nobody. The clock had stopped ticking for all the Jewish orphans. Their missing parents had either been shot or died in the ovens; or perhaps starvation or sickness had claimed them. Many children would never know exactly how and where they were killed, but one thing Lilli knew for sure: their missing parents were never coming back to hug their long-lost children. The authorities had told Lilli and the other orphans that it was time to let go of their awful past and start thinking about the future. And so they tried to do that—at least outwardly. But for some kids, Lilli told herself, like this Max, that was asking too much.

"Poor stupid kid," Lilli said, shaking her head as the boy walked on.

"Max?" Sylvie replied. "Yeah, Max still gets confused. Something awful must have happened but he's never said what it was. Most of the time he's as normal as you or me but . . ." Her words trailed off.

Lilli knew exactly what she meant. The social workers called Max's state "denial." Well, if it made the little squirt happy to live in

Never-Never Land so be it. He'd eventually learn to conceal his feelings, as Lilli and the other orphans did.

A group of neat-looking officers in sharp navy jackets arrived to check out the ridiculous round tags pinned to their jackets, which had their names and "Canadian Jewish Congress" printed on them. All the orphans wore these tags fastened with safety pins to their clothing, as though they were back in kindergarten once again. After the officers checked the tags against their list of immigration identification cards, they handed out slips of cardboard. One ticket stated a cabin number while another was for presentation in the dining room.

"Don't lose these tickets, children, or you'll have nowhere to sleep."

Lilli's group leader, who had travelled with them since their arrival in England from Germany a few days earlier, repeated this information. She spoke several languages: French, English, German, Polish, Hungarian, Russian, Czech and some unfamiliar Slavic tongues. Lilli understood five languages. She had picked them up in the three camps where she had been interned during the war. Unfortunately Lilli knew only three words in English: "yes," "no," and "okay." Her first camp, Auschwitz, was in Poland. She'd been moved from there to a work camp, Freiberg, and had finished the war in Theresienstadt, a camp north of Prague in Czechoslovakia. Certainly, no one there had spoken English.

In Auschwitz the Nazis and their foreign guards had mainly cursed at their female prisoners, who were placed in separate wooden barracks from the men. Lilli remembered how she and Feyla had been taken to Block number twenty-five in Birkenau, the work camp, where they had spent six weeks before being moved to Freiburg, in Saxony. Every morning, noon and night the Nazis took their captives outdoors for *appel* and counted them. Always they screamed, "*Raus, raus, raus!* Out, out, out!" The girls had eventually learned to remain calm when the guards poked at them with their weapons. Their captors prodded them whenever they thought the girls moved too slowly or when they tripped over the frozen soil or if they became sick or fainted because of the extreme heat. If someone kicked Lilli, she automatically got back on her feet and carried on as quickly as possible, hoping to escape greater punishment. All the girls learned to keep their heads down. Like the others, Lilli usually pretended to be invisible; perhaps that way the Germans would leave them alone instead of launching their dogs at the prisoners. No matter how exhausted they became, they worked their twelve-hour shifts making ammunition without complaint. Occasionally somebody would simply topple over. Then, unless the girl was too heavy, the other girls would prop her up so the guards wouldn't drag their victim away to the hospital—or worse.

Like the time Feyla ... *No*, Lilli decided, *I'm not going to think about Feyla today.* Instead, she took a deep breath and inhaled the sharp perfume of tar and salt coming from the dock. Delicious. Like pickles.

"These are wonderful kids, take good care of them," the group leader told one of the officers. Finally, after hugging those children nearest her, the woman hustled down the gangplank and out of their lives.

"She was awfully nice and helpful," Sylvie said. "Too bad we have to leave her behind."

"Like everyone else," Lilli responded, checking her embarkation card. It stated that their ship was sailing from the port of Dover on November 22, 1947. Full name: Lilli Blankstein. It also said she was fourteen years old, but she certainly hoped the officials wouldn't get the wrong idea: she no longer considered herself a child.

Her identification tag flapped against her powder-blue coat as they promenaded around the deck. The coat was almost new, perhaps a little large, but she'd grow into it. She couldn't help thinking that her coat was extremely smart looking compared to the shabby clothing of the other refugees. The collar was made from some shaggy fur. It felt as soft as the calico pussycat at the group home in Germany, her final transit centre before boarding the ferry for England. She was almost positive that they'd never have skinned some innocent cat to make her collar, would they? If she had thought for one second that this was cat fur she would have abandoned the coat.

She'd received the coat in the London hostel after the supervisor of that place, a chubby Englishman, had teased Lilli about her old jacket. "Don't you know its bloody cold in Canada?"

If he hadn't been the supervisor, Lilli might have taken a poke at his ample tummy to make sure it was real. Instead she gave him her merciless icy glare. (At least that's what the girls at the Kloster Indersdorf Children's Centre in Germany had called it.)

Then Mrs. Pearl, a volunteer, with pale-blue hair like the disinfectant they'd used in the camps, shushed him and patted Lilli's head. For some reason, Lilli didn't mind this. She usually became anxious and growly when a stranger tried to touch her, but not that afternoon. The social worker at the Children's Centre had already warned her, "You can catch a lot more flies with honey than with vinegar." In this instance, Lilli was really glad she'd kept her mouth zippered shut.

Blue-haired Mrs. Pearl took a liking to Lilli—or so it seemed—because she later reappeared with the fantastic powder-blue coat.

"For me?" Lilli croaked.

"Don't listen to my friend," the lady said, slipping the coat over Lilli's shoulders. It had a comforting smell of spices and mothballs. "Canada is a really fine country and you'll love it there. This coat will always keep you cozy."

What's not to love? Lilli asked herself. Although they'd never heard of Canada prior to registration, another girl told her not to worry because it was close to the United States. Everyone knew that money flowed in the streets of America, so probably this held true for the neighbouring country. If she was really lucky, somebody might meet her and say: "You're a healthy-looking girl. You belong to us and we want to educate you." She would like that a lot.

There was a thunderous belch, which sounded like the ship breaking wind. She was so startled that she almost fell over her feet. Another stunning blast and they all covered their ears. The sailors ran around frantically untying ropes. Lilli glanced up. The four red smokestacks sent forth sooty puffs of smoke. Two more blasts reminded the passengers that the crew was anxious to escape Dover. *Me too*, Lilli thought. Suddenly the narrow space separating the ship from the dock became a wide gulf of swirling water.

On every one of the open decks the passengers rushed to the railings. Some of them waved frantically at the figures down below, shouting as the people on shore were transformed into tiny dots. Lilli glanced once again at the churning grey foam, then turned away from the disappearing shoreline and leaned against the rail. She wanted to shout "Bye-bye, rotten old world!" but managed to bottle up her feelings.

"You didn't like England?"

It was the tall skinny boy from the gangplank. He had huge, deep-blue eyes that seemed to suck her right into their depths. He also had masses of dark-brown hair. His body parts looked like they were held together by string or wire; everything was loose and floppy. His raw wrists poked out of sleeves that were too short, and his long fingers were in constant motion, keeping time with his staccato speech. The younger boy, Max, who had insisted he wasn't an orphan, peered at them from behind his friend's back.

Lilli didn't reply immediately. He continued to stare. Rude.

"It was okay, but I want to get away, as far as possible," she said after a moment.

"From this continent," he finished. "Yeah, we all want to escape."

"You scared?" Sylvie piped up from behind Lilli. Sylvie was so short that she was always popping up suddenly like a *kai-auf-der-kiste*, a jack-in-the-box.

"Scared?" the boy demanded. "Of the new country—Canada? Nah. This trip isn't such a big adventure. The big adventure was surviving."

"You can say that again." Sylvie nodded. "My older sister went to Palestine but I missed the boat." She grinned and her chipmunk cheeks puffed out. "Well, I wasn't actually late for the boat, but there's lots of trouble and fighting in Palestine and I don't want anything more to do with wars." She clasped her arms across her chest.

Lilli studied her new young friend. Sylvie had an unusual pink-and-white complexion, so smooth that Lilli had been convinced she wore makeup. But she didn't. Lilli had made that discovery the previous evening when she'd patted the sleeping girl's face. She would never attempt anything like that again. Sylvie had immediately awoken and clutched at Lilli's throat. Who could blame her?

Once, long ago, when Lilli had first arrived at the Birkenau camp, she had reacted in a similar manner. She'd grabbed the arms of an old woman who'd been patting down Lilli's thin dress while she slept. Lilli presumed the woman was trying to steal the three mouldy potatoes hidden under her shirt, and she raised her fist. Her screams awoke the other prisoners sleeping above and below her. One of the women later explained that the frail lady was delusional. She believed Lilli was her missing granddaughter and was only attempting to make the girl more comfortable. A week later the old lady disappeared from their barracks; Lilli knew better than to question where she might have gone.

"I'm Danny Goffman," the bag-of-bones boy told the girls.

"Lilli Blankstein," Lilli replied. And impulsively she stuck out her hand in a very formal manner. He shook it before she could change her mind.

"My family is in Palestine," the Max boy said. "They'll send for me as soon as they settle in. We come from Lithuania."

Without waiting for their response, he turned on his heel, his shoulders rigid as those of a soldier as he stomped away to the prow of the vessel.

Danny shook his head and whispered, "Max has no family."

A handsome blond fellow, looking like some sort of American gangster in a black-brimmed hat and a loud tie, walked up and punched Danny on the shoulder.

"Hey, Danny, imagine finding you here. Congratulations. So we both passed our medicals with flying colours. I've kept my razor handy, like you advised." He grinned, and the boys chuckled.

Lilli didn't get the joke, but neither of them offered any explanation.

"My name is Kurt Goldstein," he told the girls, "and I see you've already met my friend, Max Katz. Can you imagine, I originally thought of signing up for Australia, but it's really remote. It takes four months to get there. Too long a wait."

Danny nodded. "I plan on staying in the east, in Montreal, because they speak French there and I know the language well. Don't know any English at all. "

"Well," said Kurt, "my French isn't bad, but I want to brush up on my English. I plan to be a big success in *both* languages when we get to Canada. For now I just need to figure out where they want me to sleep."

Lilli studied the card she'd been handed, with its compartment number and berth number.

After they had promenaded a few more times around the deck, Sylvie followed Lilli down the three levels to the cabins, and they stumbled along several corridors before reaching the one they were to share with two other girls. They were surprised and delighted to discover that the two levels of bunk beds were covered with snow-white sheets. It was absolute paradise after the three tight levels of bunks in Auschwitz-Birkenau. There they had slept head to heel, three high and three deep, without any mattresses. It was also a huge improvement over the crowded dormitories where the children had first been housed after their release. The officials called those places "homes" to make them sound more welcoming, but the rooms were crowded and the sheets were scratchy and wilted like they'd been scrubbed and boiled too many times.

Fingering a sheet, Sylvie gasped: "So crisp they crackle. A top and a bottom sheet. *Magnifique*." A dimple blossomed on her cheek.

The rest of the cabin appeared as orderly as the shelves of beautiful books Lilli and her sisters had rented out when her family lived in the Lodz ghetto, the books from Papa's collection. ("May his soul rest in peace," Lilli whispered to herself.) At the beginning of the war, how carefully they had tended that precious hoard of books. Lilli and Feyla had dragged them from their home when the Germans forced the family to move into the ghetto, hauled them in a baby carriage to their two assigned rooms on Wolborska Street. The sisters had rented them out for five *groschen* a week—well, the Nazis actually relabelled the money as "marks" in the new ghetto currency. The girls had an excellent inventory including *All Quiet on the Western Front*, *The Five Books of Moses* and Lilli's own favourite, *Around the World in Eighty Days*. Of course, when people "disappeared" so did the books. Their collection kept diminishing.

One hundred families had lived in one single block.

The Blankstein family had remained in the ghetto from 1940 until April of 1944, when the liquidation began. Lilli's two half-brothers, from her father's first marriage, had been the first family members to disappear. The boys were much older, since their mother had died many years earlier. A Polish officer shot Ben when he walked out of a bunker; Ben would have been a great bookkeeper. Joseph, a genius, had been drafted as slave labour by the Germans and was building an autobahn—a superhighway—for them somewhere in the east.

Lilli and Feyla worked in a ghetto factory twelve to fourteen hours a day. Five hundred girls. Feyla pressed men's pants for uniforms, while Lilli glued together ladies' hats. Feyla might have become the best doctor in the world, she had such healing hands. Every day their employers served the workers soup for lunch. Without that one meal away from home it would have been almost impossible for their mother to feed the family. Little Marisa, who looked like the Mona Lisa and was gentle as a kitten, stayed home with their mama when she wasn't at school.

They were lucky to remain together. They'd almost lost Feyla during the first roundup. She'd been visiting relatives in a small town and had great difficulty returning to Lodz. Unfortunately Feyla had a very dangerous feature—a rather prominent nose. She later told her family that she'd trembled all the way on the train trip home, trying to hide her nose behind a newspaper.

"I shook like a leaf and my newspaper kept rattling," she said. "If it wasn't for a screaming baby who distracted the conductor, I never would have made it home alive."

Looking back, it was difficult to believe that a little thing like a strong nose could endanger a person's life, but that's how it was in those days. Even before the move to the ghetto, Feyla had already suffered a whipping on her way home from school.

"*Jed-dow-vah*," somebody had shouted. "Jew." Thugs chased Feyla down the block, kicking and punching her when they caught her. She refused to return to school after that, and not much later the authorities banned Jewish children from attending public schools. Later, when the Jewish families were forced into the ghetto, their leaders organized their own schools; of course, attending these sessions was a luxury unavailable to anyone who was strong enough to work.

Lilli's thoughts were interrupted when two girls arrived to find their berths: Sophie and Pearla, new cabin-mates. Sylvie was delighted to make new friends, and she launched at once into the story of how the nuns in Brussels had kept Sylvie hidden during the war. Thousands of children in Belgium had been moved from place to place in this manner.

"So many different places and always having to hide. They gave me a new Flemish name at each place, and I learned new prayers, too. One place was called La Bas—like a fairy-tale castle, but so damp.

"We got down on our knees on cold cement floors and prayed every morning and every night. In the evening we slept in tiny alcoves—more crowded than this cabin—with thick drapes around each bed. It was lonely and scary.

"They transferred us whenever someone planned to turn us in, or when the Germans came searching. If the *directrice* got advance warning, she'd pack us up and they'd take us away to some cellar; we'd hide there until somebody else whisked us to another convent," Sylvie continued.

"Once we hid in the sewers. The only belongings I managed to keep with me all those years were a gas mask, a patent leather purse and a stuffed monkey.

"Eventually my older sister, Irenee, found me and I joined her at a place called Les Hommes des Hirondelles. Hadn't seen her in two years. When the war ended nobody came to claim us, so each day we walked miles and miles to check the lists of survivors posted in the three Brussels synagogues. The worst place was the large Hollandische Shul, close to the Palais de Justice. We had to climb such steep streets to get there and I have very short legs."

Sylvie explained that she and her sister remained together until the Congress people arrived for interviews.

"We never received any news about Mama. Irenee went off to Palestine with a group of older kids. Of course she had no choice. She was too old for Canada. She turned eighteen three months before we were to leave, so they refused her entrance."

"Will she ever come to Canada?" Lilli asked.

"Don't know. Nobody knows." Sylvie shrugged. "I wrote her about being ferried to England but I still have no address for her group. They could be anywhere . . . probably on a kibbutz—a collective farm. I leave her little notes every place I go."

A puzzled expression crossed Lilli's face, so Sylvie continued. "It's a habit. In case somebody might be alive and searching for me. You never know for certain. Right?"

Lilli found it hard to believe that Sylvie was only a year younger than her. Sylvie was so bubbly and talkative, unlike most of the people Lilli knew. Perhaps it was because the nuns had protected her? Although Sylvie had had no permanent residence during the war, at least she had not been a slave worker wondering if each hour might be her final one.

Encouraged by Sylvie, Sophie told her story. She was Romanian, and she had spent the entire war on a farm, hidden by a kind farm lady who'd told everyone that Sophie was her niece from the city. Sophie claimed her blond hair had saved her life. The Germans had shot two other Jewish refugees they found hiding in the barn.

At the war's end Sophie was twelve. If a former friend hadn't been searching for her, she'd have converted to Christianity and remained with this foster mother forever. "I thought I was the only Jewish child left in the whole world," she told them, while giving her fair hair a hundred strokes with a brush. Lilli suspected that Sophie was quite vain about that long blond hair, and who could blame her?

The fourth roommate, Pearla, had burnt-orange hair, zillions of freckles and a prominent overbite. The deep crinkles surrounding her eyes gave the false impression that she was forever smiling. They soon learned that she was actually a rather melancholy person. Pearla never looked directly at them when she talked. Her eyes skittered around like lost mice. When her cabin-mates asked about her wartime experiences, Pearla mentioned her first work camp in Germany—Klettendorf—where she'd slaved in a munitions factory.

Eventually the Nazis had transferred all the women by truck to another work camp, called Ludwigsdorff. "Those places were no kindergartens, let me tell you. We made bullets and bombs and dug ditches and cleaned toilets and weighed gunpowder."

Pearla remained in that camp until the Russian army liberated the slaves.

"After that I eventually transferred to the Aglasterhausen Displaced Persons Camp until they picked me for Canada." Beads of perspiration glistened on Pearla's forehead; she paused to dab at her face with a handkerchief. "But I do not want to talk any more about those days. Do you understand? If you keep jabbering about the past, I'll ask for a transfer to another cabin," she threatened.

This wasn't the first time Lilli had encountered a child survivor who resented discussing the war years. Perhaps it was a dangerous practice, dredging up the past? When the girls promised there would be no more questions, Pearla agreed to remain with them.

"There are some places where it is better not to go," she cautioned.

When the dinner gong sounded, Sylvie tied a perky red ribbon around her short, fair hair and the four girls climbed the stairs to the dining floor. What awaited them was so grand that it pushed aside all other thoughts.

At the entrance the staff nodded to each person and repeated a password: "Please enter."

"*Absolument*," Sylvie said.

"Why not, indeed," Lilli added in Yiddish, faking a curtsy.

Spotless white cloths covered the tables. All the Jewish orphans—there were at least forty of them—were seated in one section of the room. As Lilli and her cabin-mates sat down, she saw that Danny was also at her table. There seemed to be hundreds of other people as well—mainly refugees—seated ten to a table.

They all remained silent, gawking at the attractive tables. Everything in the room appeared clean and chalky white, almost like in a hospital. Each table had real linen napkins, stiff with starch. Perched on the tables were containers of toothpicks, bowls of sugar and loaves of odd-looking bread—pale, brick-shaped loaves. A heavy-set boy burst out laughing as he examined one of those weird lumps. Then he hoisted it aloft for the rest of the kids to see before tearing off a huge, crisp chunk from one end.

A white-jacketed waiter arrived carrying a big knife. He insisted upon slicing the loaf of bread. In fractured French, he explained that more food would arrive momentarily. Then he paused to see if the children understood his words. Nobody listened to him. They were too busy examining the sliced loaf. Not a speck of colour to the bread except for the crust, not a single rye seed or any other grain. Most unusual.

"Holler if you need more bread, kids," the waiter said as they attacked the loaf. "But don't gorge on this stuff. There's a whole meal coming."

They ignored the waiter and devoured the bread. Like a miracle, more loaves arrived, followed by platters of roast beef, peas and boiled potatoes. The orphans hadn't seen so much food in years.

Lilli found it difficult not to stare at twin brothers who remained still as statues, their hands hidden under the tablecloth. Lilli guessed they were about twelve years old. They didn't touch a morsel until that bag-of-bones, Danny, whispered something into the ear of one of them. Danny pushed plates heaped with the steaming beef and potatoes in front of the brothers and motioned for them to dig in.

The twins then wrapped their arms around their plates and gobbled down the food as if this meal would have to last them for the entire ten-day trip across the Atlantic Ocean. Perhaps they were correct, Lilli thought. Why take chances on the future? All the orphans had learned to stock up on food whenever it was available. It had been a basic rule for so many years that none of the children could imagine behaving in any other way. Lilli glanced around at the other kids at her table. Since all the children in this dining room were still alive, they must have done something right.

The brothers made snuffling noises while mopping their plates clean. A red-haired boy laughed at the twins but Danny responded with a steely glare. "There's plenty more for everybody," he snarled. "Stop gawking and leave the boys alone."

The final course was an item called "pudding." It was quite tasty, although it looked peculiar.

"Where on earth did they find all the eggs for that dessert?" Sophie asked as they left the dining room. "It was heavenly."

Back in their cabin, the four girls got ready for bed. Lilli took off her skirt and sweater and folded them neatly at the end of her bunk. While she didn't much like the bulky khaki skirt or the mouse-coloured sweater, these were her only garments for the entire voyage, so she handled them with care; she might be wearing them for several additional months.

Fortunately, the London people had provided Lilli with a change of underwear so she didn't have to rinse these out every single night. They had also supplied each child with a package that included a small bar of soap and other toiletries. What luxury not having to depend on a communal bar of soap, which was usually either a sliver or a grotesque hunk of slime from too much handling.

In Birkenau, Lilli and Feyla had learned to wash out their only dresses every evening when they returned to their barracks. Their clothes were always filthy with grime, so they'd rinse their dresses quickly, wring them out and put them back on while they were still wet. Whenever Lilli felt too tired to complete this chore, Feyla would remind her that a damp dress at night was preferable to scratching away at lice or other vermin the following day. Although some of the girls laughed at them for being so finicky, the sisters never got rashes or terrible itches like many of the others.

Lilli climbed into her bunk bed, curled up between the chilly sheets and tucked the heavy quilt around her. Sophie continued to brush her hair, counting the strokes aloud, while Sylvie circled her red ribbon round and round a wooden dowel so it would remain wrinkle-free in the morning. From Pearla's bunk there were only muffled snores. After a mumbled "good night" to her cabin-mates, and a final punch to her pillow (which appeared to be stuffed with honest-to-goodness feathers) she faked sleep. The quilt felt familiar. She vaguely remembered one from the days when she'd had a real home. Yes, it had been stuffed with goose feathers—so light. Her mother would shake it out each morning and hang it over the balcony so it would remain fresh smelling.

Eventually the cabin became silent. The only noise Lilli heard was the steady thrum and swish of the ship itself. She crept to the bottom of her bunk, grabbed her clothes and slipped them under the blanket. She was almost 100 percent sure the other girls were honest, but she couldn't afford to take any chances. It was another survival trick she'd learned in the concentration camp.

Then she opened her eyes a final time and studied the blue coat as it swung gently from a hook near the cabin door. Surely it was too bulky for anyone to risk stealing it, and she was far too comfy to get out of bed. Perhaps tonight she would sleep without waking. This would be a peaceful night with no dreams, Lilli told herself. No panic.

Chapter Three

Danny

For a moment, when Danny first awoke and stared up at the low ceiling of the overhead bunk, he thought he was back in Buchenwald again, in Barracks number sixty-six.

He felt around for Monieck's feet—always cold and bony despite the socks he wore to bed. Nothing. He moaned softly, waiting for the wake-up whistle. The dogs. The clamour of *"Raus, raus, raus!"* Only a muted droning broke the silence. He also sensed a gentle rocking sensation, to and fro, like the swaying of a giant cradle. A dream?

He slid his hand along the smooth sheet and immediately knew this was no camp. The blanket wasn't scratchy either. And space, lots of space. The ship. Of course, he was lying in a lower bunk on the ship. He stared at the life preserver hanging at the foot of the bunk and the strange cardboard box hanging above him.

Monieck? No more Monieck. Never again. They'd had three good years together, he and Monieck. They had hit it off that very first day. Lucky, because without a buddy you didn't have much chance of surviving. You stopped caring, and then you were kaput. Finished. He'd seen that happen over and over again. Those were the guys who started by losing their appetites; they'd quit eating and bumble along, pushed and pulled by the others like lifeless puppets. Eventually, they'd shrivel up like leaking balloons. Pools of discarded clothing would be the only sign they had once existed.

Unbelievable that Monieck had managed to survive captivity but the first sweets and rich canned food provided by the American troops had proved too much for him. Monieck's system couldn't tolerate all that heavy food after years of malnutrition; he died less than a week after achieving his freedom.

"What do you think they'll serve for breakfast?" Wolfe shouted from the upper bunk, interrupting Danny's thoughts.

"Not rotten potatoes or mystery soup." He chuckled. "I'd be willing to bet on it."

"If they give us that watery soup, I've still got bread. I saved it." In the bunk directly across from Danny's, Max Katz produced a squashed half loaf from under his sheet. "Do you think they'll punish me if they find it?"

"Don't fret, kid. You're not the only one." Yossel Dorfman whipped out another hunk of bread from his pillowcase.

It felt good to laugh. Immediately, five boys produced their own hidden caches of bread.

Danny was still chuckling as they filed into the bathroom. This shared lavatory was the only space that reminded him of the transit camps.

Yesterday, one of the officers had teased him about his constant frown. "Try smiling," the sailor had suggested. "Before your face freezes that way." So now, while scrubbing his teeth with the toothpowder provided by the hostel people, he also practised smiling at his likeness in the mottled surface of the mirror. Stretching those muscles was not easy. It wasn't as if they'd had frequent use.

"What's wrong, Danny? You look like you swallowed a lemon for breakfast," Max said.

Danny vowed to practise the smile only when he was alone.

His serious face in the mirror reminded him of the dream he'd had that night—the dream he had almost every night. The same dream—actually a nightmare—accompanied him no matter where he slept. It wasn't always so violent but it remained basically unaltered.

In the dream, he was reunited with his parents and his three older brothers, Zarish, Misha and Hershel. If only he'd been able to save a photograph of his parents or his brothers; instead there were only memories, and they were becoming more distorted as time passed. How he envied kids who produced photos they'd managed to hide. Lately, his parents' faces had grown dim and blurred in his mind's eye. But in the dream they were always clear and exact. He could almost touch the dimple on Mama's cheek and the grey hairs sprouting from Papa's ears.

The dream always took place during a Shabbat dinner, Friday night. Since he was the youngest child, he sat on Papa's left. The wonderful odour of Mama's chicken soup, with the delicate, thin noodles waiting to be captured in his spoon, filled his nostrils. While they ate, he hurriedly related his experiences in the concentration camp.

The family members did not believe him and accused him of lying.

"You and your vivid imagination, Danny," Papa said. "Enough of this awful nonsense."

Danny repeated the stories, stuttering, as their laughter grew louder.

"Oh, Danny, my baby, no more outrageous tales," Papa said, slapping his hand on the table.

Then the entire family, including several cousins, would stand up and march straight out the door, abandoning Danny. He always remained alone at the dining table frantically searching for his shoes.

After waking, Danny would usually drag himself around with a fierce headache. When the dreams first began, there had been a certain thrill factor because a family reunion was his most earnest desire. Recently, however, the grief he felt, knowing they were all dead, had become almost unbearable.

"What am I supposed to do with this white powder?" Chaim, standing beside him in the ship's bathroom, waved the can of tooth-powder under Danny's nose.

"For your teeth, for brushing your teeth, you poor ignorant slob," Danny replied, relieved to escape the memories.

He assumed, looking at the boys, that many of them probably faced similar nightmares. Of course nobody ever discussed his or her dreams. In the camps, and afterwards, in the children's centres, each orphan had silently ignored the nighttime groans and cries they'd heard all around them.

Danny had eventually discussed his experiences with a leader at one of the orphanages, who was also a survivor. At least this man had understood the gruesome experiences from the boys' past. But though the talks assisted the healing process, they never halted the persistent dreams.

When the boys reached their breakfast table, Danny once again noticed the striking girl, Lilli, with her mop of black curls and dark eyes. She whispered something to her friend, Sylvie, while the younger girl kept her fingers clasped in front of her. Strange, it looked as though Sylvie was praying. He glanced quickly around the room but none of the people at the other tables appeared to be praying or chanting or singing. Lilli offered him a quick smile and a nod.

Breakfast started with some mushy white porridge, which most of the guys refused to eat. Slippery, slimy stuff.

"Cream of wheat is very popular in Canada," the waiter explained as he passed around plates of toasted bread.

Scrambled eggs and fried potatoes arrived next. "Ah, much better," Berish Tannenbaum said. "Who could eat that other stuff?"

The coffee was brewed from real coffee beans. "My gosh. All the coffee we want and more sugar than you could dream of." Kurt spoke in hushed tones. After glancing round the room to make certain no waiters were present, he grabbed a handful of sugar cubes from the bowl and transferred them to his pockets. The other passengers, many of them refugee families from Lithuania, Latvia, Poland and the Ukraine, were seated far away from them. Danny wondered if they, too, were raiding the sugar bowls.

"What about this jam? I believe it's made from real strawberries." A smear of jam clung to Yossel Dorfman's freckled cheeks. Somebody tossed him a napkin to clean his face.

After breakfast Danny and his cabin-mates took a brisk walk on deck before settling into the canvas chairs grouped along the perimeter. No sooner had Danny sunk into his chair than a child's blue ball slammed against his thigh. A small boy of about eight years was playing nearby with some older children and two men. Danny returned the ball to the child, who seemed reluctant to collect it himself. Danny knew, by the way the family was dressed, that they were also refugees—but not Jewish. He guessed they were from somewhere in eastern Europe so he addressed the child in Polish.

"*Dzin dobri*, good morning," Danny said.

"*Dzin kuyah*, thank you," the boy replied, accepting the ball.

Then, without so much as a kind word, the boy's father stepped forward, grabbed the ball and dragged the child away.

"Dirty *Yude*—dirty Jew," he spat. Then he hustled the others toward an outer staircase. A single backward glance and they were gone.

"Emigrating Slavs," Danny murmured. Not since the Nazis had fled Buchenwald had he been personally confronted with such vile anti-Semitism.

Kurt spoke up. "I'll sssssssock the bastard in the jaw!" Then he shouted, "They are as bad as the Germans!"

A crew member, who had been swabbing down the deck, pulled Kurt aside. "I'm not exactly sure what got his dander up," the sailor said, "but my advice is to forget it, laddie. They're a bunch of ignorant foreigners. Don't let them start a fight—that's what they want."

"So, if they're foreigners, what does that make us?" Kurt demanded.

"Why, you kids are new Canadians, aren't you?" The sailor winked at Kurt before returning to his work.

Kurt nodded helplessly. "If I were six inches taller and a few pounds heavier, I might have knocked the guy's block off. I'd like to know why they make it so easy for those fascist pigs to get into Canada and they make it so difficult for us."

Danny only shrugged as they settled again into their canvas deck chairs. The sun struggled through thick cloud cover, and each time it managed to break through they were rewarded with a glimpse of sparkling water. Danny decided this was not a day for quarrelling. Hopefully, in Canada, the people didn't cling to such prejudices. *Please*, he thought, *no more pogroms. Don't slaughter any more of us.*

By late morning the sun had disappeared behind an impenetrable cloud blanket. The ship no longer steamed ahead on a placid course. At first it rolled forward and back, then it switched to a side-to-side action. The bow bobbed in and out of the water, appearing to wallow more deeply as each wave surged toward them. Fingers of foam turned the deck into a glassy arena. The wind skirled round the corners as Danny attempted a short walk before lunch. A few more faltering steps and he gave up the struggle. Battling the tricky wind, he finally managed to open a door and staggered down the companionway.

Although lunch featured bean soup, chicken and fruit compote, seasick passengers deserted the tables in large numbers.

"I've lost my appetite and I'm feeling light-headed," Yossel Dorfman whispered as he struggled to his feet.

"Perhaps that's what comes with having too much food?" Kurt joked.

"I'd never have believed it," one of the twins said as his brother tried to push back from the table.

The European refugee families, clustered together on the far side of the room, didn't seem to fare much better. They, too, abandoned the dining room before dessert was served.

By the time Danny, Kurt and Max had finished their meal, the exodus from the dining room had reached stampede proportions. From their perch at the top of the staircase they observed the father who had insulted them, leaning cautiously into the railing as he eased one foot slowly before the other. His face resembled a lumpy cauliflower as he struggled for firmer footing on the staircase.

"Serves him right," Max muttered as they trailed behind the man.

By evening, half the passengers were shuffling along like a group of drunks. Some people had managed the trick of swaying from one handgrip to another as they tiptoed to the dining deck but most tables remained half empty.

Back in the cabin, after supper, the boys finally understood the purpose of those strange cardboard boxes hanging above their bunks. Berish and Yossel had already made use of them. Escaping his ailing companions, Danny found his French copy of *Gone With the Wind* and returned to the top deck. He was feeling fine, and the view was truly magnificent. The ship slipped through the waves like a bobbing cork. The ocean itself remained deceptive, its hue varying from softest azure to sapphire blue.

The captain and first officer passed by, and the first officer, who spoke French, paused to chat with him.

"Here's one boy who's got his sea legs. Good for you. Never remain in your cabin when it's rough like this. Walk outdoors as often as possible even when the seas are violent." He examined Danny's book.

"Ah, a romance. You'll want to find yourself a nice Canadian girl-friend. Act friendly but not pushy. They like a guy who keeps himself neat and clean. Clean fingernails, too, although I never could figure out why that's so important. And a fresh collar. Spiffy-looking. And start smiling, boy. The girls aren't gaga for fellows who seem moody."

Danny doubted whether he could remember all this excellent advice, but he made some notes in the margins of his book to show how much he appreciated the officer's interest.

By morning, nearly all Danny's cabin-mates looked ashen. Five of them could barely wobble to the bathroom and back to their bunks. Only Danny and Kurt wanted to eat.

"Poor Max," Kurt muttered as they headed for breakfast. "He looks like a Mussel man."

Danny nodded. Mussel men was the name the SS guards gave to those prisoners who hovered near death, the guys who no longer cared about living. It had been easy to recognize a Mussel man.

"It was like they carried some sort of communicable disease," Danny said. "We learned to keep our distance from them after the first few days. No way you could help once they fell into that state of hopelessness."

Kurt nodded. "Oh, yeah. The Mussel men usually had strong reasons for caving in. There was this guy in my barracks. He heard that a guard had killed his father in a different section of the camp. That did it for him.

"Then there was my friend Grisha. Poor kid coughed up blood but they refused to take him to the infirmary. He snapped. Downhill in a hurry. Practically disintegrated. First he stopped talking. When you looked into his eyes you knew you were staring at an abandoned building. No matter how hard we tried, there was no bringing him back. A goner." Kurt sighed. "I hope Max finally stops living in the past."

"Well, I'm sure Max is no Mussel man," Danny replied. "He has his problems, but he's bound to accept the loss of his family when we arrive in Canada."

"Something really terrible must have happened to him. In our first camp he tried to jump out of a window," Kurt replied.

"A window?"

"Second-storey window. He got lucky. Some thick bushes broke his fall."

Yossel Dorfman, who shared their cabin, groaned and headed for the bathroom again. When he teetered back into the room, Danny said, "Hey, Yossel, come up on deck. You'll feel better."

"You crazy, Danny? I'm dying. Managed to survive Dachau. Always half starved. Managed not to be greedy when they freed us. Resisted the temptation to gobble down all that rich food that might have killed me with my shrunken stomach. Now look at me! We're halfway to North America and I'm going to die. It isn't fair!"

Danny spent the afternoon walking the deck with Kurt and reading. By late afternoon the storm had not relaxed its grip on the ship.

During dinner that evening the first mate requested that the passengers stop hoarding food in their beds. He enlisted the aid of four passengers, as translators, to make certain his message was clearly understood.

"There is plenty of food for everyone," he insisted. "It's not sanitary to keep food in the cabins."

"What's 'sanitary'?" somebody asked.

Kurt said, "Beats me. Probably he means it's theft."

"Oh, I get it."

Danny studied the orphans at his half-empty table. Nobody looked up.

Lilli paused on her way out. She was carrying a covered pot of chicken soup.

"It's for Sylvie," she explained. "Sick like a dog. Can't leave her for more than a moment." She left, walking hesitantly so the pot of soup wouldn't spill.

After breakfast the following morning, Kurt examined Danny's novel. "Wow, it's enormous. I couldn't finish this in a year. Hopeless, unless I kept a French dictionary at my side. How come you read French so well?"

"I lived and attended school there for two years. The book was a gift from this French family I knew. They were wonderful people. It was a goodbye present. They wanted to adopt me."

"Really? Nobody ever wanted to adopt me. Nobody even invited me to his or her home for a glass of water. You are foolish to have turned down such an offer."

Danny hesitated. "They were wonderful people, but they wanted me to take their name."

"So? So what's wrong with that?"

"I thought about it for a long time. As I said, they were a fine family. But I had to keep my family name. I owed it to my parents."

"You think Goffman is such a special name?"

Danny smiled. "No, but I'm the only family member left. The Nazis bombed Brest-Litovsk when I was nine. I got typhoid fever and my father and brothers took me to a hospital. When they finally released me, my family had vanished. This boy, Monieck, he was in the bed next to mine. We took care of each other in the camp. But all the time I kept myself alive by . . ."

"By thinking of your family?"

"Yeah. I knew for sure my brothers had survived—and maybe my papa. They were big, strong guys. I had to prove to them that the baby could stay alive, too. Me. That I wasn't a failure.

"Every time I wanted to give up I'd say to myself: You've got to keep going or they'll be awfully disappointed when they get home. They'll ask, 'What happened to the baby? Surely he didn't give up?' I kept talking to them, in my head." To illustrate, he knocked his temple with a fist. "'Hey, Papa, Zarish, Herschel. See, I'm still here. The baby is still alive.' I'd show them. I might be the youngest but I'd make it too."

"You never imagined a different ending?"

"That I'd be the only survivor? Not for a moment."

Kurt shook his head. Then he fished around in his pocket for the elusive pack of cigarettes and motioned for Danny to come up on deck. "The smoke will make poor Yossel really sick."

After lunch, when they returned to the deck, Kurt began his story.

"For me it was different. In the beginning, I didn't realize anything was wrong—until they stopped us from attending school. Their next order banned us from public places. Then they forced us to wear the yellow stars on our jackets and finally—the very worst thing imaginable at that time—they took away my blue bike.

"I know that sounds like a small punishment when compared to a lot of stuff that followed, but I loved that bike. I rode it to deliver parcels for my papa. I ran errands for my mother and grandmother. I thought I was the fastest boy in town—me on that bike. They ordered us to the police station. I surrendered my bike and my mother handed over the radio, and the silver teapot from my Baba Leah and all the other possessions they demanded.

"Those soldiers—either they didn't talk to you or they spat on you. But I'll never forget that bike. Funny the things that stay with you, isn't it? I wonder if I'll be able to buy one in Canada. Second-hand? Maybe the Canadians only ride in cars or streetcars. No telling what to expect."

"Perhaps horses?" Danny added. "We'll become cowboys." As he had hoped, his remark broke the gloomy spell. Both boys burst into laughter as they attempted to picture themselves on horses.

Danny wondered whether Kurt also felt uncomfortable about revealing bits of his personal history. Danny had made a vow to seal off the past, but somehow it kept slipping through the cracks. The future. Concentrate on thinking ahead. Wouldn't it be a laugh if the Canadians actually used horses for their major form of transportation? Perhaps they had horse-driven streetcars? Or maybe *droshkies*, the horse-driven buggies of his childhood. He'd never even read a book about Canada, only the United States. And all those books had been filled with cowboys or gangsters or skyscraping buildings.

That evening, as the storm continued to bounce the ship about, the captain made another announcement about food in the bunks. "You know you are always welcome to have seconds or even thirds. But please, the cabin stewards complain that the bread and crumbs under pillows are causing problems. Eventually the stuff will get mouldy. So please, no more food to the cabins."

Kurt defiantly tucked another roll into his jacket pocket. Then he shrugged as if to say: *Bad habit, but what can I do?*

"I know," Danny said. "We're eating for all of them."

The dining room was so empty that they could hear the echo of their own footsteps as they left the room. Kurt decided to volunteer his services as kitchen staff because the solitude made him so uneasy.

"At least if I keep busy I won't have time to think about getting sick. It's ridiculous," Kurt continued. "There's more than enough food for everybody. It's the best food we've ever eaten. But nobody is hungry tonight. They'll toss most of it overboard. An unforgivable waste. Now that just about kills me. Crazy world, isn't it?"

"Incredible," Danny replied.

Chapter Four

Lilli

Strolling along the upper deck, Lilli saw her own breath rising from her lips like puffs of cigarette smoke. She searched the horizon but saw only dense fog. Earlier in the evening, over dinner, the captain had announced that they would be landing in Halifax that night. Everyone had cheered.

"Not nearly soon enough," Sylvie had groaned as Lilli insisted she swallow another spoonful of chicken soup.

Sylvie's eyes had lit up briefly, however, at the sight of the dessert tray. "Skip the heavy stuff," Lilli warned her. She had put in enough time caring for sick cabin-mates and was thankful those days were finally past. Just when it had seemed hopeless, that the boat would wallow in the turbulent ocean forever, the giant waves had finally stopped hammering the ship. Once again the ocean had become smooth.

The children, delighted at the captain's announcement, had rushed to the decks, swaddled in jackets, scarves and blankets, but the cold air penetrated all the layers. Most of them gave up their search for land and returned to the warmth of the cabins. As they got closer to Canada, Lilli found herself alone on deck. She wondered whether her new homeland was actually an arctic wasteland. Although she found the frigid air positively invigorating, it made her light-headed.

Lilli raised the fur collar of her coat to protect her ears and, once again, silently thanked the blue-haired lady. She continued to stare through the night fog but couldn't see a darned thing. Then, for a moment, she spotted a distant light. It disappeared, then teased her by reappearing a few seconds later. This sighting was followed by a peculiar screeching sound that seemed to come from above.

"Seagulls, those are seagulls you're hearing. And that must be a lighthouse. It means we're getting close to land." Kurt spoke from behind her.

"There are probably icebergs out there, too," Danny added.

Then they heard foghorns. A sinister, mournful sound. Not the welcoming chord Lilli had hoped for. *This is silly,* she told herself. *What was I expecting—a brass band playing their national anthem, whatever that might be?*

Suddenly the bank of fog parted. Like a jewelled bracelet, billions of coloured lights studded the entrance to the harbour. Lilli stared, entranced. The lights were dazzling, far more exciting than any old band.

There had been no bright lights in Southampton or in London. When they had arrived in London, their leaders took them on a tour of the city. The damage from the Nazi's V1 and V2 rockets was still visible. Everywhere skeleton buildings confronted them with their insides hanging out. Random piles of rubble blocked the streets and the streetlights remained few and far between. England, like the rest of Europe, was a sick patient only partially on the mend.

As the ship drew closer to the harbour, all the passengers flocked to the decks. At first they were a subdued lot, leaning anxiously over the sides. Lilli was squashed against the rail. They had waited so long— so many despairing years—and now that a safe harbour glistened before them, it seemed like a hallucination. As the ship sidled closer to the pier, aided by a gaggle of honking tugboats, Lilli felt it was too good to be true. And then, as the passengers were able to pick out individual workers, bustling on the dock, it finally sank in. *We have arrived,* Lilli thought. *We have finally made it to the Promised Land.*

She turned to smile at her friends. Sylvie and Sophie wept, fat tears dribbling down their cheeks. Berish, Max and Yossel jumped up and down wordlessly like a team of crazed acrobats. A musician picked out a tune on his accordion. Kurt reached out and pulled Lilli through the crowd and swung her round and round in a wild mazurka. By the time the gangplank was in place, most of the passengers had joined in a frenzied dance of joy.

They shuffled along patiently, in snake-like queues, as the Canadians herded them into a gigantic two-storey building, near Pier 21, where they had landed. *Ah,* Lilli thought, *we still have to pass more examinations. So many things could still go wrong.* Sylvie immediately grasped her hand when they spied the men in uniform hustling everybody into the enormous dark shed. There were bars on the windows and strange cages along the back wall. At least there were no dogs. All the immigrants were seated on heavily varnished slatted benches, row upon row of silent refugees. There must have been over eight hundred immigrants, including the forty orphans.

"I think they're sending us to another detention camp," Sylvie whispered. "I thought Canada was a free country. Why are they guarding us? They lied."

Lilli attempted to soothe her friend by whispering that everything would be fine, but frankly, she wasn't feeling particularly calm herself. Fortunately she had wrapped several crackers and two chicken drumsticks into a paper napkin. She shielded the package with her coat while offering one drumstick to Sylvie. As she quietly nibbled at the food, Lilli tried to keep calm. But the sour scent of fear surrounded all the immigrants. What if the authorities sent them back to Europe? What then?

A uniformed official snapped his fingers and urged the children in Lilli's row to stand and join a line of people waiting to be interviewed by a man seated at a high desk. Lilli kept shuffling her small collection of documents as she moved forward, worried in case she had lost or mislaid some important paper. And then she was shoved before a frowning customs official. He, too, wore a uniform. Lilli hated uniforms. All uniforms.

He seemed to be examining her clothing, or perhaps he was checking on her health? She resisted the urge to cough. What did he want from her? After trying a few unfamiliar languages, he eventually addressed her in French.

"How many languages do you speak, young lady?"

"Five."

"English? A little bit?"

"Liddle bit."

"Welcome to Canada," he said.

"Liddle bit," she replied.

A clear, hard thump as he stamped her certificate.

She was so thrilled at having passed this exam that she remained frozen in place until someone gently nudged her forward. Sylvie was waiting for her and tugged on her arm.

"A lady told me we should go straight ahead. Hurry up, Lilli. Why are you hesitating?"

Lilli followed her to where a large crowd of people stood at the door of the building. They were waving signs and rushed forward as the orphans paused to get their bearings.

A tall man in a dark suit and a wide-brimmed hat stepped forward. He had a huge smile as he shook hands with Kurt, who was the first one to reach him. He spoke to them in Yiddish. "*Mein tireh kinder,* my dear children. On behalf of the Canadian Jewish Congress we welcome you to Halifax and to your new home in Canada."

The group of Canadian strangers smiled as they stretched out their hands to the startled orphans. At first Lilli found the commotion overwhelming. Finally, as one of the women hugged Lilli, she understood. These people were members of the Halifax Jewish community. They had come specifically to welcome them. It had been a long time since anyone had been pleased to see the orphans, Lilli thought. No, she corrected herself as she studied their open faces; it had been years since any group other than professional aid workers had welcomed the displaced children into their lives.

The community leader, who spoke fluent Yiddish, puffed constantly on his pipe while explaining that the orphans would be billeted in private Halifax homes for two nights. Then they'd board trains and begin their final journey to meet their host families in cities across the country. "Do you understand what I am telling you? Is it clear?" He repeated the information several times and they all nodded their heads.

The members of the greeting party were very kind, offering the children chocolates, fruit and even stamps for those who had letters to mail. Then their leader introduced a special representative from the Canadian Jewish Congress War Orphans Project. This woman, Mrs. Minnovitz, would travel across Canada with them, dropping them off at the cities that would become their permanent homes. She wore a black-brimmed felt hat with a cocky red feather and a long, matching red scarf. Lilli wondered if the lady had deliberately chosen that outfit so they'd never lose sight of her.

"Canada is a very large country and it will take several days of train travel for those of you going to the western provinces," she said in Yiddish.

Hearing this information, Lilli was instantly on her guard. Was this some nasty trick they were going to pull on the orphans? It couldn't possibly take several days to reach their destination. "Ridiculous," she hissed in Sylvie's ear. "They are playing games with us."

"No, really, children." Mrs. Minnovitz seemed to be a mind reader. "Canada is a huge country and it takes several days to cross it."

Lilli shrugged. Maybe and maybe not. What choice did they have?

Kurt pointed to several teenaged girls who giggled as they passed out bags of candy. "Somebody really misinformed us. They told us there weren't many girls in Canada but tons of bread, because they grow so much wheat. Wow. Take a look at *them*."

"So, Kurt, do you want to skip the bread and concentrate on the girls?" Sophie asked.

"I'll have both, thank you very much." Kurt encouraged the Canadian girls with a toothy grin as they attempted to communicate with him via hand signals.

Sylvie broke into loud laughter. Lilli elbowed her in the ribs. They certainly couldn't afford to insult their hosts immediately upon arrival. What was Sylvie thinking? But even as she wiped away her tears of laughter with the back of her hand, Sylvie kept staring at a particular red-haired girl, who munched away on some invisible food. The girl, in turn, kept chewing harder and harder as she held Sylvie's gaze.

"Look," Sylvie chortled. "Like a cow chewing her cud. *Une vache Espagnole*."

Lilli hushed her. "*Shah*, Sylvie. She may understand. You're being rude. Sure, she looks peculiar but you can't call her a Spanish cow. This is Canada and many of the people speak French."

"Gum, she's chewing gum," Danny said, taking note of their astonishment. He explained that the stuff in the girl's mouth was called "chewing gum" and that people actually purchased packages of it in stores.

"*Mon Dieu*, they are really crazy over here," Sylvie said.

Sophie sighed. "Haven't you seen gum before this? The American soldiers passed it out at my last camp."

Lilli had noticed something even more unusual about the Canadian girls. "Why are they wearing those old-fashioned long skirts?" she whispered to Sylvie and Sophie. "They practically reach their ankles."

"How about those heavy brown-and-white shoes—so clumsy looking," Sophie responded. "And white ankle socks?"

"All the European girls—at least those with families who can afford to buy new clothes—are wearing short skirts," Sylvie added.

"Maybe it's because of the cold weather?" Kurt said.

"Maybe."

"If this is the land of milk and honey, why is there snow on the ground?" Max asked.

As the orphans got their bearings, they were guided outside to the waiting buses that would take them to private homes. Sylvie clutched Lilli's elbow and made the older girl promise that they'd live in the same city.

"Where you go, I go. Is that a deal?" she demanded, pinching Lilli's arm as she spoke.

"I hope so. But I don't think they let us choose for ourselves."

Luckily, Lilli and Sylvie were billeted together in the home of a pleasant, middle-aged couple named Waldman. Sleeping in a private home—a house that contained only a single family—was a most peculiar event. Even weirder was sleeping in a bedroom with only one other person. Several orphans had visited private homes before leaving Europe, but this was Lilli's first experience outside a barracks or a dormitory since the ghetto days. And their host family had exact times for specific events—like when they should turn off lights and when they should get up in the morning and when they should eat. It was most peculiar.

Mrs. Waldman took the girls shopping the following morning. Lilli was delighted because everything she owned was already on her back. And she was well aware that these garments were beginning to smell a little rank. Before their departure, an older girl had warned Lilli that her skirt would shrink if she attempted to wash it. Lilli presumed the young woman had already experimented with her own garment, so she had only dabbed away at the most obvious stains on her own.

Mrs. Waldman flipped swiftly through a rack of skirts and chose a dark grey flannel jumper, which she held against Lilli's waist. It looked exactly like a uniform. A German uniform. Would the woman be insulted if Lilli refused this gift? Lilli stood very still and gazed earnestly at a pile of shoes lying on a nearby table.

"No." The lady shook her head as Lilli tried to mask her disgust. She spoke excellent Yiddish. "It's the proper size but the colour doesn't bring roses to your cheeks."

Roses? What on earth did she mean by that? She was obviously *meshugah*, crazy, but who was Lilli to argue? She simply shrugged her shoulders.

Moments later, Mrs. Waldman returned with a cherry-red wool skirt. Lilli held her breath. Was it possible that she meant this skirt for Lilli? She guided Lilli to a small room with a curtained door and motioned for her to go inside and try on the skirt and a white blouse with an enormous collar. Surely Lilli had misunderstood the lady.

"For me?"

Mrs. Waldman nodded and instructed Lilli to draw the curtain shut behind her and to try on the garments. The skirt was quite long and narrow but had slits down the sides so Lilli wasn't required to walk like a duck. Not that she cared. She twirled around on tiptoe before the full-length mirror. She'd never seen anything like this skirt. And soft too, such soft material.

"Mine?" Lilli croaked.

"Perfect with your black curls," Mrs. Waldman replied.

No one had ever given Lilli a beautiful outfit, let alone one that was brand new. She wanted the lady to know just how grateful she was but somehow she could only manage a shy thank-you. Sylvie had chosen a blue-and-gray-striped skirt with a matching grey sweater. They both smiled at their reflections in the windows as they left the store.

The following morning, when all the orphans and their hosts met for breakfast at a restaurant, the staff served something called grapefruit. Nobody knew how to eat the miserable fruit so they poked at it helplessly, signalling the waiters to remove it as swiftly as possible. Kurt, however, picked up his bumpy half globe and squeezed the juice down his throat. Everyone laughed. Even the Canadians.

"Very sour," he said. "Almost like a lemon."

Nobody could figure out why anyone would voluntarily eat such revolting fruit. "Perhaps they'll eventually come up with some *real* fruit," Yossel said. Real fresh fruit was a luxury and most uncommon in the group homes.

"Maybe apples," Yossel said. "Apples would be nice. Do they grow apples in Canada?" he asked one of the people from the Canadian Jewish Congress.

"Macintosh apples," their companion, Mrs. Minnovitz, replied in Yiddish.

"Macintosh, who's he?" Yossel asked.

His remark caused their hosts to laugh aloud although none of the children had any idea what was so amusing. They agreed that these Canadians were really very nice but rather strange.

After breakfast, the local committee divided the orphans into groups. Although they had all been looking forward to the day they would come to Canada, it felt sad. They'd been together on the ship for such a long time, almost like family, and now they had to say goodbye. Lilli wondered if they'd ever meet again—most unlikely, if

Canada was truly such a gigantic country. They began by calling aloud the names of those orphans who were being dispatched to Montreal. Lilli and Sylvie were not on that list.

Danny angrily sauntered to a table at the front of the room as the committee members motioned for the Montreal group to step aside. Another lady was already shouting out the names for another city called Toronto.

"But why is my name not on that Montreal list?" Danny asked in Yiddish. "I happen to know that Montreal is a French-speaking city and I speak French," he told the leaders gathered at the table.

"I'm sorry, young man, but the committee from Congress makes these decisions in advance, and you, obviously, have not been selected for Montreal." The man tried to pacify Danny with a smile.

"But I speak French. I've been living in France. I'd fit in perfectly. That's where I want to go."

The lady with the funny hat shook her head. "Are you very religious?" she asked.

"Not at all," he retorted.

"Well, that explains why you haven't been picked for Montreal or Toronto. We try to place religious children—those who keep kosher, follow the dietary laws—in the big cities because the Jewish communities are larger, so more religious homes are available there."

Lilli felt sorry for Danny. It seemed totally unfair. He had been the only orphan who knew exactly where he wanted to live, and already his plans were ruined.

"I'm so sorry but they don't need any more boys your age in Montreal," Mrs. Minnovitz told him. She asked his name, and then glanced quickly at the lists on the table. "Really, young man, you'll like the west. I'm going to be travelling out there with you. Believe me, you'll love it."

Lilli, Sylvie and Sophie said goodbye to Pearla, who was going to Montreal because she had distant relatives living there. Pearla promised to write as soon as they all had homes—it sounded strange to even suggest such a thing—or at least as soon as everybody had a permanent address.

The remaining young survivors and Mrs. Minnovitz boarded a train headed west for Toronto, Winnipeg, Calgary and Vancouver. As soon as she was settled, Lilli joined a group of kids who were eagerly studying a Canadian map to familiarize themselves with these unknown cities.

One of the boys was delighted when he found Winnipeg on the map. Stabbing the name with his finger he said, "I'm glad that's where I'm going to live because it's exactly in the middle of the country. It should be very safe there. Don't you agree?"

"I do. And with all those wheat fields you'll never run out of bread," Kurt advised.

The leaders had assigned Yossel to a city called Calgary because he had lived on a farm when he was very young. Of course, he hadn't been near a farm since he was ten years old but that didn't seem to matter.

Sophie said, "Just tell me, how far does this train go?"

"To the opposite side of the country. That would be Vancouver. It's on the Pacific Ocean."

"Then that's for me."

"Isn't it lucky that you've been placed there? It would take four and a half days just to reach Vancouver, even without our stop-offs," Mrs. Minnovitch said.

"Suits me. The farther away from Europe the better," Sophie responded.

When the train arrived in Toronto, several orphans who had landed in Canada a few months earlier were at the station to greet the newcomers. During the brief stopover, these children gave them advice and passed on rumours. They'd heard that several Winnipeg families had requested girls under fourteen years because they thought younger girls would be easier to raise. Certain families wanted only boys because they believed that boys would become independent faster than girls. Other people asked for toddlers and children under ten. Lilli had been astounded to hear this. Didn't they realize practically no children under ten had survived the Nazi camps? Somebody should have told these people that only those Jewish children who'd kept their wits about them, those who had been strong enough to work like adults and those who had been blessed with incredible *mazel*, luck, had survived. Probably the only Jewish babies and toddlers still alive in Europe were born after 1945, or—if they had been extremely lucky—they'd had parents who'd managed to hide them.

In eastern Canada, according to the rumours, it was customary for the orphans to stay in a group home for a few months until they learned some English, while those settled in the west were immediately billeted in private homes. Someone said that a Vancouver family had seen a photo of Kurt and had asked for him specifically.

Sophie said, "That is really disgusting. Not only will Kurt get a swollen head over this but—but . . ."

Mrs. Minnovitz was furious when the children repeated the rumour to her. "Nonsense. Don't listen to stories like that. They asked for Kurt because they thought he looked like their older daughter."

She explained that children were occasionally transferred if their foster homes didn't work out. The whole selection process seemed most peculiar, but Lilli relaxed when she was assured that she and Sylvie and Sophie would remain together in Vancouver.

It seemed as though they travelled on that train forever and a day. Lilli found the country vast and empty, with enough space for everybody. The kids admired the upper and lower berths, with their neat curtains designed for privacy. The porters simply turned their keys overhead and the upper bunks flipped out from the wall. At first Lilli found the side-to-side rocking of the train as it ate up the tracks helped her fall asleep. But as the days on the train slipped past, her nightmares returned; the trip seemed to go on forever, and a final destination seemed beyond her grasp.

Some kids played card games to pass the time. Others settled for chess or used the game boards their chaperone provided. A small group concentrated on their English-language dictionaries in order to speed up the learning process, but English appeared to be a most difficult language. They all eagerly anticipated the meals in the long, narrow dining room.

The twenty-six remaining orphans had been arguing over whether to play card games or study some western Canadian geography after dinner when their waiter suggested they wait for dessert. Kurt, who had been waving his turkey drumstick in everyone's face, dropped it immediately. Lilli, who was seated with Kurt, Danny and Max, was eager to try another of the delectable sweets. Their waiter, Jerome, had been exceptionally helpful in offering assistance and advice whenever the kids were unsure about various foods.

Jerome slid through the service door separating the cooking and dining areas and plopped the first dessert plate in front of Max, who sat closest to the kitchen. On the plate, with a paper doily underneath, sat a silver pedestal bowl full of some bright red stuff that shivered and shook as if it were alive. Lilli was horrified to see this frozen blood trying to shimmy free of the bowl. Before she could say anything, Max jumped to his feet and knocked the bowl of shivery stuff to the floor. Loose specks of the stuff clung to his pant leg. He screamed, "Help me, Mama! Help me!"

He lurched down the corridor, smashing against the people at neighbouring tables. *"Rateveh mir!"* he shouted. *"Ich darf hoben heelf. Es kumnt noch mir."*

"What is he saying?" Jerome asked Lilli, clutching at her arm. "What is the poor boy shouting?"

"'Help me. I need help. It's after me.'" Lilli translated. "He thinks the stuff is chasing him."

Lilli and the others seated with Max jumped to their feet, causing the tablecloth to slip out of position, plates to tumble and cutlery to clatter. Mrs. Minnovitz ran frantically down the aisle, trying to catch Max. Lilli was astonished to see her running so fast in those spike-heeled pumps. Her black hat with the red feather flew off her head but one of the other diners rescued it before it settled in his roast beef and gravy.

The other orphans didn't move; they were dumbstruck as they inspected the slippery stuff pulsating on the floor.

The commotion didn't shake Jerome one little bit. He simply shook his head. "Poor little boy, poor, tragic little boy," he whispered as he bent down and shovelled the pulpy mass into a dustpan.

"What is that stuff?" Danny asked.

"Jell-O," the waiter explained. "Haven't any of you seen Jell-O before?"

"Afraid not."

Lilli listened to the murmurings of the other diners. They whispered to each other, leaning forward across the little lamps that sat on each table. They obviously considered the foreign children insane.

Kurt finally asked, "What is that stuff made out of? Calves' blood?"

A lady explained that the strange dessert was frozen gelatin. "Like you freeze ice cream. You have seen ice cream, haven't you?"

Everyone nodded. What did she think they were? Morons? Of course they'd eaten ice cream.

Lilli told her, "Lots and lots of ice cream but never this stuff. Why does it jiggle?"

Nobody answered, and so they agreed to leave the dining room before another disgusting dessert arrived. Who knew? Maybe the next dessert would prove even more repulsive. The kids excused themselves so they could search for Max. Not that there were many places to hide on a moving train.

Before departing, Danny paused and scooped up a tablespoon of the stuff from a bowl on their abandoned table. He held it up for everyone to see, like a magician who was about to perform some daring act.

"Now you see it, now you don't."

His friends gasped when he shovelled it down his throat. One swallow. A brief pause as it slid down his gullet. "Not bad, not bad at all. Tastes rather like strawberries might if they were alive." Then he carefully returned the spoon to the plate and followed the others down the aisle, pausing to nod politely at the startled diners before he fled through the door.

"To think I rejected the United States because I was scared of gangsters—you know, Al Capone and people like that. This place is really crazy too," Kurt complained when they had finally located Mrs. Minnovitz and Max.

Of course everybody understood that Kurt was trying to make up for not being as courageous as Danny.

Poor Max. Mrs. Minnovitz tucked him into his bunk and told him not to worry. Tomorrow nobody would even remember his experience with the Jell-O and, if they did, the other passengers wouldn't know which of the orphans had run away from the fearsome stuff. Unfortunately Max couldn't stop talking about the monstrous dessert for at least another couple of hours. That night he insisted on sleeping with his curtain open.

The following day, in Winnipeg, everybody got off the train—even those who were continuing on to cities farther west. Lilli was told that Winnipeg was recovering from a blizzard. To her, it was definitely the coldest place in the entire world. The kids wondered if the climate would become progressively colder as they journeyed west. Several kids stayed at a Jewish community centre. Each night they were served turkey with stuffing, mashed potatoes and cranberries; a heavy dark fruitcake also appeared frequently on the menu. They studied the local people and noticed that turkey and chicken were always eaten with a fork and knife—not with fingers.

Kurt said, "Turkey must be the national dish of Canada."

"Oh, no, you misunderstand," Mrs. Minnovitz replied. "This is the Christmas season and turkey is the most popular meal at this time of year."

Although she insisted that Canadians ordinarily ate a wide variety of foods including chops and chicken and ground beef and roasts, the kids remained skeptical. Mrs. Minnovitz also claimed that the beautiful multicoloured lights, looped gracefully around the windows of many houses and stores, were seasonal decorations. "Did you think they remained there permanently? They hang them especially for the holiday season. For Christmas. After the New Year they'll take them down."

"Imagine that! Seems really stupid to me—wasting all that effort for such a short time," Max said.

They listened carefully, trying to comprehend the customs of their new homeland. Lilli couldn't stop thinking about the time—very soon, she hoped—when she'd be a pupil in a real school. It had been many years since she'd received any formal school training. Well, they'd offered some training in her camp, but it had consisted primarily of practical skills for future employment. She hated being so ignorant about Canada. She'd learned several words and phrases during the journey, even if the real Canadians occasionally made jokes about her heavy accent.

They remained in Winnipeg longer than expected. Three weeks. The local kids were polite but Sylvie, who had already frozen her nose twice, felt it was time to move on, despite the hospitality. There had been a minor skirmish with the local committee when they tried to separate the Novak sisters. Kurt accepted an invitation to remain with a Winnipeg family and had to be reminded that he'd already been promised to somebody in Vancouver.

It seemed the shipments of orphans to Canada were quite irregular, depending on which vessels had space for them. Also, the number of children who arrived in any given shipment never balanced exactly with those initially listed, so the project planners were always juggling either too many or too few children for the designated areas and foster families. This problem made it difficult for everyone involved.

Lilli overheard one lady say, "This time they short-shipped us. Some doctor in Germany required duplicate paperwork on several cases so they refused to let those children leave, even though everything else was in order."

"What do I say when a woman prepares her family and fixes up a special room for an eight-year-old girl and, instead, I ask her to take a hulking fifteen-year-old boy?" Mrs. Minnovitz asked another social worker, not realizing that Lilli and Sylvie were standing nearby.

While the girls recognized the problems faced by their chaperones, it was most unsettling. They agreed that nobody wanted to be sent to a house where they were not welcome. Those orphans who had not yet been placed were anxious to continue on to the west coast as originally planned. Eventually the committee resolved the problems and the final fifteen children boarded a train for the prairie communities and Vancouver.

"Suits me fine. This is such a windy city. Snow and more snow," Sophie said.

"Warm people, cold place," Danny agreed. "If I can't live in Montreal, why not another city by the water? Don't forget that being near an ocean offers more possibility for escape in case something goes wrong."

"You are right, Danny." Max nodded. "We can always take a boat back to England—or go home from there."

"What nonsense! Next you'll insist on swimming to China," Kurt responded. "And you certainly can't call those transit camps home." He studied his profile in a window as they proceeded across the flat plains. Actually, Lilli had noticed that he inspected his appearance in any mirrored surface he happened to pass.

"Oh, oh," Sophie said. "Kurt is looking at himself again."

"I'm just checking out my nose—to make sure it hasn't changed. I'm sure I froze it that day when they took us sleighing in Winnipeg."

"Oh, don't be so vain, Kurt," Lilli replied.

"One of the reasons I survived was because of my looks. Did you know that I was chosen to deliver messages for the Underground because of my small nose and my blond hair?"

Lilli had had enough of his bragging. She nodded at Danny and Sophie and the three of them dove for Kurt's nose; he immediately buried his head under a pillow for protection.

"Well, I've heard that noses sometimes get larger as you mature, so you'd better watch out," Danny warned Kurt when they finally let him up for air.

Lilli laughed, then settled herself back in her seat and stared through the window at the passing villages; only their lofty burgundy grain elevators stabbed through the unvarying acres of snow. *Now me*, she thought. *I'd just like to get to this Vancouver place and start school so I can become somebody.*

After five of the kids disembarked in Calgary, the train swung into a land of craggy mountains and awesome valleys. Lilli settled in for the final lap of her journey through the vast, untamed country with its huge, empty spaces. Enough space for thousands of orphans, she told herself.

Chapter Five

Marilyn

Standing beside her mother on a platform at Vancouver's Cordova Street railway station, Marilyn Becker was becoming more disgusted as each minute ticked away. That afternoon her mother had insisted that she come along to greet the arriving refugee children. The train had still not arrived, and Marilyn was fuming at having to be there when her own family wasn't even getting an orphan.

Originally the local committee had promised the Becker family an orphan. They had all been delighted once they'd reached the decision to take a child, especially Marilyn's dad. They'd put in for a boy, a foster son for Pops so there'd be a second man in the family. Marilyn didn't find her parents' choice insulting, nor did she blame Pops for wanting a boy. Women had always surrounded him. He'd been squished, suffocated, outvoted and, yes, even banned from the upstairs bathroom except for his early-morning shave. First in line, naturally, was their mother, followed by Marilyn's three older sisters, Rosemary, Sally and Helen, and finally Marilyn.

Her mother and father had become interested in the idea when the Canadian Jewish Congress mailed pamphlets to communities all across Canada asking Jewish families to take in war orphans. The first pamphlet featured a picture of a smiling boy on the cover. It said: "That spare room in your home can fulfill a promise for David. He has come a long way from war-torn Europe. He needs a home, a room in your home. David most likely will soon be working and will be able to pay his own way—but he needs a home—now!"

Marilyn had stared hard at the pamphlet. "Just looking at his face makes me so sad," she'd declared. In the photo, the boy had a huge smile and freckles but, somehow, the smile hadn't worked its way up to his eyes.

Her parents had attended a community meeting regarding the orphans. Although Jewish refugee children had been begging for sanctuary long before the war started, the Canadian government had previously barred them from entering the country. According to Marilyn's parents, the government had imposed an exceptionally restrictive immigration policy during the war. The authorities had wanted to keep out what they labelled "undesirables"—the waifs and strays of Europe—and racial groups that it felt "would not assimilate easily." Recently, however, after receiving many urgent petitions, the Canadian government had passed a measure called an Order-in-Council. This order permitted one thousand Jewish orphans to enter the country. A Canadian Jewish Congress spokesman had made it clear that all responsibility for these children would be borne by the Jewish communities, not the Canadian government.

Another poster had appeared in the front hall of the Jewish Community Centre, two blocks above Broadway on Oak Street. Marilyn remembered it was a Sunday afternoon because that day she'd attended a Young Judea meeting at the centre. That poster was a real heartbreaker. It featured a snapshot of a girl and it said: "If there is room in your heart, there is room in your home for a Jewish war orphan."

Her parents felt the family should provide a home for one of those children, and because Marilyn's three older sisters had already left home, there was plenty of available space.

Rosemary was married now. "Thank goodness she's out of my hair and into someone else's," Pops had murmured to Marilyn during the wedding reception. Sally attended university in Seattle and only returned to Vancouver for vacations. Helen was the family musician and studied violin at the Royal Conservatory of Music in Toronto. That left Marilyn. Once her parents had made it clear that she wasn't expected to relinquish her newfound privacy, she'd readily agreed to the plan. Maybe that condition sounded selfish, but she certainly didn't want some outsider mucking up her life by sharing her bedroom.

Pops owned several pharmacies in Vancouver—five of them. Becker's Pharmacies: "Your health is our business." He had been disappointed when Marilyn's sisters had shown neither talent nor any particular interest in pharmacy. He'd always spoken of someone in the family carrying on in his place. (Marilyn was refusing to make any major commitments while attending grade nine.) Although he yearned for a refugee boy who liked chemistry and all that stuff, he'd agreed that there were no guarantees that their assigned orphan might be interested in pharmacy as a future profession. Both her parents did make it clear, however, that they were prepared to assist in long-term education if the orphan assigned to them showed interest in continuing his schooling.

A refugee boy would have been just the ticket, as far as Marilyn was concerned. Number one: it would have kept Pops off her back—no more guilt. Number two: they'd be doing a *mitzvah*—a good deed—by taking in an orphan. And, finally, it would have created the perfect opportunity for Marilyn to figure out what actually made boys tick; they were such weird creatures.

Unfortunately there had been a mix-up. Two boys had refused to be separated when they'd arrived in Winnipeg, so some kind family had taken them both in. Now there was nobody left over for the Beckers. Marilyn guessed it was bye-bye to any future Becker pharmacist.

Given that there was no refugee for the family, Marilyn wondered why she was being dragged along to the Cordova Street station. Her mother spoke excellent Yiddish. She also happened to be a retired social worker, so the committee was counting on Mrs. Becker's help. But why Marilyn? Mrs. Becker had mumbled something about Marilyn handing out treats and showing the orphans that the Vancouver Jewish children welcomed and supported them.

"That's plain stupid," Marilyn had told her mother on the way there. "How about we wear cheerleader skirts and shout: 'Give me a *D*. Give me a *P*. Displaced Persons—rah, rah, rah!'"

Unfortunately her mother lacked a fully developed sense of humour and called Marilyn's attitude "unfeeling." She knew it was useless to argue when Mom had made up her mind about something. So they stood together on the platform, shivering in their boots.

None of those close-mouthed adults fooled Marilyn. Not for a second. She was sure the host families were more frightened than the refugees themselves. They were probably quaking because of all the gossip about foster families having problems with certain refugee children. They'd heard rumours that some of the children were "damaged goods." When Marilyn asked her mom if that meant "damaged" like a parcel that fell off the back of a truck and smashed, Mrs. Becker told her not to be so silly. End of discussion.

The welcoming committee had been warned not to ask any questions about the orphans' past. The immigrants, they were told, did not wish to discuss their years in the internment camps. That decision seemed odd to Marilyn—wouldn't everybody prefer to talk about it immediately just to get it over with?—but people were always insisting that she asked too many questions. She vowed to remain silent as a Dodo bird on this occasion. It was *"Shah, shtill"* as her grandmother kept telling the family during her infrequent visits from Toronto. In other words: "Keep your trap shut, Marilyn." Fortunately, her grandmother usually spoke Yiddish to the Becker children, so Marilyn was also fluent in that language.

Mrs. Karr, a local social worker representing the Canadian Jewish Congress, stood beside the train while a porter placed a stool under the bottom step. She absently tapped her prepared list with a pencil. Marilyn was stuck behind her, waving a huge sign that said: WELCOME TO VANCOUVER, JEWISH ORPHANS. It made her cringe just holding it. So *gooey*. But again, nobody was asking Marilyn's opinion.

First off the train was someone identified as Mrs. Minnovitz. The lady wore a very silly hat. Right behind her came a tall, handsome blond boy who was immediately claimed by the Goodman family. (Since Mr. Goodman headed the local committee, Marilyn imagined he got first pick.) The boy sauntered right past Marilyn without so much as turning his head. Marilyn flushed a little.

Then a long-jawed, sad-sack boy of about twelve appeared, clutching on to a taller guy. He shrank back as Mrs. Meltzer attempted to embrace him. Mrs. Karr explained that the Meltzers spoke Russian and Lithuanian; this orphan had been born in Lithuania. Marilyn pitied the boy. He looked as though he expected one of the Meltzers to take a bite out of him.

Next in line were two girls. The first one was short and blond with a sparkling dimple. Her friend, a black-haired girl with smouldering dark eyes like a Gypsy—not that Marilyn had ever seen one in real life—simply stared past the line of smiling people and strode down the platform. Marilyn could imagine the dark thoughts going through the girl's mind as she searched the faces of the committee members. The girl was probably thinking to herself, "Loves me, loves me not," as the bystanders failed to reach out to her. Meanwhile the crowd kept pushing goodies at the blond girl the way they'd throw peanuts to the monkeys in the Stanley Park Zoo.

"This one is ours. You're ours," Mr. Elman said as he and his equally tiny wife leapt at the little blond. "Oh yes you are. We've never had a daughter. You are Sylvie, aren't you?"

The girl smiled again and allowed them to take her by either hand and waltz her away.

After consulting with Mrs. Minnovitz, Marilyn's mother spoke to some of the children in Yiddish. Marilyn stepped back to admire her mother because Mrs. Becker was not just fluent in Yiddish but also gentle and reassuring. The newcomers seemed to relax around her.

Just then a deep, piercing voice shouted "Hello" to her mother. Oh, no. What on earth were the Chandlers doing here? "Mom," Marilyn whispered. "Oh, Mommy, not the Chandlers? Please don't give anybody to the Chandlers."

Mrs. Becker gave Marilyn her number-one shut-your-mouth-instantly-or-I-will transform-you-into-a-pillar-of-salt expression. Then she advanced to greet the Chandlers.

Marilyn shrugged. Well, perhaps she was exaggerating. The Chandlers were a perfectly nice couple—if you saw them only once a year. They played bridge with Marilyn's parents every Thursday evening. Smart, too. Both of them. But they had no children and— how to explain the Chandlers? Well, at her cousin Aaron's bar mitzvah, they'd given the thirteen-year-old an electric razor as a gift. Aaron didn't even have any peach fuzz sprouting on his cheeks! And Mrs. Chandler had once told Marilyn: "A pity those wide nostrils spoil the look of your little nose."

According to Marilyn's parents, the Chandlers were "salt of the earth," but Marilyn and her sisters had always thought of them as stiff and starchy.

Mrs. Karr kept crossing names off her list. She turned to the girl with the curly black hair. She had a coat with a fur collar that she'd raised so high only her dark eyes were visible. Marilyn was sure the girl couldn't possibly be cold because it was a beautiful January day—at least fifty degrees Fahrenheit. The girl looked like she was about to bolt back onto the train. Mrs. Minnovitz grabbed her coat sleeve before she could take a step. A tall, gangly boy whispered something into the girl's ear and she reluctantly turned back.

"Lilli? Are you Lilli Blankstein?" Mrs. Karr said.

A reluctant nod from the girl.

"Welcome to Vancouver, Lilli. Lilli, meet the Chandlers." Mrs. Minnovitz motioned for the Chandlers to approach Lilli.

Lilli put out her hand, tentatively, and instead of throwing their arms around her the Chandlers stuck out their gloved hands. Marilyn suspected that this relationship was going to take time— lots of time—to unfold. Marilyn voiced her thoughts to her mother as they watched the last refugees meet their foster families.

"You talk too much, darling," her mother whispered while smiling and nodding to the people. "Stop thinking overtime, my sweet one. Today we must think only positive thoughts."

Easy for her to say. Of course Marilyn's mother was disappointed because she'd been hoping that someone wouldn't show up and there'd be an extra boy for the Beckers to take home. As the crowd dispersed her mother's smile became more fixed. She'd also bitten off all her lipstick.

"Oh, Rose," Mrs. Karr said. "Another group is arriving in the next few months. I'm sure there will be someone suitable for your family." Mrs. Minnovitz said goodbye to the children as Mrs. Karr moved off to calm the Jacobsons, another disappointed family.

"But they promised, they promised us a little girl of five or six years. We requested her several months ago," Mrs. Jacobson kept murmuring.

The Chandlers' orphan was listening to the Jacobsons as she walked past. She stopped so abruptly that Mr. Chandler almost tripped over her.

"A little child?" the girl asked the Jacobsons. "You wanted a young girl of five? A *kleineh maideleh*?" She spoke in Yiddish.

"We've been waiting for such a long time."

"Don't you people understand? There are no young Jewish children left in Europe," the Lilli girl continued in a strong, icy voice. "They killed all the people who couldn't work. That meant little children along with their mothers."

Mrs. Jacobson turned to Mrs. Becker for an accurate translation. Marilyn's mother gripped Lilli's shoulders and hugged her briefly before turning back to Mrs. Jacobson. Her voice was soft but very clear.

"She says that all the young children were murdered by the Nazis."

The adults sucked in their breath. Marilyn's mom had mentioned the unmentionable. Mrs. Jacobson's black kid gloves fell from her hands to the platform.

As Marilyn bent forward to pick them up—anything to avoid prolonging the awkward moment—she knocked heads with Lilli, who was also attempting to retrieve them. They both started to laugh, but Mrs. Jacobson spoiled the moment.

"Oh my, I simply can't bear to hear such violent stories. How can such a young girl speak so freely about this brutality?"

"Please, Lilli," Mrs. Chandler admonished her charge in Yiddish. "No more discussion about such matters. We must all look forward to the future and not dwell in the past. Don't you agree?"

Mrs. Chandler didn't wait for a response. Clutching Lilli's elbow, she led the girl away from the group.

The Vancouverites and their orphans rapidly dispersed. The station was half empty and the mood no longer festive. Marilyn paused to dump her crumpled banner in a metal garbage bin. Then the Beckers followed the Chandlers out of the station and into the parking lot. Marilyn watched as Lilli stared straight ahead and allowed the Chandlers to direct her into the back seat of their gleaming green Nash car.

Chapter Six

Danny

When he finally had a free moment to compare notes with the other newcomers, at a drugstore soda fountain, Danny decided he probably had the best host family in all of western Canada. He luxuriated in the knowledge that the Halperns allowed him to make frequent calls to the other orphans on the family telephone and gave him a great deal of freedom.

The Halperns had two children: a son, Ben, aged nine, with whom Danny shared a bedroom, and a daughter, Betty, approximately his own age. He loved their older rambling two-storey house. He'd been astonished to discover how large it was, and that a single family occupied the entire space. It seemed that most homes in Vancouver were built on separate lots, so unlike the crowded apartments of Europe. Even the Balsam family in Paris had lived in a modest apartment. And each house here had its own garden. Amazing to have all that space for a single-family dwelling.

While some of the kids found their host families confused by their demands and expectations, Danny praised the Halperns. Lilli, on the other hand, wasn't totally at ease in her situation.

"Although the Chandlers try very hard to make me feel at home, so far it isn't clicking. Something is missing."

According to Sophie, when her foster father brought her home, his wife simply nodded hello and continued to feed their toddler. No special greeting whatsoever. Sophie worried that her invitation to share their home was based on her future talent as a babysitter.

"Don't make any snap decisions," Danny told Sophie.

"Easy for you to say," Sophie replied. "Instead of shaking my hand the mother dropped a baby and a bottle into my arms."

"Well, at least it means she trusts you."

"Everything will get much better. After all, it's not easy for them either," Kurt added.

Both Sylvie and Kurt gave glowing reports. Ever-cautious Max believed it was too early to pass judgment on the Meltzers. "At least I can communicate with them," he concluded. "Their family came originally from Lithuania so that makes things a lot easier."

Danny didn't tell them that Mrs. Halpern, who was a tall, vivacious lady, had requested that he call her "Mom." He had been taken aback when she suggested it. There was no way, definitely no way he'd ever call another woman "Mother" no matter how generously she treated him. He'd tried not to stiffen up. Even the Balsams had eventually realized that nobody could replace Danny's own family. He knew he'd have to deal with this uncomfortable incident sooner or later and opted for the present. As she showed him to the shared bedroom he hesitated, then decided to broach the subject with her. "I think you're a wonderful, lady, Mrs. Halpern, but far too young to ever be considered my mother."

She paused while directing him to the closet and drawers. Then she looked directly into his blue eyes. "Of course, that was thoughtless of me. You had your own mother. I'm sure she was a fine lady.

Naturally nobody could or should ever take her place. Call me Bess, how about that?"

He was still not comfortable, and it must have shown on his face.

"Unless you prefer to call me Auntie Bess?"

"Auntie Bess, I never had an Auntie Bess. I'd like that. It suits you. If that's okay with you?"

It had been a week full of surprises. He found the language quite tricky to absorb. There were so many expressions that didn't follow the rules. Most confusing. He tried to communicate with Ben in English, but even with the assistance of his dictionary, sometimes the response he got made no sense.

"I haven't got a clue what you're saying," Ben said to him one day. "It's no big deal."

"Beeg deal?" Danny repeated. "What means a *beeg deal?*"

The boy laughed, almost choked to death while snorting at Danny's use of the language. Then, reverting to sign language, because what he now had to explain was extremely important, Ben pointed to two huge piles of comic books. His Yiddish was garbled and atrocious.

"See," Ben advised. "These are my comic books. Those I've already finished," he continued, pointing to a tattered pile. "You're welcome to read them. This other pile is brand new. These I have not yet read. Don't touch them. Get it?"

Danny got it all right and admired the child for his honesty.

The Halperns took him to a barber and then they bought him an elegant new suit. Brown pinstripes. A grey felt hat completed the outfit.

"Double-breasted," the tailor said.

Danny said, "Double *tzitzes*," like the vests religious Jewish boys wore under their clothing. Mr. Halpern slapped his thigh and laughed out loud.

When Danny tried on the whole outfit—including a white shirt and bronze tie—and stared at himself in the floor-length mirror, he decided he looked like Humphrey Bogart, the film star. Well, perhaps he was a little too thin, but Mrs. Halpern's scrumptious food would soon correct that condition.

He stood very straight and added the hat, angling it sharply on his head. Aha. Much better. All he needed now was a cigarette dangling from the side of his lip and they'd think he was the star of *The Big Sleep*, a Bogart picture he'd seen in France.

"Wow, wow," Betty said. "Now you're a real hep cat."

Naturally there was no Lauren Bacall to appreciate his new look. So far Betty Halpern was the only young woman he'd met in Vancouver, and she certainly was not his idea of a dream girl. An extremely cheerful person with sharp features and a harsh laugh, she was an unbelievable chatterbox.

The Halperns provided a second set of clothing, which they insisted was a requirement for more casual times at school and eventually for work. That was when he learned that the older refugee children would attend school for a brief time to learn basic English prior to seeking employment. The younger children would attend school full-time.

"The sweater must have a V-neck," Betty advised her mother. "We don't want Danny to look like a war refugee, do we? Make sure you follow the list I gave you so he'll come across like one of us and not stick out like a sore thumb." Mrs. Halpern selected dark-coloured serge trousers, a white T-shirt and a grey pullover sweater.

While too polite to point out that he actually *was* a war refugee, Danny found it comforting to know that in school he wouldn't be mistaken for a sore elbow . . . or was it a sore finger?

Mrs. Karr explained how the system was supposed to work. Six months after they became wage earners, they were expected to pay 25 percent of their salaries for room and board. The younger children would all attend school full-time. In Danny's case, it was suggested he attend school for a short time and then seek employment, probably in a Jewish-owned furniture store or another place that manufactured lamps.

Bess Halpern was an excellent cook, although Danny wished she wouldn't serve cornflakes for breakfast each morning. The very first morning he'd picked up the box and tried to eat the dry cereal by itself. Ben had chuckled as Danny doggedly crunched away at the ghastly stuff; then Ben finally passed him a pitcher of milk. The stuff tasted horrible even when he drowned it with milk, but he certainly wasn't about to complain.

Mrs. Halpern had also given him a banana that first day. He couldn't remember when he'd last seen a banana. He took it gingerly in his hand, peeled it, took a bite and started to gag.

The sick, sweetish odour was overpowering. Nauseating. His tongue puffed up as it made contact with the pale yellow flesh; his skin started to itch. Dropping the banana on the table, he rushed to the bathroom, where he perched on the edge of the bathtub. As he did so, he became aware of that dreadful swishing sound that often overwhelmed him when he felt anxious, panicky. It lasted only a moment, and afterwards, stricken with embarrassment, he had difficulty finding the proper words of apology. What must they think of his bizarre behaviour?

"Sorry, Mrs. Halpern—Auntie Bess—I don't know what happened . . ." he began. Unfortunately his tongue, which was swollen, refused to form solid words.

"Perhaps you have an allergy to bananas?" she said. "I've never heard of anyone being allergic to bananas but it happened so quickly that must be the case. I suppose you don't—you don't remember anything about some previous experience with them?"

"I really don't think so. I never saw a banana in the concentration camp or in the children's homes after the war."

"Before the war?" She looked questioningly at him but he had no answers for her.

He'd obviously eaten bananas at some time—he was certain of that—but he had no clue as to where or when. This banana was like so many other things that provided him with glimpses of the past, images that flashed by him briefly, then faded. There was no one left to supply answers to his questions. And he definitely did not want to examine his reaction any further.

Mrs. Halpern stood very still, nodding gently as her hands pressed against the flower-printed skirt of her apron. So young. Not at all a typical mother. No resemblance whatsoever to the mother he remembered. For a moment he desperately wanted to sit down at the kitchen table with Mrs. Halpern and talk about Mama. Maybe if he talked about her it might help to make Mama real again—sharpen his focus, which had become shadowy. No, no, that would be a calamity. No sense chasing after stolen memories. He might fall apart.

Oh, he knew that something from his past had triggered this response to a banana. But how had Ben phrased it? "Danny didn't have a clue." It was one of those things he couldn't account for, like his dreams, or that swishing in his head that plagued him.

Eventually, when his tongue shrank back to normal size, he turned to Mrs. Halpern. "I'm sorry but I can't account for it."

She promised she'd never offer him another banana. "From now on I'll keep the bananas in a brown paper bag so you'll never be directly exposed to them."

Another day the Halperns took him on a city tour in their private car. As they travelled, Danny noticed the city-operated buses and streetcars and some noisy commuter trains called trams, but Vancouver had no underground transportation like the Metro in Paris. He asked Ben about this but the boy didn't understand what he meant.

They travelled across the Granville Street Bridge and through the downtown business district. Turning left on Georgia Street, they followed it until they reached an immense park called Stanley. Vancouver was truly an amazing place. He could only gasp at the silver-tipped mountains with skirts of evergreen forests and an ocean lapping at their toes. And a gentle climate, as well.

Betty pointed to a man-made lake called Lost Lagoon, situated on their left as they entered the park. They followed a road that edged the seawall. The road was several miles long, circling the entire park. He'd never seen such a huge park. It was very informal, with huge stands of untamed trees, totally unlike the manicured woods of the Bois de Boulogne or the exact grass pattern of the Jardin des Tuileries. Betty identified the gigantic evergreen trees with unfamiliar names like "hemlock" and "cedar." "Fir" was the only name he recognized. Mr. Halpern pointed to various beaches along their route and Ben bragged about a zoo in the centre of the park.

They also passed the Lions Gate Bridge that connected Stanley Park to the north shore. Although it was January, only a sprinkling of snow decorated the mountains that framed the city. Ben pointed to a formation of two peaks and said they were called the Lions. On their route home, they crossed yet another bridge, called the Burrard Street Bridge. When they paused by a deserted beach called Spanish Banks, which looked over the city, he decided he loved this glorious place.

Danny sniffed the delicious salty air and laughed at the jeering seagulls as they swooped and circled above him. Spanish Banks: what a romantic name, he thought. Listening to the birds caw overhead, he knew that he wanted to belong here. So clean and new and untouched by wars.

Their final stop was the University of British Columbia. It was built on a point of land. Point Black or Grey or something like that. Ben said he planned on attending that university when he was old enough. It certainly didn't resemble a Parisian university. All the buildings were quite new and plain. *And why shouldn't I go there, too?*

Danny mused. Of course, right now, the idea was nothing more than a dream, but perhaps someday, some way . . .

That evening the family listened to several radio programs. Ben's favourite was a program called *Fibber Magee and Molly*. It was really peculiar. Danny found it extremely difficult to understand. The show started with somebody opening up a closet door. Immediately there was a huge noise as everything tumbled out of the closet. He couldn't understand why everyone laughed. Ben claimed the program opened exactly like this each and every week, although Danny thought that most unlikely.

The program Danny liked best was something called *Lux Presents Hollywood*. It came on every Monday night and featured a different movie story every week. Mrs. Halpern wasn't big on radio and read a book called *East Side, West Side* while the others followed the radio programs. She'd borrowed her book from a library and promised she'd take Danny there and help him obtain his own library card as soon as he became more fluent in English.

Taking the streetcar was also an unusual experience. When Betty had first volunteered to teach him how it operated, he'd rushed to his room for his papers.

"What are you searching for?" she'd shouted. "Mother already gave me money for our tickets."

"My papers. ID card and my Canadian visa."

"Don't be a dope. You don't need to carry special papers when you leave the house."

"Don't you carry your passport?"

"Don't be silly, Danny. I don't even own a passport. For someone who seems so smart you sure can be a birdbrain. Did you have to carry papers in Europe?"

"Everywhere." He produced his travel card: *Titre D'Identité et de Voyage* from France. He also took out his immigration identification card from the *Aquitania*, which had been stamped "Landed

Immigrant. Canadian immigration, December 1, 1947, Halifax, Nova Scotia."

Betty shook her auburn curls in astonishment.

However, the most intriguing experience was his visit to a grocery store with Mrs. Halpern. The sight of all that food, stacked shelf upon shelf, overwhelmed Danny. Foods that were packaged and foods that were fresh were all openly available. He couldn't believe how the Canadians all seemed to take this abundance for granted. In fact, it was one of the first things the refugee kids all talked about the next time they got together. They stayed in a coffee shop for hours, talking about the people, the food and their own hosts.

"You're allowed to touch the fruit and vegetables before you buy anything. Nobody slaps your hand for handling the stuff," Lilli said.

"*Incroyable,*" Sylvie added.

Kurt bragged openly about his foster parents. The Goodmans had allowed him to borrow their older daughter's bicycle the very first day he arrived. Even Max felt at ease now with his foster family; he already had his own paper route. And after an uncertain beginning—Mrs. Elman had seemed rather chilly that first week—Sylvie seemed pleased with her situation. Only Lilli was openly disappointed.

"They're not bad people, but they don't understand me," she said.

"What do you mean? Don't they talk to you or feed you or take you out?" Max asked.

"Of course they feed me," she snapped. "Do you think everything in life is about food?"

"It sure helps." Everyone laughed.

"Okay, okay, I should be satisfied to have a full belly, but it's not enough."

"Didn't they buy you any new clothes?" Sylvie asked as they admired her pleated plaid skirt with its matching yellow sweater set. The Elmans were wealthy, judging by what Sylvie said about their two-storey Tudor-style home, which was crammed with elaborately carved furniture and heavy velvet drapery. They had no children. Obviously they'd been indulging Sylvie with gifts since the day of her arrival. In case any of the others had doubts on that score, Sylvie made certain they got the picture.

"Sure, my clothes are lovely, although Mrs. Elman insists on picking out everything herself like I'm a five-year-old."

Lilli said, "I've no complaints about clothing. It's—"

"It's what?" Danny asked Lilli very gently.

"She keeps saying: 'I'm sure you'd rather forget the past.'"

"So?" Danny said.

"So, so nothing. What do I say when she complains about my silence—when she insists I'm sulking? What should I talk about to her? You tell me. There's really nothing to say. "

"You look really nice," Sylvie said.

"Yeah, despite this dreadful orange lipstick. She won't even let me pick out my own lipstick. She insists that young girls wear only this stuff—it's called Tangee Natural. Coral instead of red. Like I'm a child. I suppose things will improve once we start school and I have more privacy."

"Well, I've also got a confession to make, so don't feel so bad, Lilli," Kurt said, putting his arm around her shoulders.

"Not you, Kurt," Sophie shouted. "Not our perfect Kurt!"

Kurt launched into a story of how he got lost when he went on a bike ride his very first day.

"Mrs. Goodman suggested I take the bike they own to a service station several blocks away and put more air in the tires. On the way back I got confused and lost my way. I tried to ask questions but nobody spoke any language other than English. I wandered around the streets for at least a couple of hours looking for a familiar house. I'd been really stupid, not memorizing their address. By then I was feeling quite desperate, and it suddenly came to me that perhaps this request had been a deliberate trick by the Goodmans to dump me permanently. Maybe they didn't like me. I suppose I'm still suspicious of everyone.

"I sat down on the curb trying to figure out my next move and suddenly I saw Mrs. Goodman, driving down the street, looking for me. I started jumping up and down, shouting and waving at her as she passed by. Of course the whole incident was my own stupid fault. A misunderstanding. She was frantic. They really like me and they weren't trying to abandon me after all."

"So you decided Mrs. Goodman was like a wicked stepmother," Danny said, "attempting to lose you at a service station?"

"Yeah, I know it sounds stupid but that's exactly what I thought at the time. It takes a while to get used to living a normal life again."

Danny waved his arm for the bill. *"L'addition, s'il vous plaît."* The waitress stared at him as though he were an imbecile and he swiftly switched to broken English. "The bill, if you please."

Of course he loved life in Vancouver. Hadn't he just written his Parisian friends a glowing letter? But despite his good fortune he still missed old friends like the Balsams and the ability to express himself without sounding like an absolute newcomer.

Chapter Seven

Lilli

It was Lilli's first day at a school called Totem Point Junior High. She was thankful to be entering grade nine, grateful that she hadn't been held back and therefore was going to be with kids her own age despite the fact that she'd certainly be behind them in many subjects. And it was a relief to learn that Sylvie would also be attending the same school, in a lower grade. Although the school wasn't far from her home, Mr. Chandler drove her there before going to his office.

"Gee, I really don't like the look of this place. It sort of gives me the creeps with those spy towers perched on all four corners," she told Mr. Chandler as his car approached the hillside school. "Do they have guards spying on all the kids from up there?"

"No, no, my dear. Don't worry," Mr. Chandler replied. "You have some imagination! The towers are simply part of the architect's design. I assure you, there is nobody up there."

Although Lilli was usually apprehensive when faced with new and unfamiliar situations, she was certain that meeting the Canadian students would be a relief after sitting at home all day learning the Chandlers' five hundred rules of proper behaviour. Mrs. Chandler had rules for everything. When she wasn't attempting to teach Lilli proper manners—"We must cover our mouths when we sneeze and then say excuse me"—she was lecturing her about speaking properly. On answering the phone, one was supposed to say: "May I pull-eeeze esk who is calling?" She also scolded Lilli about her flyaway curly hair.

The Chandlers were okay as foster parents—they weren't mean or malicious—but she felt they were monitoring her behaviour all the time. Mr. Chandler worked hard at making her feel at home, but Mrs. Chandler made Lilli feel that everything she did was wrong.

Unfortunately she had got off to a bad start the very first day. They had entered the Chandler bungalow together by the back door. Lilli learned quickly that the Chandlers never used their front door themselves; it was reserved strictly for guests. As they entered the house, she heard a dreadful growling. A giant black beast lunged at her. At first she remained frozen in place. When the creature placed his huge paws on her new red skirt, she started to scream. She continued shrieking until Mr. Chandler finally dragged the dog off her and shoved him through a door that led to the basement.

"What on earth is wrong with you, child? He's only a dog. You are becoming hysterical," Mrs. Chandler said.

At first Lilli didn't reply because her lungs were burning. Gasping for air, she was unable to control the spasms that rocked her body.

"That terrible wheezing. Is she asthmatic, do you think? Nobody told us to expect an asthma patient."

Lilli eventually managed to shake her head back and forth and reply, "No, I am not asthmatic. No. Never ever." Perhaps they would return her to the authorities before she'd set down her suitcase? Could they deport her back to Europe? She realized she'd better find out about her rights as quickly as possible or she'd be whisked away to another internment camp.

At least Mr. Chandler seemed more approachable then his wife. He led her to the kitchen table and seated her on a chair. Then he offered Lilli his big white hanky.

"There, there," he said, patting the top of her head as if she were an obedient dog herself. "I'm sorry Rex frightened you. He's really quite harmless. Very old. He wouldn't do anything more dangerous than slobbering on you. He was trying to be friendly."

Lilli nodded once again, like a mechanical doll. She could still see that miserable black Doberman pinscher guard dog tearing at her sister Feyla's arm. Feyla had merely stepped forward as one of the guards called out her number. The dog had ripped away at her sleeve while the *kapo* stood by and laughed. Then there was that poor Tzigun—the Gypsy girl who didn't escape the animal. On that occasion the guard had waited too long to call off his dog. Lilli took a deep breath. *Forget it happened,* she told herself.

Mrs. Chandler handed her a damp cloth to place on her forehead. She spoke in Yiddish. "Control yourself, Lilli, and no hysterics, please. You must develop some restraint, my dear. Control. And no more shrieking like a fishwife. Do you understand?"

Yes, she understood. Again, Lilli could only nod because she was shaking too much to reply. She almost blurted out the reason for her extreme reaction but stopped herself. The Chandlers wouldn't want to hear any brutal tales from the past.

She looked up at them, trying to appear very calm and well behaved on her first day in their home. They had probably already made up their minds that she was one of the wild ones. She saw the bewildered look on Mr. Chandler's face and the anxiety in Mrs. Chandler's hazel eyes.

"Sorry, Mrs. Chandler." Lilli finally got the words out. "I've never been near any dogs except guard dogs and they were used strictly for disciplining inmates—for punishment."

Mr. Chandler looked shocked, and then he squeezed Lilli's shoulder very gently.

Mrs. Chandler said, "Lilli, perhaps it's a good idea not to talk about such things. They are best forgotten as soon as possible." She patted Lilli's shoulder. "You must look ahead. Now, let me show you to your bedroom and explain our house rules and hours."

Mr. Chandler, who was lighting his pipe, gently chastised his wife. "Fanny, don't make our home sound like the army, my dear. Can't the rules wait until tomorrow after Lilli's had a good rest?"

"Lou, you know how I am. My motto is 'Do not postpone for tomorrow anything that can be done today.' I like things neat and tidy—everything in its place—and I'm sure you will, too, Lilli?"

Lilli nodded. "Certainly, ma'am. You'll find I'm very tidy."

Mr. Chandler suggested they have some coffee before starting a house tour.

"I'd love some." Lilli smiled. "We drank a lot of coffee on the ship. It was delicious."

Wrong answer.

Mrs. Chandler gave her husband a dirty look. "Coffee for a child? Ridiculous. Children in North America do not drink coffee. It will stunt your growth, Lilli. You wouldn't want that, would you?"

Stunt Lilli's growth? Who was she kidding? All those years in the camps the orphans had been lucky to receive bowls of thin soup or potato peels for their main meal and now, with all the abundance of food in Canada, this woman was worried about her growth? It took all of Lilli's self-control not to snap back that she wasn't a child. That she had lived by her wits all these years with no adult to help her. That rules about food were about the most insane thing she'd ever heard. For years, during the war, they'd all eaten anything and everything that looked halfway edible.

She held back. She might be impulsive but she was not a total idiot.

"We'll have some cookies and milk as soon as we get you settled," Mrs. Chandler said. "Would you like that?"

Mr. Chandler and Lilli both nodded as Mrs. Chandler led Lilli down the hall.

The bedroom was lovely, like a garden. Everything was pink and green with a design of printed roses—big as cauliflowers. They sprouted all over the bedspread, the curtains and the heavily starched flounces edging the bed. So crisp and perfect that Lilli was afraid to sit on the bed in case she crumpled the beautiful spread. Mrs. Chandler had even hung a shelf with some dolls. Dolls? Perhaps they'd been expecting a younger child. Again Lilli kept her thoughts to herself. *Sorry to disappoint you folks, but I was all they had left.*

"Well?" Mrs. Chandler waited for a reaction.

"I've never seen a room this springy—this pretty," Lilli replied. That response seemed to satisfy her hostess, at least for the moment.

The living room chairs and sofas were covered in plastic or thin blankets—"throws" Mrs. Chandler called them. Later Lilli learned the special routine. Whenever guests rang the doorbell, Mrs. Chandler and Lilli immediately dashed to the living room and frantically tore off the throws and stuffed them into a back closet. Clear plastic hoods also protected the lampshades but, for some reason, those remained in place even when company arrived.

Things improved on Lilli's second day. They took Lilli shopping and were most generous, although Mrs. Chandler insisted on selecting Lilli's wardrobe. Afterwards they visited a delicatessen and Mrs. Chandler ordered Lilli the most scrumptious corned beef sandwich on real rye bread.

With a dill pickle!

She was pleased when Lilli cleaned her plate. And Lilli was happy to discover that not all the bread in Canada was doughy and white. She told the Chandlers that the rye bread was delicious. The meal reminded her of something good from the past but she couldn't remember what it was or when it had happened. Perhaps before their move to the ghetto, Lilli's family had shared food like this.

"When do I start school and really learn English?" Lilli asked Mrs. Chandler. "I want so much to go to school and learn the language."

A pause. "Well, first we take you for remedial lessons at the Peretz School—they speak Yiddish there—and then perhaps Totem Point Junior High after a few weeks."

"Sounds great," Lilli replied. "What grade will I start at?"

"Well, we'll leave that decision to the school authorities. Depends how quickly you learn English. You need to learn enough of the language to be understood at work. I'm sure you want to get started on a trade, don't you?"

Another long pause. "A trade?" Lilli gulped. "I want to get as much schooling as possible so I can better myself. So I belong here."

Although Mrs. Chandler absently patted Lilli's hand, Lilli sensed they were a long way from understanding each other. "Lilli, you do want to become independent as soon as possible? Right?"

Lilli nodded her head once again.

"Tell me, do you have any particular trade—have you some talent or training which you developed, before coming to Canada? Something you'd want to continue?"

"I don't understand."

"Perhaps you sewed in the factory or worked with your hands? Maybe you'd like to be a hairdresser?"

"I worked in a factory with all the other girls. When we lived in the ghetto, my older sister worked in a factory pressing men's pants and I glued feathers on ladies' hats. Mine was an easy job compared to most. But I was quite young, you see? Next I learned to sand baby cribs and toys. Everybody worked because otherwise we wouldn't get the rations of soup and bread for lunch at the factory. That was our main meal of the day.

"But I was never very good on the machines. I was too small and not particularly quick."

Lilli avoided telling Mrs. Chandler that she had developed some additional talents that made up for her awkwardness on the machines. How could she tell Mrs. Chandler that within her own family she was called "the Little Spy" because she could sniff around on the street and pick up valuable information? Nobody had paid any attention to a curly-headed little girl loitering near the gossips. Lilli's small talent had saved the family on several occasions.

There was the day she'd rushed home from the factory, scrambling in her wooden clogs over the slippery wooden bridge.

"Mama, Mama!" she'd shouted. "Today the police will be loading up people on our street so we must hide far away." She had been standing at the back of a store when a member of the *Judenrat*, the governing council, whispered this information to a friend.

On another occasion, she'd overheard someone at the market announce: "Tomorrow there will be onions for sale." The following day, Lilli and Feyla had run behind the trucks as they slowed for delivery and swiped a few onions that happened to fall off the back.

No, Mrs. Chandler certainly wouldn't care to hear about those memories.

Mrs. Chandler paid for the meal and snapped the catch on her black purse open and shut over and over again. "Any other trades, Lilli?"

Lilli found herself babbling. "In the camp? Block number twenty-five in Birkenau? We didn't work there. When they moved us to Freiberg, in Saxony, that's where I learned to make ammunition— bullets and bombs. At first I was supposed to weigh the gunpowder for the bullets. I also dug ditches and cleaned toilets and barracks for the SS women guards. That was a privilege because I could occasionally smuggle out a piece of bread." She stopped. She could tell from Mrs. Chandler's expression that she'd said too much.

"That's enough, Lilli. I was merely inquiring what type of work you had done in the past."

Lilli shook her head. "I don't want to do that kind of work ever again. I want to stretch my mind."

Mrs. Chandler laughed as she took one final sip from her coffee cup.

"Interesting. We'll see what you're capable of. Don't worry, you won't be making any bullets here. But I'm sure, above all, you want to bring home your own paycheque so you can eventually take care of yourself."

"Well, sure, of course I want that, but not now—not right this minute. Right now I want to learn. Learn to read and write and express myself easily so I'll eventually be like all the other Canadians."

Surely Lilli had misunderstood Mrs. Chandler's meaning. There couldn't possibly be any question about her remaining in school.

Chapter Eight

Marilyn

Marilyn had just nudged the school office door shut with her hip while balancing a pile of mimeographed sheets for her homeroom class in her arms when she spotted the refugee girl heading up the down staircase.

"Hey, you." She couldn't for the life of her remember the girl's name. It had been almost a month since they'd welcomed those kids at the station. "Hey, stop, you can't go up those stairs," Marilyn shouted. "It's forbidden."

The refugee girl didn't even turn around, so Marilyn lunged after her and, switching her load of papers to the crook of one arm, she grabbed the confused girl's left wrist.

"*Loz mir tzu-ruh*, leave me alone. Let go," the refugee girl hissed, switching to English.

A sharp chop to her wrist and Marilyn almost lost her balance.

"Ow!" Marilyn clutched her wrist, which stung from the blow. "Why did you do that?" she demanded in Yiddish.

The newcomer turned inscrutable black eyes on Marilyn. "Don't do that again," she replied in English. The words were thick and mushy, as though her mouth were stuffed with mashed potatoes. Her voice had a singsong inflection. But her eyes—they were scary. They looked like twin icicles ready to pierce Marilyn's chest.

Marilyn was too astonished to reply. What a bad temper this girl had! As she massaged her aching wrist, the pile of paper slipped from her grasp and fluttered to the bottom of the stairs. Marilyn sighed, then turned back to the girl, trying one more time.

"Sorry, kid, real sorry, but you're climbing up the down staircase. You don't want to get a detention, do you?" she said in Yiddish.

There was a moment's hesitation, then the sly creature moved up another step, trying to distance herself from Marilyn. Foolish but gutsy. The girl seemed puzzled but not at all apologetic. She obviously didn't know what Marilyn was telling her, nor did she show any signs of embarrassment.

"That was some rabbit-punch. Where did you study karate?"

Marilyn could tell the newcomer found her remark confusing and she obviously wanted Marilyn to go away. Marilyn pretended to chop her own neck. "We call that move 'karate.' Hey, I'm really sorry if I startled you but I've forgotten your name. I know you're new to this country. I was at the station when your train arrived."

While the girl still didn't get it, at least she hadn't run away. Progress, of sorts.

"You must remember the rah-rah brigade at the station? I don't bite. Honest, I don't. I'm sorry I grabbed your elbow but I wanted to save you from a detention—for breaking the rules. It's no skin off my nose but in Totem Point Junior High we have 'up' and 'down' staircases. You broke the rules."

Still nothing. Marilyn decided to give the newcomer one last chance. "No speek-a-ta Anglazee? *Comprenez-vous anglais? Farshtay?* Do you understand what I'm trying to tell you? Get it?"

She didn't speak Yiddish very often, so she had to pause while attempting to dig up the proper words in that language.

The girl nodded. "Sure, it's clear. But how do you remember me from the station? Do I look foreign?"

Marilyn risked a shrug. "Let's say you have a little ways to go. You spoke in both languages. Actually, it's rather cute."

"Cute?" She frowned.

Marilyn switched to Yiddish. "Let's start over. I recognized you on the staircase. You are holding a yellow admission slip. I met you once before. At the station when you arrived. The station?"

At that point Marilyn felt so frustrated that she did a *chug-chug-whoo-whoo* manoeuvre, the kind of mime one might perform for an infant.

"Oh." The refugee girl finally cracked a smile. "You're a choo-choo train, and you are Jewish?"

"Yeah, sure. Glad you finally got it."

The girl stared at Marilyn as if trying to work out a puzzle. "Do I look like a foreigner?" she suddenly asked.

"Beg your pardon?" Marilyn gulped. At least those eyes no longer flashed danger signals. "Not really, that is . . . not until you open your mouth."

That admission prompted a brief smile.

The orphan girl wore a soft grey sweater over a white blouse with a Peter Pan collar, a red wool skirt and bobby socks. Everything about her was correct, until Marilyn glanced down at the shoes. What repulsive shoes! Nut-brown oxfords with black laces and pointy toes. Little perforations swirled around the toes and the stacked heels. Yuck! Quite impossible, as Marilyn's mother would have phrased it. Marilyn wore saddle shoes herself, white oxfords with contrasting brown saddles. Mrs. Chandler had probably selected those hideous orthopedic shoes.

"The shoes?" the refugee girl murmured. Marilyn flushed. "I

know," the girl continued. "Disgusting. Mrs. Chandler decided they were good for my feet. They'd straighten them out."

"Oh, yeah, no doubt about that. So you've got crooked feet?" Marilyn cleared her throat. Oh dear, she'd criticized the girl's deformity. She wanted to bite her tongue. So stupid. "Too bad," she croaked.

"No. I have good feet."

They both smiled.

"Actually the shoes aren't really so terrible." Marilyn smiled to cover her lie. "Penny loafers or saddle shoes, like mine, are more—uh—popular over here, but those lace-ups will certainly support your arches." Marilyn couldn't help thinking that apple crates wouldn't be any worse. "They'll keep you on the straight and narrow. Through thick and thin." Why did she keep on babbling? It only happened when she was dreadfully embarrassed. "Otherwise you look just fine. Great. The mostest."

"Like everybody else in this school?"

"Hey, don't judge by me. I'm no expert," Marilyn replied, staring down at her own pink wool sweater and the rose print scarf tied around her neck. She'd borrowed the scarf from Helen's drawer and reminded herself to eat lunch with greater care today—she couldn't afford to spill tuna salad on it. Helen wouldn't tolerate even the smallest grease smear on any of her possessions.

"By the way, my name is Marilyn Becker. Nice to meet you." She didn't offer her hand. Once bitten . . .

"Lilli Blankstein. But what's wrong with your nose?"

Marilyn was startled. "Nothing is wrong with my nose," she snapped back. "Why do you ask?"

"You said it had no skin on it."

Marilyn laughed. "Sorry. Just a silly expression we have. No skin off my nose means—it's like saying that something is not my problem. By the way, most schools—especially the smaller ones—don't have 'up' and 'down' staircases. Totem Point has all these rules because we're such a large school."

"Most strange. Yes?" Lilli scrunched up her face.

Marilyn wasn't certain whether that meant the girl thought Marilyn was telling a fib or maybe that she found the school rules and regulations slightly overwhelming. On second thought, Marilyn decided it would take a lot more than school rules to overwhelm this girl. Just a gut feeling she had.

Lilli was very attractive with that long, black curly hair tumbling around her face. Her short, turned-up nose and sparkling eyes gave her a pixieish expression. She was already quite curvy. Yeah, she was wearing a bra. So was Marilyn, but Marilyn's was a French bra that laced up the back—the kind that was supposed to pull you up a bit and shape you. So far that purchase had proven worthless. It was a nuisance trying to adjust the laces in the morning and she still could pass for a twelve-year-old.

For a moment Lilli's cheeks were covered with a rosy flush. Then she glanced down at her shoes once again.

"I am sorry for hitting you. My first day here."

Each word was drawn out, like somebody had been giving her elocution lessons. She managed a small hiccup of a laugh. "Sorry if I hurt you. I was afraid you were a . . ." She snapped her fingers, searching for the elusive word.

"A bully? A monitor?" Marilyn suggested.

"Someone chasing me."

"Chasing you? Whatever for?" Marilyn asked. But Lilli was correct. Marilyn had been pursuing her. The jangle of the second bell interrupted their conversation.

"We don't want to be late for roll call," Marilyn said. "Which one is your classroom? Maybe I can help."

"Room twelve," Lilli replied.

"Oh, great. That's my homeroom, too, although I don't think

Mr. Peabody, our homeroom teacher, is so great. He also teaches us English. Did you know that? Follow me."

"A great teacher? He's very tall?"

Obviously she hadn't understood half of what Marilyn had told her. "We're running out of time, and Mr. Peabody is definitely a dangerous man if you're late."

Lilli helped retrieve the papers. Together they dashed down the main hall until they reached the "up" staircase at the opposite end of the corridor.

They reached the classroom just as Mr. Peabody was about to shut the door. Marilyn placed the papers on the left-hand edge of Mr. Peabody's desk and hurried to her desk on the window side of the room. Lilli handed in her admission slip. Mr. Peabody kept her standing while he studied the note. Then, after tapping his ruler against his thigh, he raised it and directed her to a desk in the second row.

Mr. Peabody had masses of faded brown hair that spiked upward like the crown on the Statue of Liberty. Although his milky blue eyes and sharp pointed chin gave him an elf-like expression, students learned not to be deceived by his outward appearance. The man had orbs that could peer around corners and an antenna that quivered at the slightest breach in conduct, even when he stood at the blackboard facing away from the class. If students were late more than once, they immediately received double detentions.

Following the class recitation of the Lord's Prayer, he absently introduced Lilli Blankstein. He didn't mention anything about her being a new immigrant, Marilyn noted. Maybe he didn't know, she thought. Catching sight of a boy whispering to a friend, Mr. Peabody called out, "Eric, would you like to step forward and present this lecture in my place?"

"No, sir," Eric Hill replied automatically.

"I thought not. Now, who will tell us what wonderful event occurred yesterday?" No hands were raised. If a student gave a wrong answer, he'd make sure that person felt as worthless as a wad of discarded chewing gum.

"Come now, come now. You can't all be a bunch of addlepated nincompoops."

After a little prompting, Marilyn's close friend, Barbara Deutsch, raised her arm. "Yesterday, Canada's own Barbara Ann Scott won the gold medal at the Olympic Games figure skating championship."

"Very good, Barbara. February 6, 1948. This is the first time Canada has ever won the gold medal. Barbara Ann also won the European championship. Now, tell me class, where were the Olympic Championships held?"

"St. Moritz, Switzerland," Murray Armstrong shouted.

"Right on the button," Mr. Peabody said. "And, incidentally, Dick Button of the United States won the men's figure skating championship."

He produced a newspaper photograph of Barbara Ann Scott. The headline read: "Our Barbara Wins It!" Barbara Ann appeared to be floating free in space, her arms crossed in front of her with one leg bent underneath her and the other leg extended behind her. The girls in the classroom oohed and ahhed.

"She's not only Canada's first queen of the ice, she is the first woman to bring the world figure skating crown to North America. Now, before we open our poetry books, one final current events question. What can you tell me about Mohandas Gandhi, known as the Mahatma?"

He directed the question at Lilli. "Well, Miss Blankstein?"

The whole class looked at Lilli. She remained still as a tombstone; not an eyelash flickered.

"Miss Blankstein, has the cat got your tongue?"

She didn't speak. She stared down at her desk, her hands clasped together. Marilyn felt sorry for Lilli. For a moment, she wanted to stand up and explain to Mr. Peabody that Lilli couldn't possibly appreciate the question, but then, her courage drained away.

"Surely you can tell me his homeland? Lilli? This is not a difficult question."

Silence.

"My, my, you are certainly an ignorant one, aren't you, young lady?"

She nodded.

"Speak when I address you."

"Yes, sir."

"Yes, sir, you're a dunce?"

"Yes, sir."

The class giggled.

"Well, I'm sure the other class members know that he was the Hindu spiritual leader of India and that he fasted for 121 hours. He did not quit until 200,000 Sikhs and Moslems had signed a peace pledge. Unfortunately a Hindu fanatic assassinated him. Last week."

Everyone tittered and stared at Lilli. She scowled back at Mr. Peabody but refused to open her mouth.

"What a simp," Eric murmured from the desk behind Marilyn.

Marilyn swivelled around in her seat to glare at Eric, then quietly swung forward again before Mr. Peabody turned his attention to her. She wished she had spoken up on Lilli's behalf. She wished Lilli had said something herself. She was thankful when Mr. Peabody turned away and directed them to open their poetry books at page seventy-three.

She'd neglected to tell Eric that Lilli hadn't enough English to respond. Should she have explained that, or would the information only make things worse for Lilli? If only Lilli had spoken up, they might have recognized her problem.

While Marilyn pondered her next move, Mr. Peabody read a few lines from the page and told them to write their interpretations of the poem. Marilyn was making corrections to her work when the bell rang. The students gathered their loose-leaf binders and textbooks and stampeded out the door. Marilyn considered stopping Lilli, but Lilli didn't look back as she stomped down the hall.

"What a numbskull," Lois Fraser said. "And those hideous shoes? A real country bumpkin. Did you notice her loose-leaf binder? It doesn't even have a zipper. She'll never fit in here."

"She's a refugee, just arrived from Europe," Marilyn replied. "Give her a break. You can't expect her to understand how we do things yet."

"Oh, come on, Becker, she's a jerk, a real drip. That much is obvious."

Chapter Nine

Marilyn

Since that first morning, Marilyn hadn't seen much of Lilli except for exchanging a casual hello during English class. Lilli held her tongue in class—behaved as though she were mute—but Marilyn assumed she took remedial English after school since she no longer sounded as if she were swallowing heaps of mashed potatoes.

But other than nodding at each other in the hall, Marilyn and Lilli avoided each other. Lilli obviously had her own group of friends and her own private life, and didn't seem to give a hoot what the rest of her classmates thought.

Marilyn had heard, via the grapevine, that Lilli was the smartest person in French class. Marilyn had been studying Latin for the past two years instead. If she decided to become a pharmacist, like her father, she'd need to translate doctors' prescriptions, written in Latin, into English. Marilyn assumed Lilli was born in some country where they spoke French, which probably explained why she was doing so well in that particular subject. That's what Marilyn's friend

Lois thought, too. She made it sound as though Lilli were cheating somehow, but Marilyn actually felt more at ease knowing Lilli was comfortable in at least one academic subject.

Lilli had recently transferred to Marilyn's home economics class. Home economics was not Marilyn's favourite subject. She detested the sewing part, while Lilli was an absolute whiz at it. She zipped away at the sewing machine with total confidence. The previous week the home economics teacher, Miss Jeffries, had actually held up Lilli's apron—the first project of the season—for everyone to see. According to Miss Jeffries, it was "a perfectly finished" piece of work.

To her dismay, Marilyn's apron had come out cockeyed. The pockets bulged when they were supposed to lie flat. Even pressing them with a hot iron had failed to flatten the bumps. The orange rickrack stuff had ended up festooning the whole blasted skirt instead of merely outlining the edges. Marilyn told Miss Jeffries that the machine had simply run away with her, but the instructor didn't crack a smile. Actually, that was exactly what had happened.

"Sewing machines really do have minds of their own, at least when I'm doing the pedalling," she told the teacher.

She'd sneak the miserable apron into a bag and bring it home so her mom could repair the mess before Marilyn submitted it for a final mark. Unfortunately, one of the sashes that tied around the waist appeared to be several inches shorter than the other one. Marilyn had her doubts whether even her mother, of the magical hands, could fix that mistake.

Last term, the subject of home economics had been cooking. While Marilyn had found the cooking classes more fun than sewing, they were also a little yucky. Lilli was lucky to have missed the fall session, particularly the class where they made a concoction called Mustard Pickles. When Marilyn opened her sealed jar at home, her father called for a gas mask. The next item they'd made was a dessert called Floating Island. Somehow her island had sunk leaving a large crater in the centre of the bowl.

Marilyn arrived home from school one day to be greeted by her mother waving an invitation at her, as if Marilyn were incapable of opening her own mail. It was an invitation for a party at the home of her best friend, Barbara Deutsch. Since Barbara's parents belonged to the same bridge group as Marilyn's parents, Mrs. Becker must have felt entitled to open Marilyn's mail.

"Hey, Mom, this letter was for me, not you," Marilyn said as she studied the invitation. There was something odd about it. Barbara had never hinted that she was planning a party.

"Since the Chandlers live down the block from Barbara's parents, Mrs. Karr, the social worker, asked them to organize a get-together for the refugee children," her mother replied.

Marilyn decided to phone Barbara to get the "real" story. Barbara explained that she'd invited all her usual friends plus the European orphans—those who were the same age as the girls or slightly older.

"The Greenies," she said.

"Greenies? Who's green?"

"Didn't you realize that's what people call them? My mother says it's an old Jewish expression meaning 'new.' Like the green shoot of a plant? They've always used it to describe newly arrived Jewish immigrants. Newcomers. Greeners."

"Sounds peculiar to me. Greeners? Greenies? Like they're green orphans—instead of black or white or orange or purple. How about Dappled Bronzes or Pinkies?"

"Don't be silly." Barbara went on to explain that the party was to make the refugees feel more at home. She'd even squeezed in a few of the younger European children "so they'll all have somebody to talk to in case they're still uncomfortable speaking English."

During lunch break the following day, Marilyn's closest friends, including Barbara, Marion Walker and Lois Fraser, decided what they'd wear to the party. Lois had a new pink cashmere twin set that she would wear with a white Peter Pan dickie collar.

"Cashmere?" red-headed Marion gasped. "Wow. Well, my sweater is only lamb's wool but I'll tie a scarf around my neck and knot it with a big ring. Sound okay?"

Since Barbara was tall and slim she'd chosen a plaid pleated skirt, a wide belt and a ruffled white blouse. "And pearls, of course," she concluded.

"Of course," they all agreed. "What about you, Marilyn?"

"Well, I have a new grey gabardine skirt and Mom finally let me buy those red penny loafers, and you remember my baby-blue angora sweater? Probably a lariat of long fake pearls. Should work, don't you think?" They nodded in agreement.

The party was held the following Saturday. When Marilyn arrived that evening she heard the blast of the record player from the basement rumpus room. The song being played was a silly one called "The Too Fat Polka."

Despite the semi-darkness, she knew trouble was brewing the minute she hit the bottom step.

On one side of the room, holding up the knotty-pine-panelled wall, were all the local Jewish kids from various schools around the city. She knew several from her school. Some of the other guests attended nearby schools like Prince of Wales in Old Shaughnessy, Point Grey or the Model School. There was also representation from high schools like Magee, Lord Byng, John Oliver and King Edward. A few boys Marilyn recognized from functions at the Hebrew School or the I. L. Peretz Institute on Broadway. There were also kids who attended the Beth Israel Synagogue Sunday School with Marilyn. Her mom insisted she continue until her confirmation the following year. Only two of Marilyn's friends attended the same synagogue as she did.

Ranged along the opposite wall were the refugee kids. You couldn't miss them because they were so formally dressed. Instead of wearing pullover sweaters and cords, the boys wore suits. *Yikes,* Marilyn thought. Vancouver boys never wore suits except for holidays or bar mitzvahs or weddings. She pitied those poor guys. Surely their foster families could have warned them? They looked like a bunch of stuffed shirts. And they'd all chosen similar suits: double-breasted ones with pinstripes. Geekish.

"Maybe they bought them by the carload, or someone got them wholesale?" a Magee boy whispered.

"The girls are dressed like they're going to The Cave nightclub for cocktails and dancing. Too agonizing for words," Marion Walker whispered.

Not only had they chosen dresses, they wore nylon hose and Cuban heels. The only missing ingredients were hats and gloves.

Barbara pointed to one girl who had combined the worst of both worlds. Dressed in a dramatic green velvet jumper and a white satin blouse with huge bishop sleeves, she'd added short white socks stuffed into suede high-heeled pumps. The bows on the pumps looked like giant dragonflies about to take flight.

"How could she? Nobody wears dress shoes with bobby socks unless they're still in kindergarten," Marion said. "Unbelievable."

"Maybe that's how they dress in Europe? Christian Dior and the New Look?" Marilyn suggested.

"Dream on," Marion replied.

Smack in the middle of this group, perched on the arm of a club chair, was Lilli. She looked both beautiful and unbelievably sophisticated, except for dark red lipstick that was way too thick. Marilyn was positive that it was that fancy Chen-Yu brand that came in a showy black plastic tube with an attached elastic that you pulled back to raise the lipstick itself. In the Chen Yu ads they always showed an exotic lady with long fingernails. Lilli also appeared to be wearing pancake makeup. Their mothers usually allowed the girls to apply a daub of colour to their lips but nothing beyond that.

Lilli's dress was a black wool, full-skirted number. A matching bronze-studded belt showed off her tiny waist. She, too, sported nylon stockings and black patent leather pumps with ankle straps and high heels.

"Isn't that something? I kid you not. It must take heaps of practice for her to keep from teetering over and twisting an ankle in those shoes," Ruth Silverstone said.

They all watched as Lilli leaned over a boy sitting in an armchair. She whispered something directly into his ear.

"Can you believe it?" Barbara added. "That getup? My mother says she looks like a tramp. Probably is one, too."

Marilyn interrupted her. "That's no tramp. That's Lilli Blankstein. She's okay."

Marilyn kept staring at Lilli's dress. She'd die for a simple black sweater. A dress like that was beyond the realm of possibility. According to her mother, everybody knew that girls under eighteen did not wear black. But that outfit made Marilyn's baby-blue sweater look like something stolen from a playpen. She waved at Lilli, but Lilli didn't notice because she was making eyes at that boy.

"Black is hardly a trampy colour," Marilyn told her friends.

"My mother says this Lilli has Mrs. Chandler at her wits' end. According to Mrs. Chandler, she's a strange duck."

"It wouldn't take much to send Mrs. Chandler off the deep end. Hey, who's the good-looker she's talking to?" Marilyn asked.

"Kurt somebody. A real wolf, that one. He practically bowed when we were introduced. Too slick for words. He lives with the Goodman family," Marion said.

"Now he is a real Casanova," Marilyn whispered. Both girls started to giggle.

"Smooth."

"Bedroom eyes."

Marilyn eventually chatted with everyone she knew and nodded politely to the less-familiar faces.

"I thought this was supposed to be a mixer but nobody seems to be mixing," she told Barbara.

"So, Marilyn, do something to improve the situation," Mrs. Deutsch replied as she entered the room with a tray of Coca-Cola bottles. A glazed doughnut perched on the neck of each open bottle. While Mrs. Deutsch was setting her tray down on a corner table, all conversations came to a standstill. Heading back up the staircase, she nonchalantly snapped on the overhead lights.

Barbara moved to the record player and chose the really soppy "Dance Ballerina Dance" played by Vaughn Munroe and his orchestra. She dimmed the lights again and immediately the hum of voices became stronger.

"This one is a spot dance. There'll be a prize for the couple that is standing on the secret spot when the music stops. So let's dance, everyone. If you don't know someone, introduce yourselves." Her voice became slightly edgy as she encouraged people to mix a little.

Herbie Wilder grabbed Marilyn's hand and they moved to the middle of the bare hardwood floor. Somebody had already rolled back the large oval carpet. The dancers glided easily across the floor because Barbara had scattered some soap flakes to make it slippery.

Herbie's fair hair was worn in a brush cut, held at attention with a little Brylcreem. In addition to being a snappy dresser, Herbie was never at a loss for words. And he always managed to make Marilyn laugh. He told her how wonderful the ski season had been up on Hollyburn Mountain. Herbie's family skied every weekend. And he had an older brother with a car so he didn't have to take the long bus trip over to the north shore. Marilyn had skied only twice during the season but remembered seeing Herb flash down the twisty ski-out.

Marilyn peered over Herbie's shoulder as Kurt urged Lilli to join in the dancing. Although he took huge steps, twirling Lilli around abruptly, then snapping her away from him, Lilli had no trouble following him, despite those unbelievable high heels. The other refugee kids remained slouched against the wall. They whispered among themselves in a variety of peculiar languages and seemed to ignore the Vancouverites. The dancing wasn't helping at all.

The music stopped and Barbara announced that Kurt and Lilli were the winners. Barbara handed them each a rabbit-foot key chain. "The next dance is 'Ladies' Choice.' So mix it up, everybody—choose new partners."

Herb told Marilyn, "This party is going nowhere. The foreign kids—those orphans—probably think Ladies' Choice is a brand of food."

Marilyn recognized the gangly-looking guy from the train lurking in the shadows by the far door and swung over in his direction. Standing at his side was the younger boy with that thick shock of unruly hair and the long jaw. He delivered the Beckers' newspaper every morning on his bicycle. His name was Max Katz. He seemed a sweet guy but he was still a kid.

As she approached, both boys tried to perform a disappearing act behind a Chinese-style screen. The older guy was too tall to make it, so he stood stiffly against the wall as Marilyn approached.

"Hi." Marilyn spoke a little too loudly. "Dance?"

"Not well enough," he said.

"I wasn't expecting Gene Kelly."

He looked puzzled.

"Gene Kelly is a dancer in the movies like, uh, like Fred Astaire. A star. I suppose you haven't heard of him, either?"

"A star," he repeated slowly. "What kind of star? Like the Big Dipper or Andromeda drifting somewhere in the galaxy?"

At first she simply glared at him. Creep.

"Like in movies—movie star. Like in motion pictures?" Marilyn frantically searched the room for someone to free her from this dope but everyone else was either dancing or, like most of the newcomers, had moved across the hall to the ping-pong table.

"Ah," he said. "Movies. Where people speak?"

She caught on fast. A joker. Ha, ha. A real funny bunny, this one.

"Brilliant," she said. "However, I refer neither to the Andromeda galaxy nor to the wife of Perseus, who was rescued from the sea monster."

Gotcha, she thought triumphantly. He was momentarily stunned, so he allowed her to drag him onto the dance floor. Once there he tripped over her shiny red loafers, but she wasn't giving up so fast. Let him sweat a little, this wise guy.

"Come on, genius," she continued. "I realize you're no Fred Astaire but you're probably not Tarzan of the Apes, either. Get with it."

That remark brought a smile to his lips. "How come you know about the stars?" he said as they bumped against another couple.

"Why? Think we're all a bunch of idiots over here? Have you cornered the market on brains?"

He shook his head and they stumbled into another couple, who glared at them. Marilyn suggested maybe they should stop the conversation and concentrate on their feet while dancing. He freed his hand to waggle a finger at her.

"Didn't I warn you?"

"You did."

Eventually, after they'd slammed into every couple on the dance floor, like a misguided bumper car at the Pacific National Exhibition, they agreed the results were not worth the effort. Instead they settled into a corner to talk.

Marilyn noticed that several local girls were swarming around Kurt, so maybe the ice was starting to break up. Marion smiled at Kurt as he led her to the dance floor. Perhaps there was still hope for the party.

Although his English was frequently fractured, her new acquaintance expressed himself easily. His name was Danny Goffman and he was really smart. He took several hours of classes each day because he wanted to start working as soon as possible so he could become independent.

"So I can be my own person," he told her. "And become like everyone else."

When Marilyn asked him why he wanted to become like everyone else, their conversation ended abruptly and his smile faded.

"Sorry," she said quickly. "You'll have to forgive me. I'm not making fun of you, really I'm not." He didn't understand, so she tried again. "I always talk too much and ask too many blunt questions."

He was framing a reply when Lilli arrived at his side and jerked on his arm. She spoke only to him, as if Marilyn didn't exist. She addressed him in some guttural language, which Marilyn obviously didn't understand. She was practically shouting. Little Max appeared from nowhere and tried to shush her. Then Danny placed his hand on Lilli's cheek, very gently, and whispered into her ear. Whatever he said, it seemed to have a magical effect. Lilli grinned at him.

The threesome continued their heated conversation, using their hands for greater effect. It was as if Marilyn had become invisible.

When they eventually stopped motioning with their hands, Marilyn decided to join in.

"Hey, Lilli. Are you enjoying the party?"

"Terrible party." Lilli snapped off the words. "We are leaving now because nobody wants us here. Right, Danny?"

"Don't be ridiculous. It's early. People are just getting to know each other and soon there'll be food." Marilyn pointed to a crowd of girls surrounding Kurt. "Look, your friend Kurt is dancing."

Lilli frowned. "Food? Somebody asked whether I'd ever seen a hot dog! Do they take us for backward children? No, it is time to leave."

"I'm really sorry to hear that," Marilyn muttered. "But please don't go. It's still early."

"I can't figure out why you Canadian girls chase after our boys when you actually look down on us newcomers," Lilli said.

Before Marilyn could muster a reply, Lilli turned on her heel and shouted something to her friends.

The group reacted as though a drill sergeant had blown his whistle. They immediately dropped their ping-pong paddles and returned their unfinished Cokes to the nearest tables. Mrs. Deutsch arrived with another tray from the kitchen and watched in bewilderment as they slinked past her.

"But children," she said in English and broken Yiddish, "you haven't had anything to eat yet. I've brought a tray of hot dogs— kosher hot dogs. With mustard and ketchup and fried onions. You can't possibly leave until you've eaten."

After lowering her heavy tray to the largest table, Mrs. Deutsch placed a hand firmly on Kurt's shoulder as he tried to slip past her. The Vancouver teenagers watched to see how this drama would unfold.

"Certainly you are not going to turn down my hot dogs, young man?" She smiled as she tapped his shoulder.

"Thank you for your hospitality, Mrs. Deutsch, but we are no longer hungry." Kurt made an abrupt bow and continued walking toward the staircase.

Mrs. Deutsch stood quite still. She no longer made the slightest attempt to halt the mass departure.

"Now, tell me that wasn't ridiculous," Barbara whispered to Marilyn and Marion.

"Like a scene from a 'Theatre Under the Stars' production. Imagine bowing! I'm surprised he didn't click his heels together like in one of those costume movies. But it was impressive," Marion said.

Danny paused to thank Marilyn for the conversation. No bow. Using exactly the same flat tone, he thanked Mrs. Deutsch and Barbara for "your kind hospitality to us refugees."

The party wound down. As soon as they'd demolished the food, the local kids made a less organized exodus, leaving Marilyn, Marion and Barbara in the basement.

Marion said, "What happened, Marilyn? I don't get it. What did we do wrong?"

Barbara pointed her finger at Marilyn. "Did you say something awful to that boy? Ask him questions about his past? You know we're not supposed to ask them any personal questions."

Marilyn was frankly baffled and a bit humiliated, too. She actually thought her discussion with that Danny character had been successful. She'd found the conversation stimulating, until the moment Lilli began to spit nails. Up until that point, he'd seemed almost friendly. Then he'd knuckled under like all the others. What a spineless jellyfish.

"*Emess Hatorah*, on my honour I didn't ask a single personal question, unless one considers a conversation about the galaxy a personal subject."

"The galaxy? Come on. Nobody is that boring."

"Maybe Lilli thought you were trying to steal her boyfriend," Barbara suggested.

Marion Walker was getting a ride home with Marilyn, and she was staring out the window, watching for Marilyn's dad. Now she swivelled round. "Could be. She was really furious. Sizzling. Maybe she expects us to stick with our own kind and leave them—the DPs, that is—to themselves?"

"That's what she said. But it would not only be boring but impolite," Marilyn replied.

Marion started a long discussion about which boy, Kurt or Danny, actually was Lilli's boyfriend. Someone else suggested perhaps they both were.

"Now that would be impressive," Barbara said.

Mrs. Deutsch, who was stacking dirty plates and listening to the last part of the conversation, asked worriedly, "Oh, children, you didn't ask them anything about their past, did you? They're very sensitive and it's off limits."

Why did people always ask that question? Marilyn wondered a little impatiently. What was wrong with having a past, and why was theirs—the orphans' history—forbidden territory?

"You've been warned—we've all been warned—to steer clear of that explosive area."

"Who cares about their past? I don't care and I don't want to hear anything about it," Marion insisted. "If you ask me, they're a bunch of misfits. Most of them are just stuck-up, although that Kurt seemed rather nice, don't you agree?"

Marilyn spotted the headlights from her father's car as it pulled into the Deutsches' circular driveway. He didn't like to be kept waiting. "Hey, Marion, hurry up," she murmured while reaching for her raincoat.

Her stomach churned as they settled into the car. She was certain that it had nothing to do with the fact that she'd just polished off the last forlorn hot dog. Her mom should be pleased, she thought. Mrs. Becker always insisted that it was criminal to waste food when there were so many starving orphans in the world.

Somehow the sour taste refused to disappear. She couldn't stop thinking about those refugee kids. Although they had displayed unbelievable arrogance, she knew that something had upset them.

"How did the evening go?" her father asked. "A good mixer?"

At first no one replied. His question dangled in the air, making them squirm a little as they tried to find the right words.

"Could have been better," Marilyn said when it became obvious that Marion intended to remain silent.

"Oh," he said. "Well, that's the way it goes sometimes."

"Mmm." She nodded, grateful that he'd accepted her answer without additional questions.

Marilyn wondered what those immigrants were actually thinking. Sure, they were different, but so were her eastern Canadian cousins. And then it came to her. *If we think they are different, what must they think of us?*

Marilyn suddenly realized that the newcomers probably thought the local kids were a bunch of spoiled snobs. This new concept was most disturbing; as she mulled it over in her mind her nausea increased. Had they treated the orphans like outsiders? Possibly. Had they frozen them out of the party? Probably. And how could they ever become friends if they couldn't even talk to each other?

Chapter Ten

Danny

He awoke from another of those terrifying dreams. Would they never stop plaguing him? At first he was back in Buchenwald with Monieck. But this nightmare was more disturbing than usual. All those worlds colliding. Chaos. His Auntie Belbina shouting at him to leave the fish alone—the live carp for Shabbat that were swimming in a metal tub in Mama's kitchen.

Of course there'd never been any fish in Buchenwald. All that remained of Buchenwald now was a grainy photo somebody had taken of the boys after their release. They looked like skeletons, so emaciated it was impossible to tell their ages. The only way in which they differed from the piles of corpses was the fixed smiles on some of their faces. And the alert, watchful eyes.

In the dream, a guard was shouting at Danny, demanding he say his name aloud, and all he could remember was his number. For the life of him, Danny couldn't remember his proper name. He knew he'd once had one, but it had disappeared, stolen forever. Then somebody else started singing that new song—something about a four-leaf clover—and he awoke. These Canadian songs had the most ridiculous words. Where had he heard that one? Oh yes, at a meeting for all the newcomers at the Jewish Centre, following their session with Mrs. Karr.

He'd also met a very nice Vancouver girl there. She attended the I. L. Peretz Institute, which was another of the local Jewish schools. The Peretz School taught their students Yiddish rather than Hebrew, so she spoke it fluently. This girl, Riva, spoke easily with him, as though he actually belonged in Vancouver and hadn't dropped down from some remote planet. There was only one minor problem: when they walked together to the streetcar stop on Oak Street, she told him she was going steady with a university student.

While dressing for breakfast, he attempted to banish his latest dream. "Shazam!" he whispered. Wasn't that the magic phrase Billy Batson (a hero in one of Ben's comic books) produced when he wanted to escape an unpleasant situation? "Shazam!" and the boy Billy automatically became the hero, Captain Marvel. Danny suddenly remembered that other Canadian girl, the one at that flop of a party the previous month. She, too, had been rather interesting, although not much older than fourteen. How did they phrase it here? Oh yeah: "Petite and peppy." Marilyn, that was her name. Marilyn Becker. Seemed quite friendly at the time, but Lilli had insisted she was bossy. To be fair, Lilli thought most of the Vancouver kids were poison.

Poor Lilli. For some reason she was having a really rough time. First there was that party with the Vancouver teenagers. How had she explained her feelings to Sylvie and Sophie after the event? Oh yes, she'd felt that the boys, Danny and Kurt, were about to disappear, blend into the crowd—as if such a thing were even remotely possible—while she remained a total outsider. She felt her relationship with Mrs. Chandler was spiralling downward. She still hated that slobbering dog, Rex. The animal gave her the shivers. She appeared to be plunging from one perilous situation into another. Mrs. Chandler had set a curfew and Lilli continued to test and break it, along with any other rules she considered highly restrictive.

Sylvie, on the other hand, was loving it in Vancouver. The Elmans adored her. They took her everywhere with them. They'd enrolled her in Sunday school and had recently invited several of the other refugees to their home for cake and drinks. Kurt, too, was constantly bragging about his host family including him in everything. Sophie was even dating a survivor who had recently arrived from eastern Canada with his family.

And Max? Given Max's fears it was no wonder that he had so many down days. For some reason, Max felt most comfortable sleeping on the carpet in his bedroom, rather than on the bed. But while this had at first upset his sponsors, they no longer viewed it as a major calamity.

Without a doubt, the orphans were working hard at carving out normal lives for themselves. For some children it was a greater struggle than for others, but all of them attempted to fit in, even if that meant cutting off or reshaping bits of their personalities. Perhaps that was the most suitable expression for their condition: reshaping. Danny and the others had received several letters from friends they'd met on the boat coming over, those who'd settled in other communities. Sure, they occasionally complained about the complexities of North American life, but they all seemed to be gradually getting the hang of it. Danny also wrote regularly to the Balsams in Paris.

The Calgary bunch was already planning a reunion with the Edmonton kids. They didn't mix much in the general community, although one friend had written that they were always included at large communal parties. Two Winnipeg boys had switched foster families, and one of the Toronto girls had written that she was getting married as soon as her boyfriend turned twenty-one. That letter had been a stunner.

Danny absently filled his bowl with the ever-present cornflakes, giving the box an extra shake before he poured the milk over the cereal.

"My, my, you certainly have an appetite as big as a horse," Mr. Halpern said as he joined Danny at the table.

Danny looked down at his bowl. It was very full. There was no possibility of shovelling the stuff back into the box as he desperately desired, since he'd already poured milk on it.

His face burned. His hands, resting on the oilcloth table covering, were sticky. "Sorry, I didn't mean to waste food like that."

"S'okay," Mr. Halpern mumbled as he buttered a piece of toast. "As long as you eat all of it."

"Mr. Halpern," Danny said before he had a chance to change his mind, "you recently mentioned a warehouse job? When could we go for an interview? I'd like to start as soon as possible."

"Oh, no, Danny, not yet," Mrs. Halpern murmured as she entered the kitchen with a basket of laundry balanced on one hip. "Too soon. First you must get a little more education under your belt."

"A great idea, boy," Mr. Halpern replied enthusiastically, overriding his wife's concerns. "How about tomorrow morning? It'll make a man out of you. You'll see."

And what am I now, Danny wanted to shout, *if not already a man?* Instead of replying, he stared down into his cereal bowl. The crisp sugary flakes were already disintegrating into a disgusting mush but he forced himself to choke the stuff down, one spoonful after another, before Mr. Halpern could again accuse him of wasting food.

Mrs. Halpern frowned at her husband as she placed the fresh laundry on the countertop. "I don't see why there's a rush for him to start work."

"Please, Bess, this is men's business." Mr. Halpern swiftly flipped through the pages of his newspaper.

Danny started his job two days later. They paid him eighteen dollars a week at a furniture store, five dollars of which he applied to his room and board. When Kurt later questioned him, Danny explained that he also planned to attend night school. After he mastered English, he hoped to earn a diploma, maybe as an accountant. The firm's owner, a pleasant enough man named Block, claimed there was a shortage of accountants in the city.

"But why the big rush to work, Danny? You told me you wanted to go to university and become an engineer," Kurt said when the newcomers met the following Saturday afternoon in the Rexall drugstore at 41st Avenue and Granville Street. It was a convenient meeting spot, and they all favoured the ice cream delicacies served at this particular soda fountain.

"Maybe someday that will happen," Danny told Kurt. "But right now, more than anything else I would like to earn a living. I want to become a normal human being. In order to become a proper Canadian I'll even learn to bowl, if that's what it takes."

"Oh, no, not that," Max said, as he scooped up some chocolate from his ice cream float.

"I can't expect any more assistance from the Halperns. They're not wealthy and they have two children of their own to educate."

Kurt didn't get it, but maybe it had something to do with his particular foster family. While Kurt admitted to struggling with the English language, his host family seemed to pamper him like a child. Kurt claimed he was the fastest runner and the most valuable member of the basketball team at his school. Next on his list was ping-pong; he was determined to star in that sport, too. The only sport that appeared beyond his abilities was a strange new one called lacrosse, which was played with a net on a stick on an outdoor court. An indoor racquet game called badminton was also peculiar. It involved playing with something called a birdie.

Danny thought both games sounded weird but he was pleased for his friend. There had been no opportunity for sports during their childhood, so he admired Kurt, who was making up for lost time.

"The older guys, like Shmulik, already have jobs. He's working in the back room of a meat market. Very cold and the work is really strenuous but he says they don't pick on him. They offer helpful advice and the guys are a friendly lot," Danny told Kurt. "I'll be independent a lot sooner if I go this route," he concluded. Of course he regretted leaving school—he'd received excellent marks while attending school in France. And secretly he still hoped to attend a university someday, but right now it was vital that he strike out on his own and become a *mensch*—a good person.

Max, who was slurping down the dregs of his chocolate float, turned on his stool and said, "Then you'll forget all about us. I know you will. Or you'll be so tired on the weekends that you won't want to take a bike trip like we did last Sunday—to that out-of-the-way place in the woods."

It was the first time Max had spoken since they'd taken their seats at the counter. Danny turned to study his young friend. He worried more about Max than the other kids; somehow Max seemed less able to adjust to his new circumstances.

"You really liked that isolated spot, didn't you, Max," Sylvie said, patting his shoulders.

"It was kind of like stepping into a different world," Max said. "So peaceful down there by the ocean."

The two boys had followed 41st Avenue west to where it intersected with Marine Drive. They'd continued down Marine Drive, past a neighbourhood of huge homes overlooking the water, and then onto a narrow, two-lane road that led them away from civilization into rough, heavily wooded country. Surrounded on either side by stands of giant trees, they'd travelled until reaching a viewpoint on the left-hand side of the road, where they'd stood in silence, staring down the cliff at the log booms that formed a ragged patchwork quilt on the surface of the river.

After pausing briefly to check out the university, which was situated smack in the centre of the untouched forest preserve, they'd headed toward Point Grey Peninsula, travelling through a dense parkland with evergreens guarding both sides of the road. Max had wanted to stop and eat their sandwiches at a hidden beach on their route but Danny had insisted they continue down to Spanish Banks and then cycle home, because he was unsure whether the good weather would hold.

"It was incredible." Max managed a brief smile. "But we'll never do it again. And we'll never see you again, Danny."

Danny detected a note of desperation in his last words.

Danny promised Max that they'd always keep in touch, although Max, too, attended school full-time. "Don't be ridiculous," Danny said. "We'll go on more bike trips when it stops raining, Max. And I certainly won't work on Sundays. Are you trying to get rid of me?" He nudged Max with his elbow. While the younger boy finally acknowledged the gesture with a friendly shove of his own, he still seemed out of sorts.

"Mr. Goodman says that the only way I'll get rid of my accent is by having a tutor after school," Kurt told them. "'Total immersion' he calls it."

Kurt was always quoting Mr. Goodman as though his foster father were the ultimate authority, his words carved in granite.

"Well, I guess I'll just have to live with this accent," Danny replied.

"Never mind," Sylvie said as she licked round and round her diminishing scoop of strawberry ice cream. She was really plumping up.

"You sound like Charles Boyer or Jean-Pierre Aumont or some combination of the two and they're really hubba-hubba movie actors."

"*Hubba-hubba*, what's that?" Max said, pushing his new beanie hat further back on his head.

"Don'tcha' know?" Sylvie said. "An expression. Also a song."

Everyone groaned, but Sylvie was very pleased with herself. She started to recite one of the popular "knock-knock" jokes, but they insisted that they'd heard more than enough from her.

Danny didn't mention that Betty had offered to assist him with his schoolwork at night. Or that he'd refused the offer. Mrs. Halpern kept handing out extra money so they could attend movies together. Somehow it didn't seem fair to accept these favours. Danny felt uncomfortable because he couldn't—what was that giant word? Oh, yes, he couldn't reciprocate.

In addition, Betty's suggestion that they become closer friends made him extremely jittery. He'd rejected all her recent invitations. She'd made hints about couples who were "going steady." "Pinned" was another of her favourite expressions. That one required the boy to give his club pin to the girl, like a high school fraternity pin. The idea made him cringe. He had neither the time nor the money to get involved in such nonsense. But living in the same house made him feel guilty, as though he was insulting the Halperns if he refused their daughter's requests.

She'd invited him to some dance called a "Sock Hop." He'd wriggled out of that event by suggesting he was loaded down with homework for his night class. And, as he reminded her, he was hopeless on the dance floor. Anticipating that she might volunteer to give him instructions on the two-step or jitterbug, he spoke solemnly of the necessity to "put first things first" on his agenda. His words were so pompous that he almost gagged as he said them.

However, while Betty perhaps questioned his refusals, she didn't take offence. At least he thought not. He almost cheered out loud when he overheard her call another boy.

Max dug into the bottom of his tall, tulip-shaped glass, trying to ferret out the last bits of melting ice cream. "I love this stuff," he announced for the fifth time that afternoon.

"You can't imagine what they snack on," Sylvie said. Everybody knew to whom "they" referred.

"Oh yeah, remember that bowling alley experience?" Lilli added.

Sylvie jumped in. "The students from my Sunday school class at the Beth Israel Synagogue went bowling and I brought Lilli along."

"After knocking down the required number of pins, the girls ordered soft ice cream covered with canned fruit salad," Lilli continued. "It was disgusting. Why they'd want to melt down perfectly hard ice cream and turn it back into slush is beyond me."

"Don't forget the toast points," Sylvie added. "They served toast with that stuff. Everyone simply gobbled it up. Don't they realize that you only eat toast with breakfast?"

"Did you enjoy the bowling part?" Danny asked Lilli.

She groaned. "An absolute disaster. Somehow my bowling ball bounced across three lanes before it stopped. I interrupted everyone's game, so, never, never again. They were horrified," Lilli added. "The girls insisted that nobody had ever done anything like that before."

Max, who had remained silent during this conversation, managed a smile. "My English is improving. I read lots and lots of comic books. I think that's the best way to learn English. The manager of the drugstore helps me whenever I get stuck on a word. And the people on my paper route give me big tips when I collect." He paused to sip at his drink. "Did I tell you that I saw a hockey game?"

"Lucky you!" Kurt said.

Max was anxious to describe the game he'd attended with the Meltzers. The other children all envied him that experience.

He paused to push a shock of his straight, thick hair back from his face. "We drove to New Westminster where they have a team. Playoffs against the Camrose Maroons. Our team was called the New Westminster Royals. It was a wonderful evening, until I asked the wrong question."

"What was the question?" Kurt asked.

"I wanted to know why all the guys were chasing the same puck."

"You didn't," Kurt wailed.

"Yeah, I did," Max admitted.

"So what happened next?" Danny demanded.

"I asked Mr. Meltzer: 'Why don't they give each of the guys their own puck so there won't be any more fights?'"

Kurt tried to hide his smile as Danny prompted Max. "So what happened then?"

Max blinked and blinked again, making his deep-set eyes almost disappear. "They started to snicker." He was stammering now, so they all leaned in closer.

"Take it easy, Max," Kurt said.

"Yeah, Max, relax. It's not important. It's just a hockey game. You had fun while you were there, didn't you?" Danny said.

"Everyone sitting near me started to howl with laughter. You'd think I'd said something funny," Max continued. "They kept repeating my words to their friends. Some rude people pointed their fingers at me like I was an idiot. I don't ever want to attend another hockey game because I hate it when people laugh at me. And, come to think of it, I'm never going to a sports event for the rest of my life. Not after that game. And that's definite."

"Oh, Max," Danny whispered, patting the younger boy on the back. "They weren't making fun of you. You didn't understand how hockey is played and—"

"You're wrong, " Max said, turning his stool to face them. Tears streamed down his cheeks. "No, I know when people are laughing at me. If I can't be a real Canadian then I've decided not to be any-thing."

Danny said, "Maybe it's going to take a lot longer than we expected. Don't give up so quickly, Max."

Max stood up from his stool at the counter. "No, you're the ones who don't get it," he continued, wiping away a tear with the sleeve of his shirt. "I want that no one should think of me as a survivor. I want to forget all of that forever. I don't want to be a Greenie any more. If I can't do that—well—well, what's the point in being here?"

"But, Max, we're not just Greenies," Danny replied. "We're new-comers to Canada, but we've got friends here. Remember, friend-ship is the most important thing."

Chapter Eleven

Lilli

Lilli paused to study her image in the hall mirror, and then she gave her hair a final swipe, trying to get the curls to stay behind her ears. It wasn't an easy task because the humidity from the ocean made her hair extra curly, even on days when it wasn't damp and raining.

And suddenly Mrs. Chandler entered her space, her nose practically nudging Lilli's ear.

"You have too much vanity, my girl. Vanity is a bad thing, as I've told you often enough. And that dishevelled mop of hair. It's messy and time-consuming. If you can't control it, it's time to chop it off. I want you home immediately after school today. No dilly-dallying. I'll take you to Mr. John's of South Granville for a proper haircut."

"I will not cut it," Lilli told Mrs. Chandler. They glared at each other in the splotchy face of the antique hall mirror. "It's my hair and I'm not cutting it off."

"Oh yes you are, my girl—if you're remaining here, you'll trim that wild mop."

Before Lilli could protest, Mrs. Chandler vanished.

Mrs. Chandler always complained about the time Lilli "wasted" looking at herself in the mirror. Admittedly, Lilli couldn't stop herself when she passed by a mirror. There had been no mirrors in the camps. And what harm was there in occasionally glancing at oneself in a mirror? Surely it wasn't such an awful sin?

She ran her fingers through her thick curls, remembering how they had treated the girls when they'd first entered the camp. The *kapos*—the Christian and Jewish prisoners overseeing the girls— had first insisted they undress. Then, wasting no time, they'd shaved off all their hair. Lilli still pictured those gigantic multi-coloured piles of hair stacked throughout the room.

And she remembered that beautiful girl, the one with the long auburn curls. The spiteful *kapo* had shaved off her eyebrows, as well as her hair, because that girl remained gorgeous even with a bald skull.

From the day they were taken from the ghetto and were separated from Papa, Mama had never stopped crying. After that it was just Mama, Lilli's two sisters and Lilli herself. Lilli remembered standing at the gates of Auschwitz, in that long, twisting line, and how a woman behind them whispered, "Do something with that child. Cut off her hair right away."

Mama turned round and said, "Why should I cut off my Marisa's beautiful braid?"

"To make her look older," the woman hissed.

Mama didn't understand what the woman meant. At twelve years Marisa could have been mistaken for eight because she was so thin and petite. She'd had typhoid fever in the ghetto and had barely recovered.

The woman passed Mama a pair of nail scissors and said, "Listen, lady, don't be foolish, do it now."

Mama chopped off Marisa's thick, golden braid, but it didn't help when they reached the front of the line. A German officer took Marisa's heart-shaped face between his thick fingers for just an instant, and then motioned for Marisa to go to the left. He directed the rest of the family—Mama, Feyla and Lilli—to go to the right.

"No," Mama said. "She stays with me."

So the man shoved them both to the left and pushed the two older girls to the right.

"Why are you crying?" one of the workers asked as Lilli stumbled into the huge room where they ordered the bewildered girls to remove their clothing in preparation for the showers.

"They took away my little sister and my mother," Lilli told the woman as she added her clothing to a pile of garments in a corner.

The attendant, who wasn't much older than Lilli, smirked. Several of her side teeth were missing so it looked as if she had wolf fangs. Lilli took a step back for fear the *kapo* might bite her.

"Stop snuffling, you stupid cow," the woman scolded. "I don't have a mother, so why should you? Heh?"

Before Lilli could reply, another *kapo* pushed her toward the showers.

"Don't worry," she said. "Your mother went to work in a match factory. Where you're going you don't need a mother."

The woman and the *kapo* started to laugh.

It was several days before the sisters understood the joke. "Match factory" to the workers meant the crematoriums, the ovens where bodies were burned after the prisoners had been gassed to death.

Now Lilli looked into the Chandler mirror one last time. She was definitely not cutting off her hair, not for Mrs. Chandler or for anybody else. She reached for her pile of books. Mr. Chandler watched silently as she headed for the door. Then, putting down his paper, he motioned for Lilli to approach his chair.

"Why argue with her, Lilli?" he said. "You only make things more difficult for yourself."

She managed a lopsided smile and a shrug. He was a sweet man, a caring person, but she'd already decided there were certain things she had to fight for and her hair was definitely one of them.

She had a fairly good morning in school. She'd completed her homework so she hoped there'd be no hassles.

When she reached Mr. Peabody's English literature class she took out her copy of the novel *Ivanhoe* by Sir Walter Scott. They had recently completed *The Lady of the Lake* and now she was slogging through *Ivanhoe*. It seemed to be a very talky book—lots of big words. Lilli was only mildly nervous that day because she'd plugged away the entire weekend reading about the Lady Rowena, Isaac, Cedric the Saxon, and all those knights like Athelstane and the other Templars. She rather liked the heroine, Rebecca, although Rebecca was sort of timid. With some coaching from Danny, who was a really fast reader, she'd digested the specifics of the story, although the writer, Mister Sir Walter Scott, sure used fancy phrases.

She was still thinking about how best to handle the hair appointment after school when Mr. Peabody called her name: "Lilli Blankstein, please stand up and read aloud for us from chapter ten where it begins . . ."

Lilli remained seated at her desk. She twisted her head to look at the students sitting behind her. Then she glanced at the kids seated on either side of her, deciding he must mean some other person. As a last resort, she slumped down in her seat hoping to be hidden by the tall boy who sat in front of her. Nothing worked. Mr. Peabody continued to point his ruler at her.

"Lilli Blankstein," he said. "Please stand."

Sliding out of her seat, she stood at attention still clutching the edge of her desk to maintain her balance.

"Is something wrong with your hearing?" he asked.

Lilli's classmates giggled, relieved, no doubt, because at that moment Lilli was the object of his persecution, and thankfully not one of them. She hated them all then, every last one.

She shook her head.

"Please read aloud, Lilli. Chapter ten, page one hundred and twenty."

She grasped the small red book and looked up at him, beseeching him to choose some other person. After the first week, he had realized, from her heavy accent, that she was a foreigner and had difficulty with the language.

Mr. Peabody nodded his head and, with great reluctance, she began to read.

"But faaaaah-zir, said Webecca, you seemed to give the gold to Pwince . . . Pwince John villingly. Villingly? The blotch of Eejump upon him! Villingly, sayest dow?"

"Willingly, sayest thou! And it's not *he jump*—its Egypt, girl. You are mocking Sir Walter Scott and the English language."

Lilli could hear her classmates start to snicker. Just saying the princess's name aloud was painful. *Lady Rowena.* Who could pronounce such a name? In addition, Mr. Peabody had chosen a section with paragraph after paragraph of Jews versus Christians.

And he would not allow her to stop.

She tried again. Her mouth was very dry. "T'ink not tus of it, *mein vater*," said Rebecca. "A-sewer-id-lee . . ."

"Assuredly," Mr. Peabody corrected Lilli. "'Assuredly' is the word. Nothing to do with sewers. Disgusting thought," he added.

The class laughed out loud.

He showed no mercy, nodding as Lilli continued to struggle. She wanted to shout out loud that she wasn't a total idiot. She realized that the words tumbling through her lips were pure gibberish but the more she struggled, the more her tongue refused to co-operate. At that point the words were dancing up and down the pages, heckling her with their contortions. Some words slid cheekily right off the margins as she tried to blink back her tears. To concentrate. Her voice dropped. Then her voice faded out altogether. She slammed the open book on her desk, cracking its spine. She stood stock-still but the laughter in the class continued.

Mr. Peabody had removed his glasses and wiped them with a checkered handkerchief. He leaned forward, his hands clasped together under his chin while he continued to gaze at Lilli. He was waiting, with bated breath, for her to continue.

It was unbearable, the way he taunted her. His behaviour reminded her of Dieter, one of the *kapos*. She could see Dieter standing at the door, waiting for her to explain why she was late getting back to the barracks. Once again she could feel the stolen vegetable hidden under the instep of her shoe. Would the rubbery carrot suddenly make a crunching sound when she stepped forward and reveal her theft? That thought did it. She refused to become a victim again. She would not take it any longer. No: she couldn't and she wouldn't. Instead of sinking into her seat, Lilli marched straight to the front of the room and paused beside Mr. Peabody's desk. Then she kicked him as hard as she could right in the shin. He gave a rusty shriek and fell backward into his chair.

The class members gasped.

Somebody whispered, "Unbelievable," but she no longer cared what they thought. She could only think of escape. Lilli scurried down the nearest staircase. She had no idea whether it was an "up" or "down" staircase. And she didn't give a darn. Hurtling through the heavy double doors of the school and out into the crisp winter air, she swiftly covered the twelve blocks to her foster parents' house.

Fortunately the place was empty. The Chandlers' beast of a dog came to see who had arrived, but he wisely stayed out of Lilli's way. She went directly to her bedroom and shut the door. Actually, she slammed it hard. She had always wanted to do that but had never dared before. It felt so good. Only then, as she rubbed her aching hands together, did she realize that her precious coat was back at her school locker.

When she heard somebody enter the house, Lilli considered hiding in the closet. Instead, she remained in her room, curled up in bed still dressed in her school clothing.

Nobody disturbed her, although she heard the phone ring over and over again.

At dinnertime, the Chandlers whispered in the hallway outside her door. Mr. Chandler opened Lilli's door and probably noticed the lump she made huddled under the covers. Without saying a word, he closed the door very gently. Perhaps he thought she was asleep.

After dinner she heard them mumbling again in the living room, but it was late evening before Mr. Chandler knocked on her door. He eventually persuaded Lilli to leave the room and together they walked to the kitchen, where he directed her to a seat at the table. He pointed to a cold roast beef sandwich. She told him she could not eat a bite but he insisted. Mrs. Chandler did not appear.

"Ah, Lilli, Lilli, Lilli, what are we going to do with you?" he said, watching as she nibbled at the sandwich.

She had no answers.

After she finished the meal, he guided her to the living room, where Mrs. Chandler sat waiting in the big gold brocade armchair with the high back and the claw-like legs. Mrs. Chandler perched there, rigid as a queen, for at least five minutes. Only when Mr. Chandler tapped his pipe several times against the side of a brass ashtray did she finally open her mouth.

"Explain this—this barbaric behaviour if you can, my girl," Mrs. Chandler demanded. "Totally unacceptable. Normal people in Canada do not behave in this manner."

"Please, Lilli, exactly what persuaded you to—to kick your teacher? Did he hit you first?" Mr. Chandler asked Lilli. "Threaten you in some way?"

Lilli attempted to describe her classroom experience but words failed her. How could she make them understand that Mr. Peabody's actions had been deliberately aimed at demolishing her—that she'd snapped because she was never going to let that happen again? She, too, was perplexed by her own behaviour but she certainly was not admitting that fact in front of Mrs. Chandler.

Mrs. Chandler said, "This is the end."

"I don't understand," Lilli said. She was far too frustrated to offer a response. What could she tell these people? That she really was a very nice girl, not a monster; that she had never struck another human being in her entire life? Sure, she'd told a few lies and stolen food in the camp whenever it was possible, but only to keep her sister and herself alive for one more day.

Mrs. Chandler sighed but refused to explain. Instead, she told Lilli to return to her bedroom.

The following day Mr. Chandler insisted that Lilli get dressed and return to school with him. "You've got to face the music," he said. Then, seeing her confusion, he added, "Be prepared to accept the consequences of your behaviour."

Fortunately for Lilli, Mrs. Chandler remained at home. She stood by the door, tight-lipped, with her hands on her bony hips, as Mr. Chandler marched Lilli to his car. Lilli was quaking beneath the old jacket he'd placed over her shoulders.

They entered the office of the principal, Mr. James, and there, in a back room at a long table, sat Mr. Peabody, the lady guidance counsellor and two strange adults. A pair of crutches stood by Mr. Peabody's chair and a white cast encased his ankle. Lilli was petrified by what she saw. She certainly hadn't meant to hit him that hard. To crack his ankle! His complexion paled when he saw her but he remained silent.

They asked Lilli loads of questions; everyone did—except Mr. Peabody. He sat as far away from her as possible. Whenever she spoke, he looked past her at a faded sepia photograph of the school. There was some talk about finding a translator because, on this occasion, Lilli had great difficulty expressing herself in English.

"Does anyone know somebody who speaks Polish?" Mr. James enquired. "Perhaps there is someone in the school who speaks Russian or Czech? A translator?"

Lilli had no intention of assisting them by making any suggestions.

At the close of the session, Mr. Chandler tightened his grip on her shoulder. He didn't need to give her any hint. She understood exactly what was expected of her.

She whispered an apology to Mr. Peabody. "Sorry for cracking your ankle, sir."

He corrected her. "It is not broken. A torn tendon."

They ordered her to return home once again while the school board pondered her case.

Two days later, the authorities sent for her again. Again Mr. Chandler accompanied her. Much to Lilli's surprise, they returned her to Mr. Peabody's class. She was no longer seated in the second row. Her new place was at the very back corner of the room.

The only positive result from this calamitous event was that Mrs. Chandler seemed to have forgotten all about Lilli's hair. Lilli had worried that Mrs. Chandler might equate Lilli with the biblical hero Samson, and decide that she might lose her strength—her mean streak, to be more exact—if they chopped off Lilli's hair. Fortunately for Lilli, Mrs. Chandler was probably not a big Bible reader. Lilli didn't know whether word of her "abominable behaviour" (as Mrs. Chandler kept phrasing it) had become public. She remained ignorant because she was forbidden to make telephone calls. She was also confined to her room.

That evening, after her first day back at school, there was another family conference in the living room. Lilli realized that she was in really big trouble when she saw the social worker, Mrs. Karr, perched on the edge of one of the spindly chairs.

"Lilli," Mrs. Chandler began, "it is obvious that you are not meant to be a student, and you take discipline very badly. Most unruly. We have decided, Mr. Chandler and myself, that if you are to remain in our home you will have one additional month in school, then you will get a job."

"A job?" Lilli cried. "I do not want a job. I want to finish school."

"That is simply out of the question. After that unforgivable behaviour, why would you want to continue in school?" she shouted. "You obviously have no respect for authority or for learning."

Mrs. Karr tried to interrupt the conversation at this point but neither Lilli nor Mrs. Chandler allowed her to speak.

"I must go to school. That is the only way I can better myself, the only way to become a real Canadian," Lilli murmured.

Mrs. Chandler pointedly arched her thin eyebrows at the other two adults, showing her contempt for Lilli's demands. Then she wrinkled her nose in disgust, as though Lilli had been guilty of making a terrible smell that was polluting the room. "This is quite unbelievable. After all this, I cannot comprehend your total lack of appreciation."

"I don't want to quit school—not now—not yet," Lilli mumbled again, hanging her head.

"By now it must be clear to everyone that this child is incorrigible," Mrs. Chandler told Mrs. Karr.

"I think it might help if Lilli were able to talk about this with somebody else. Perhaps an outsider could help Lilli, perhaps all of us, understand what happened. Maybe even why," Mrs. Karr suggested.

After the meeting broke up, Lilli looked up "incorrigible" in her dictionary. It said: "beyond reform, unruly, not easily swayed." Ha!

Although she agreed that she was not easily swayed, she didn't for one moment believe that was necessarily such a terrible fault.

The following day, Mrs. Chandler announced, "Lou will pick you up right after school."

"Not an appointment with a barber?" Lilli whined.

"Ha! A hairdresser is too good for the likes of you, young lady. No, Mr. Chandler is taking you to see a psychiatrist. We can no longer deal with your obstinate behaviour."

"Because I kicked Mr. Peabody?" Lilli asked. "I know it was a dreadful thing to do and I'm really sorry for that."

"That, young lady, is merely the tip of the iceberg," Mrs. Chandler responded. "Your total conduct is in question. Quite unbelievable. Given your past history, why do you wish to continue school? Your reasoning is quite beyond me. It is futile—useless, for a child like you to waste more time in school."

For the first time since her arrival in Canada, Lilli sensed that doors to the future were slamming shut before she could reach them.

Chapter Twelve

Lilli

Lilli agreed to meet a psychiatrist. All the newcomers knew about psychiatrists, of course, as they'd faced a barrage of them before coming to Canada. This doctor, whose office was downtown in a tall building on Granville Street, looked and sounded like all the others. His name was Dr. Steiner. He had an abundance of white hair, thick tortoiseshell glasses and a voice so soft Lilli had to lean forward to hear him. His office had no sofa to lie back on, just two stuffed chairs cozying up to each other across from his desk. Mr. Chandler remained in the waiting room during her session.

To begin with, the doctor consulted a whole sheaf of papers that supposedly contained Lilli's history. Lilli hoped the doctor would be called away by his secretary, so she could slip over to his desk and take a quick peek at what those files said about her. After she'd completed the usual tests, the ones where patients explained the meaning of a slew of ink blobs, the serious questioning began.

Lilli had trouble understanding Dr. Steiner. "I'm sorry," he said, "sorry you're having difficulty understanding my Yiddish, Lilli. It's a little rusty."

Finally, after they'd gone over the Mr. Peabody story a hundred times, she insisted, "*Emess Hatorah*, I swear on the Bible—the gospel truth—before this Totem Point incident, I had never hit or kicked another human being in my entire life. Really, Dr. Steiner."

The psychiatrist managed a small smile, and Lilli's expectations soared. Perhaps this doctor was different. She almost trusted him. During the entire session he hadn't once peeked at his clock or watch. At least, if he had, Lilli hadn't caught him doing it. Not like the other doctors she had visited. And he never left the room to attend to "more important business."

"Okay, Lilli, I believe you, I really do. I don't think you're a violent person. I understand that anger and stress can sometimes make us do things that we later regret. I don't imagine that there will be another episode like this?"

"Definitely not," Lilli replied, although she no longer was certain about anything.

"So," he continued, tiptoeing around the vital question. "So, I understand your hosts—the Chandlers—wonder why you wish to continue your education. Is that stating the question fairly?"

She nodded and wrapped both arms around herself. "To begin with, they treat me like I am a baby," she said. "Don't misunderstand. They have been very generous to me. Mr. Chandler, in particular, has been wonderful. I am very grateful. But you've got to understand . . ."

How was she going to explain her past circumstances to this stranger? It was impossible, quite impossible to put into plain words the horror of the camps. Lilli coughed, fidgeted with the pleats of her skirt and finally spoke again. "Although I am only fourteen I've . . ." She stopped.

"Assumed responsibility for yourself for many years?" he suggested. "You were forced to grow up very early if you hoped to survive the camps."

"Exactly." Lilli let out a great gust of air. "In order to survive. And Mrs. Chandler—she—they—can't accept this."

"They were under the impression they were getting a fourteen-year-old child who would obey them all the time?"

"Yes." Lilli nodded. "Don't get me wrong." She raised her arms in a gesture of surrender, and then dropped them to her lap in defeat. "I'm grateful to them, really I am, but in order to stay alive in the camps you had to be strong and—and have a buddy. I had my sister. And you had to have nerve and be prepared for pretty well . . ."

"Anything?"

"Absolutely anything," Lilli replied, relieved that perhaps somebody understood her side of things for a change. "You've got to appreciate that this place is—well, it is a different world over here. Nothing, nothing you can possibly imagine is similar to the camps."

She paused as the memories welled up again. They were most unwelcome. She dug frantically into her purse, then fished around until she found a stick of gum. At least the fumbling manoeuvre had killed a few moments.

He didn't push her. He waited. "You lost most of your family during the war, didn't you?" he asked at last.

"My parents and two half-brothers and a sister. My other sister, Feyla, has gone to Palestine. I do not wish to speak about them. Not here. Not now."

"I'm so sorry, my dear."

"When we arrived in Canada, well, I believed they were promising us an education. That's what I need. I don't want to cause them money problems nor be a burden to anyone—but isn't public school education free? I must have an education if I'm going to get ahead over here. Otherwise, why don't they send me back?"

Dr. Steiner nodded again and waited for Lilli to continue. And waited. And waited.

Lilli maintained the silence for a very long time, angry that he wouldn't tell her what to do next or at least offer some suggestion. And then she finally asked the crucial question. "Do you think I am crazy, Dr. Steiner? Crazy for wanting more education?"

"No, Lilli Blankstein, I do not think you're one tiny bit crazy. I think you are very sane." He smiled a second time.

She heaved a great sigh but was too choked up to continue.

"But you must realize that what I think and what the Chandlers feel are not necessarily the same thing. . . ." He paused to clear his throat. "I'm afraid that Mrs. Chandler doesn't follow your way of thinking. And I must warn you—despite my recommendations, she might not allow you to remain with them unless you are prepared to obey her rules. Are you ready to face that situation?"

Lilli nodded. At least this doctor didn't think she was crazy. She clutched his words tightly to her chest; he had given her a prize and she couldn't risk losing it, no matter what happened in the future.

She was so wrapped up in her own thoughts that it was a moment before she realized that he was still talking—talking about the necessity for Lilli to make peace with Mrs. Chandler if she hoped to remain in their house. Of course, along with his advice there was an implied warning. Without the Chandlers' agreement, she would be sent away, perhaps to a place where she'd be simply a boarder or required to assume additional responsibilities such as housework or baby care. Pearla had written from Montreal about a new friend who had been removed from her foster home after running away twice; they'd placed the girl in a boarding house and enrolled her in a hairdressing course.

Lilli, however, was not prepared to think beyond this moment. All that mattered was Dr. Steiner's faith in her dreams.

"Thank you, Dr. Steiner," she said, knowing that she was no longer considered hopelessly wilful. If someone as important as Dr. Steiner believed her needs were not outrageous, it would be all right. It might be a struggle, but she'd muddle through. Somehow she would find a place in this new country where she would feel comfortable and—and valuable.

When she returned to the waiting room, Mr. Chandler went in and had a brief, private meeting with Dr. Steiner. When the door opened again, she heard Mr. Chandler say, "I'm really sorry but I just don't think it is going to work." Neither Lilli nor Mr. Chandler discussed the visit to the psychiatrist's office while driving back to the Chandler house.

The following day the Chandlers made an announcement over breakfast. Mr. Chandler did the talking. "Lilli, I am sad to tell you this but you will be packing up today. Then Mrs. Karr will take you to another home where, perhaps, you will be more comfortable."

Lilli was stunned but could only nod her head.

"They have children in that home, and maybe you'll be happier with more people around," he added as he nervously straightened the cutlery around his plate.

At school, Lilli chose the very back corner of the cafeteria to have her lunch. She needed to disappear into a silent, dark place to mull over the disturbing news. Yes, she was happy to escape Mrs. Chandler and all her strange rules, but she had no idea what to anticipate from the next foster home. She certainly hoped they weren't dog owners. Before she'd even placed her lunch tray on the metal table, a group of grade nine girls surrounded her.

Marilyn Becker was the first girl to drop her tray down beside Lilli's. "Mind if we join you, Lilli?"

Lilli shrugged. "Suit yourself."

Marilyn motioned for two of her friends to join them and eventually the table was full.

Marilyn waved a french fry in the air as she spoke. "Well, Lilli, how does it feel to be the talk of the whole school?"

Her words startled Lilli, but she certainly wouldn't allow these girls to see her embarrassment. How could they already know about her transfer? Even here, news didn't travel that fast. Then Lilli realized what they were referring to. "You mean because I kicked Mr. Peabody?"

"Yeah, you'd better believe it," Marilyn said. "That is exactly what I'm talking about—what everyone is talking about." The other girls joined in with nods and giggles.

Lilli felt an overpowering need to escape their questioning. What did she have in common with these snotty girls with their smooth, glossy hair and twin sweater sets? They were so self-confident and shallow.

She picked up her hamburger and tried to choke it down as swiftly as possible, before they could ask her more of their nosy questions. The bun tasted like raw dough. It gummed up between Lilli's teeth, forcing her to stop chewing and reach over to sip from her soft drink.

"How did you have the nerve?" Lois gushed. "We've all been dying to ask you."

Lilli couldn't speak as she was still trying to finish chewing. Maybe if she remained silent Lois would leave her alone? Lois was so . . . so Miss Dream Girl. So different. She had a cute turned-up nose with a dusting of freckles, a short, blond pageboy hairstyle that stayed in place even on rainy days, a fuzzy pink sweater and a matching pleated skirt.

And then Lilli's gaze settled on Barbara Deutsch. There wasn't a single scuff mark on Barbara's saddle shoes. And her hands—smooth hands, not a blemish. The nails were painted a pale pink.

Miss Perfect. All Lilli could think of was her sister, Feyla, and Feyla's raw hands permanently scarred by the dreadful lye they'd used in the factory. She'd have to send Feyla her new address immediately, although Feyla didn't write that often. She was probably busy settling into her own new life in Palestine.

"What happened in the principal's office?" Barbara asked.

"What did your foster parents say? How did you manage that dragon lady, Mrs. Chandler?" Marilyn demanded.

Lilli grinned, she couldn't help herself, although she wasn't prepared to disclose her new situation—not right now. "Dragon lady? I like that expression. You really think she's a dragon too?"

"Everyone knows how difficult she is," Marilyn replied. "My mother says—no, I'd better not quote my mother. I'll get in deep doody."

Another of their strange expressions. They'd finished eating and were taking turns getting up to place their trays back on the side table. Those who had brought lunches from home crumpled up their paper bags and tossed them in the garbage can. Lilli could tell that they were the type of girls who always obeyed the rules.

"So, tell us," Lois demanded.

"Tell what?"

"About how you stood up to Mr. Peabody!"

Lilli was startled to hear that they cared. "What's to tell?" she asked.

"Oh, come on, we're dying to hear everything. The whole school is talking about you and your run-in with Mr. Peabody," Marilyn insisted.

After absorbing that last remark, Lilli was no longer merely perplexed but anxious to escape. She felt like an exotic fish trapped in a huge, glass tank, like the one in the Chinese restaurant they had once visited. Everyone was peering down at her, watching each flutter of her gills and tail. Was there no escape?

"Hey, we'd better hurry up if we're going across the street for treats before school starts," Marion said.

"Sure, right away," Marilyn agreed, looking down at her wrist. She sported a tiny watch on a red band. "Lilli can tell us all about it while we're walking. Okay, Lilli?"

Lilli wasn't quite sure what they wanted from her. Was she the curiosity of the day? Would they humour her with ice cream in a Dixie cup so she'd spill some gossip? Was that how it worked with these girls? Without giving it further thought, Lilli managed a brusque shake of her head. No, no, she decided. Let them get their kicks some other way.

"No thanks, afraid not."

They looked so startled at her refusal that she felt the need to add something more.

"I'm really sorry, I have so much catching up to do that I can't join you. Perhaps another time."

That silenced them.

"Bye-bye." Lilli picked up her tray, deposited it with all the other empties and headed toward the hall. Her pace slowed as she reached the door.

"Can you believe that?" she heard Barbara say as the other girls made their way down the corridor. Lilli slipped through an open classroom door. "Lilli Blankstein just dumped us. Those Greenies are definitely not normal."

"Aw, guys, forget it," Marilyn replied as the girls strolled down the hall toward the double front doors leading to the Kerrisdale shopping district. "She probably thought we were snooping."

"For sure," Lilli mumbled to herself. The door slammed behind the girls, blocking off the remainder of their conversation. But Lilli had heard enough. She'd heard enough to know that, with the possible exception of Marilyn, these girls were not to be trusted.

Chapter Thirteen

Danny

Danny was thrilled with his first paychecque. The crisp piece of paper made up for all sorts of things he'd been missing. At first he even thought about framing it and hanging it on the wall—an outlandish idea. When he presented Mrs. Halpern with the rent money he was bursting with pride. She tried to refuse it but he insisted that he'd move elsewhere if she didn't accept his contribution.

Danny's boss seemed to like him, and he'd already been transferred from shipping, in the back section of the warehouse, to the front showroom. Mr. Block claimed that Danny was a whiz at adding and subtracting figures, so he was teaching Danny bookkeeping. He allowed Danny to perform many tasks in the office. Naturally, that often resulted in working overtime, but that surely was the swiftest route to getting ahead.

These extra responsibilities kept Danny away from the house, so Betty stopped pestering him to go out with her and her friends and he no longer had to make up excuses. And Danny had struck up a conversation with an interesting girl he'd met when he went to hear a speaker at the Jewish Community Centre. Two weeks later they'd attended a movie together—a double feature. Unfortunately, the next time he called Arliss, she declined to see him.

"I suppose you already have another date," he said, innocently enough. "I'll call again."

"No, Danny, don't bother. That's not the reason."

From her cool tone of voice he sensed that it would probably be safer not to probe; unfortunately, his curiosity got the better of him. Being naive—no, he corrected himself, being a natural-born idiot—he simply had to complete the intimidating conversation.

"Then why not?" He immediately knew that he had asked the wrong question. There was an awkward silence. Then he could hear Arliss take a deep breath.

"Because," she responded, "you are too difficult to be with—I mean, for a long time, for a whole evening. You're so serious," she continued. "Sometimes you are a real pill. I have no idea what you are thinking and really, I don't much care."

"Oh."

"I don't want to hurt your feelings, Danny, but I go out with boys to have fun and a good time. And frankly, you're no fun."

Those words really jolted him. She didn't want to hurt him? What a joke! At the very least she had taught him a lesson in absolute rejection.

"Well, I guess that covers everything. So long, Arliss. And thank you for telling me about my bleak character. Your explanation of my many faults will save me from paying a psychiatrist for his advice."

She retorted with: "Ha-ha."

Surely she could have come up with something a bit more original? Maybe his dismissal wasn't such a huge loss after all. Danny vowed to resist all girls—particularly North American girls—for the next couple of months. Too dangerous and too expensive. At least for his ego.

When the newcomers met at the Vancouver Jewish Community Centre that Sunday, Kurt confirmed Danny's decision. Kurt told them about his own strange dating experience the previous week. The girl, Irene Gilbert, had invited him to a special family party at the Commodore Ballroom. During their initial conversation, she had made quite a point about the dress requirements for the event: was Kurt prepared to wear a suit and tie?

"Of course, I have a beautiful suit," he had responded with great impatience. "Why do you ask?"

"Because it is a formal family affair, and many people will be wearing tuxedos. There will also be dancing with a band, so you should know what to expect in advance. Just so there are no surprises."

According to Kurt, the first inkling of trouble occurred when he rang the family doorbell.

Her mother, who answered the door, stared down at his empty hands as though she expected him to produce some package. Mrs. Gilbert then led him into the family den where the father, dressed in a tux, looked up from his newspaper briefly and said, "You certainly look a lot older than seventeen to me."

Kurt was too stunned to give an answer right away. After a few minutes of silence he said, "In my family we all—we all mature early."

"You don't say," Mr. Gilbert muttered, giving Kurt the evil eye.

Did this man think Kurt was some sort of imposter or a European menace out to ruin his daughter? Whatever the old man was thinking, it was obviously negative. And Kurt was unaccustomed to people who resisted his charm.

Kurt reached for the gleaming white handkerchief in his breast pocket and mopped his face, grateful that Mrs. Goodman had stuffed the stupid hanky into his pocket prior to his departure. He was getting more and more nervous. He was also thankful, he told Danny, that he'd shaved a second time that evening. But where was his elusive date hiding?

He was almost sure that the father was studying him closely from behind that newspaper shield.

Ten minutes later, the father bellowed at the mother, "Tell that daughter of mine to get down here immediately. She's making us late for the party. Enough of her primping."

The reaction was instantaneous, as though someone had set off a fire alarm. First he heard a rustling sound, then his date swept down the staircase.

"What did Irene wear?" the girls asked as Kurt continued his story. "Was she beautiful?"

Kurt paused for a moment. "Oh, yeah, she was really stunning— like that girl, you know the one on the cover of those chocolate boxes with that rainbow behind her?"

"Pot of Gold, that's what they call those chocolates," Sylvie said wistfully.

Kurt attempted to describe Irene's dress, using hand gestures to show the puffed sleeves and the sweetheart neckline. The girls lapped it up.

But it was all downhill from that point, as Kurt explained. When Irene arrived in the den, hoisting up the hem of her long gown, she immediately asked: "So, where is my corsage?"

"Your what?" Kurt replied.

"My corsage of flowers. Boys always bring a corsage to girls when they are invited as guests to such a formal event."

"I'm afraid I've never heard of that custom. Is it important?"

"Important? Everyone will laugh at me. I'll be the only girl there without a corsage," she wailed.

Kurt was crushed. Finally her mother solved their mutual embarrassment by picking a white camellia from a bush in the garden and making it into a wristlet for her daughter.

"And then?" everyone asked Kurt. "Was everything okay after that?"

Kurt shook his head as he continued his tale.

"Everything was swell during the party."

They arrived just as the soup course was being served. The dinner and the dancing went okay, because, as Kurt boasted, "One of the nurses in the camp taught me how to dance the jitterbug, the foxtrot and the waltz, so we got along great, as long as we kept to the dance floor."

"So, so what else could go wrong?" Lilli asked.

His friends held their breath as Kurt picked up his saga. It was strange, Danny thought, how the kids seemed to feel that the event was happening to them personally. Each of them—like Danny himself—was probably taking mental notes in case they faced a similar situation in the future.

"Disaster. Her parents went home early so we had no transportation."

"What do you mean, no transportation? Weren't there buses or streetcars?"

"Of course there were buses and streetcars."

"So?"

"It was snowing."

"What? Like the time it snowed a couple of weeks ago?" Sylvie said.

"What's that got to do with anything? There's hardly any snow here, and when there is, it melts immediately," Sophie insisted.

Lilli asked, "So, was Miss Pot of Gold going to melt?"

"She was wearing new satin shoes and she said they'd be ruined. She refused to take a streetcar. When I made the suggestion, she exploded."

"No kidding? So what happened next?" Lilli said.

"I called a taxicab. Just my luck she lived way out near Jericho Beach. I kept watching that meter go up and up and up. It took every last cent I had to pay for the trip. And she didn't even thank me when I escorted her to the door. She slammed it in my face."

Danny guessed that Kurt had been anticipating a good-night kiss, or at least a peck on the cheek.

"So that's it, that's the story of my Canadian date. It took me two hours to walk home in the drizzle and I ruined my best shoes."

"Serves you right for going out with one of *them*," Sylvie said.

Lilli remained silent but nodded her head—in a gleeful manner, Danny thought.

They argued for a while about the Vancouver teens and whether they should try harder to understand them or give up the effort altogether.

"They think we are aliens," Sophie said.

"Or else most of them dislike us," Lilli suggested.

"Come on, Lilli. You just don't have enough faith in people," Kurt admonished her.

"I suppose it's also our problem not understanding the way things work over here," Danny insisted. "I feel ignorant and strange at times, but I'm very grateful for being here. We've all got to look on the positive side of things."

Kurt agreed. "There are many people like the Goodmans who are willing to do anything to help us fit in."

They spent the next half hour listening to Kurt brag about how he had been elected captain of yet another team in his school.

Max had remained unusually quiet during their discussion but insisted that everything was fine. His paper route was growing and the Meltzers were taking him with them to their cottage in Penticton in the summer.

"Lucky you," Lilli told him. "At least you get paid for your work. At my new place, the Davidsons never pay me for babysitting at night. They go out, both of them, practically every evening. Their kids are really cute but spoiled rotten."

Sophie claimed the whole town was still talking about what had happened between Lilli and her English teacher, but that was a month ago now, and Sophie exaggerated everything. Lilli still attended Totem Point School so it couldn't have been that bad. Lilli and the Chandlers had parted company the previous month. She hated talking about it, so Danny hesitated to ask too many questions.

"At least I haven't lost my hair or my schooling," Lilli said. "Mr. and Mrs. Davidson don't give a hoot whether I keep my hair short or grow it out until it reaches my knees. Now that's what I call a positive note. Of course, I don't have much spare time to wash it any more. And it's a smaller house. But I'd rather be living there than with the Chandlers."

She glanced up at the wall clock and gave a long whistle. "Oh boy, I'm going to be in deep trouble. I have babysitting duties in ten minutes." She jumped to her feet.

Sophie objected, "But it's Sunday."

"Sunday somewhere else." She was gone before Sophie could think of a response.

After they separated, Danny stepped into the community library to check out a book. He bumped into Marilyn Becker as he was leaving, and she asked how he was getting along at his high school.

"What do you mean, you're no longer in school?" she insisted. "How come? You're so smart!"

"Think so?" Danny said. "How could you tell when we only talked for a few minutes?"

"There are certain things I just know," she replied. "And I know—for certain—that you're no stupe. I'm really sorry to hear you gave it up."

Danny explained that he still attended night school, and before he knew exactly what was happening, they were both seated in the library. They talked for at least an hour. Danny came to the conclusion that Marilyn was no dummy herself—very opinionated, but certainly smart.

Chapter Fourteen

Marilyn

Marilyn woke up one morning and heard her parents squabbling downstairs, which was a rare occurrence. They were arguing about something Marilyn's father seemed to have misplaced. Their conversation was difficult to hear because the radio in the den was blaring away, but she thought she heard her father mention "chains." After struggling to find her clothing and misplaced homework, she glanced in the bathroom mirror before heading downstairs. Just her luck, another pimple had sprouted beside her right nostril. By the time she arrived in the den, both parents had disappeared.

She turned down the sound on the large radio, standing in its shiny mahogany cabinet. The announcer boomed out his message in a clipped British accent. The Arabs had attacked a Jewish convoy, taking forty-five lives in a place called Kabiri in northern Palestine, and he warned of renewed tensions.

"An earlier Arab attack against another food convoy moving between Jewish communities was counterattacked," he continued.

Marilyn paused to scrawl a few notes just in case Mr. Peabody questioned them about current events. She received A's in most subjects but she was always competing for top marks with Eric Hill, so she tried to keep ahead of the game whenever possible. Last week Mr. Peabody had asked whether the American president, Harry Truman, was going to run again on the Democratic ticket. Eric's arm had flailed in the air while Marilyn remained clueless. Taking a few notes couldn't hurt.

Then she plunked herself down on the fake-leather banquette in the kitchen nook and dug into her bowl of puffed wheat. Only after she'd demolished half of the cereal did she look up. She was so startled by the view from the window behind her that she spoke aloud to the empty room.

"Unbelievable! Look at the snow." It was March 27. A snowfall this late in the season was almost unheard of in Vancouver. As Marilyn raised her spoon again, a gust of frigid air streamed through the kitchen. Her parents entered through the back door.

"You'd better hurry," her mom said. "You're going to have trouble getting to school on time today."

"What's going on?" Marilyn asked as her father dragged a dusty pile of heavy chains behind him. "Do you plan on capturing your own prisoner today, Pops?"

"Really, Marilyn, didn't you look outside? You can't ride your bicycle to school in these conditions."

She glanced outside again and noticed that the lawn was already heavily blanketed in the white stuff. The camellia bushes that had bloomed in riotous colours only the previous day were doubled over in frostbitten grief.

"Ohmygosh, no wonder Pops needs chains."

"Your mother found them hidden in the very back corner of the garage under the lawn furniture," he said, giving his wife an accusatory scowl.

Mrs. Becker flicked back a wet, grey curl and zipped off her black, fur-trimmed overshoes, carefully placing the boots on an old newspaper. "They were exactly where you left them three years ago," she answered breezily.

"Perhaps I'll ask someone from the service station to put them on." Mr. Becker stared down at the heap of rusting metal.

"In that case, will you please drive me to school?"

Mrs. Becker said, "It will be impossible to find a serviceman this late. They're probably overwhelmed with emergency calls."

Mr. Becker nodded. "I suppose you're right. Sorry, Marilyn, I can't drive you today. I'm already running late for work."

"By the time your father manages to fit the chains on the tires, you'll be late for school. Forget that idea, miss," her mom said.

"But it's cold out there."

As if on cue, the radio broadcast was interrupted by a flash bulletin. The announcer talked about the freak snowstorm. "We are facing near-blizzard conditions this morning—weather that is blanketing the Vancouver area in heavy snow. Traffic is almost at a standstill in some areas as workers try to get snow equipment out on major thoroughfares."

The announcer repeatedly warned about slow traffic conditions and mentioned especially hazardous spots, including the small hill at Granville Street and 16th Avenue.

"Granville Street is treacherous. The buses are having problems getting up all hills today, so please look for alternate routes if you are heading downtown."

"That does it," her father said. "Why is Vancouver never prepared for even the smallest snowstorm?"

"Because they so rarely happen and we don't have the proper equipment for snow removal," Mom replied. "Now, back when I was a child in Winnipeg . . ."

"Maybe I should stay home today?"

"No, you are not made of sugar, Marilyn. Why, when I grew up on the prairies . . ." Mrs. Becker was off and running with her familiar tales about her own difficult childhood years in the province of Manitoba—all that stuff about how easy life was for Marilyn's generation, the stories Marilyn had heard over and over again.

"Enough," Marilyn's father replied. "Dress up warmly and go to school. You won't melt."

"Sure I will. Just like the wicked witch in *The Wizard of Oz*," Marilyn snapped back as her dad folded her into one of his bear hugs.

Her mother returned from the front hall closet and handed her dad an old coat, which smelled of mothballs, a pair of her own gardening gloves and his grey felt snap-brim fedora. He plopped the hat on at a perky angle and then headed outside, rattling his load of chains as he walked. Mrs. Becker quickly inspected her daughter's outfit. Marilyn was wearing a sweater and skirt under her everyday navy wool jacket.

"You are not going to school with bare legs today. In this weather you'd risk getting frostbite." Her mother snapped her fingers and ordered Marilyn back upstairs to change into a pair of wool trousers.

"You might be right, Mom. Yesterday, when the weather started to change, the school furnaces didn't give enough heat. We all wished we'd kept our coats on during class."

"See what I mean? That's all you need—a case of pneumonia. In this weather nobody will complain about appearances. The main object is warmth. After all, you have a ten-block walk to school."

Mrs. Becker concluded a second inspection when Marilyn returned. "That's better. You look fine. Now cover your nose with my red scarf. This old toque of Helen's will protect your ears."

Her mother plunked the toque so low over Marilyn's forehead that she practically couldn't see. Giving Marilyn a brief hug, she sent her out into the storm. Marilyn waved goodbye to her father, who was honking the car horn, apparently hoping it would bring Mrs. Becker outdoors again to assist him with the wretched chains.

It took about three times longer than usual to walk to school because the snow was so deep and mushy. Marilyn's rubber boots squeaked and squelched as she plunged through the mounting drifts of snow. She arrived just as the first bell sounded. Dashing to her locker, she dumped the boots and hung up her outer garments. It was then that she realized she'd forgotten to pack a skirt to wear in class. Girls weren't allowed to wear pants in school, but she decided nobody would care on such a miserable day. She ducked into her homeroom just before the conclusion of roll call.

Looking up, Mr. Peabody shot Marilyn one of his piercing stares. Fortunately no sarcastic remarks followed. After the prayer reading, he called Marilyn up to his desk and nodded when she explained why she was late. Since three of her classmates had arrived even later, she didn't feel particularly guilty.

Next, it was home economics. When she entered the sewing room, Miss Jeffries gave her a sharp look. Then, after pointing to a list of instructions on the blackboard, the teacher excused herself and left the girls alone to copy down their new assignment. It was a horrendous one. The girls were supposed to choose dress patterns and fabrics in order to sew "suitable" spring dresses for themselves—whatever that was supposed to mean.

Marilyn groaned. While several girls chattered on about the special fabrics they would purchase, she fantasized about next fall, when she would enter Magee High School. Once there, she'd finally have a choice of options and would never again be forced to study home economics. She'd have a choice of drama, art, typing, some additional languages and maybe even journalism. Anything but home economics.

Marilyn, who was seated at a table directly behind Lilli's, overheard Lilli ask her partner: "Are we allowed to do all our sewing at school? There is no sewing machine in the house where I live."

Lilli did not mention the fact that she had no mother to help choose her pattern or her fabric. Although Marilyn knew that Lilli was no longer living with the Chandlers, she had no idea where the orphan had moved to. Mrs. Becker had mentioned some falling out with the Chandlers and Marilyn decided the girl was better off away from the dragon lady. Surely Lilli's new foster mother would offer some assistance.

"I can't wait to go shopping with my mother. I know exactly what I'll purchase," Lois gushed. "I'm going to make a scoop-neck peasant dress with a broomstick skirt. That's the latest."

"How can you talk about spring dresses on such a cold day? Gee, Marilyn, aren't you the smart one to think of wearing pants?" Barbara said. "I'd like to give that old radiator a kick. It's freezing in here."

Marilyn looked down briefly at her trousers and nodded her agreement. Troubled by the immensity of the new assignment, she wasn't prepared to think of much else.

"Do you think I could fool her with a sheath dress—two pieces of plain material with a small hole for my head at the top and a wider one for my legs at the bottom?" she asked. "I'd call it the 'New Look' . . . something like the designs from that Dior guy in Paris. Do you think Miss Jeffries would care?"

At that moment, Miss Jeffries returned. "Marilyn Becker, you are to go to the office, immediately," she announced.

Marilyn looked up, puzzled. "Why is that, Miss Jeffries? I already explained to Mr. Peabody why I was late this morning. Because of the snowstorm."

Miss Jeffries clapped her hands and the long bishop sleeves of her beige silk blouse rustled as she motioned. "Please don't argue. To the office with you."

Giving Lois a shrug, Marilyn left her loose-leaf binder sitting open on the wide table she shared with five other girls. Then she headed down the hall and up the stairs to the school office on the main floor. She stopped at the high counter there and spoke to one of the secretaries.

"I'm Marilyn Becker, but I don't know why they wanted me to report here."

Before replying, the secretary studied Marilyn closely from the top of her head to the bottom of her red penny loafers. "Oh, yes, the principal, Mr. James, is at his desk, talking on the telephone. Please wait here." She pointed to a bench.

Mr. James eventually called her into his office. "Good morning, Marilyn," he said.

Extremely tall, even when seated, Mr. James appeared old enough to be Marilyn's grandfather. He had a huge head that was completely bald; the way it shone, you'd almost think he deliberately polished it each morning before school. Marilyn knew that he'd served as principal of their school for many years, but she'd never been singled out by him during the two and a half years she'd attended Totem Point.

"Pardon me, sir, I'm sorry I was late this morning. I'll bring a note from my mother tomorrow. But the snow and the traffic . . . and . . ."

He didn't appear to be listening to her but quickly motioned to a hard wooden chair. "Sit down, please. This has nothing to do with tardiness. It has to do with the fact that you flouted our dress code."

"Beg your pardon, sir?" What did "flouted" mean?

"Do not interrupt when I am speaking, young lady. You have broken the Totem Point Junior High School dress code. I am sending you home to change out of those despicable trousers." He looked directly at Marilyn as if daring her to disagree. "Do you understand?"

Marilyn struggled to make sense of this. "No, sir, I really don't get it. I mean I don't . . . understand. What is wrong?" She searched the room as though anticipating the entrance of another student, the real culprit. He couldn't be talking about her, could he?

"Those trousers, those impossible pants." He pointed toward her navy gabardine trousers with a finger that shook, his expression one of total disgust.

"Oh." The word slipped through her lips accompanied by a whistling sound. "My pants, sir? You object to my trousers, is that it, sir?" Despite her nervousness, she steeled herself to look directly up at Mr. James.

His tone of voice became even more intense. "Of course that is it. Don't play innocent with me, young lady. You have broken one of our primary rules. Nobody, in all my years as principal, has ever broken that regulation."

"But it was snowing hard and my mother insisted."

"Then I shall also speak to your mother. Nobody breaks the rules in this school, Marilyn. Your behaviour is totally unacceptable for a properly brought-up girl. Now return directly to your classroom, pack up your belongings and go home. You are suspended from this school until tomorrow. As you are well aware, every girl in this school is specifically forbidden to wear trousers on school property."

"But my mother . . ." she murmured. "My mother said that it was okay."

He opened the door and stood stock-still, expecting her to slink out of his sight. As she passed the front desk, the three secretaries peered over the counter to get a glimpse of the girl wearing the abominable trousers.

When she entered the home economics classroom, Marilyn sensed twenty-four pairs of eyes focused on her. She felt like a human dartboard. Miss Jeffries had obviously known the situation when she'd first dispatched Marilyn to the office; perhaps it was she who had informed Mr. James about Marilyn's crime. On the other hand, the other teachers would probably have done the same thing. Marilyn supposed it was their duty to rat on her. It might even have been a fellow student who blabbed, although she found that idea particularly infuriating.

She shuffled her notes into a single pile and packed them into her zippered loose-leaf binder.

"What is going on, Marilyn? Why are you leaving?" Barbara asked.

Marilyn mumbled something about being suspended.

"You're what?"

By that point Marilyn had packed up every item she owned. She was practically dizzy from embarrassment but attempted to remain cucumber-calm in front of her gawking classmates.

"I've been suspended from school for wearing pants," she hissed.

All eyes immediately settled on her lower torso, as if some fearsome aliens had clamped on to her bottom half. Perhaps extraterrestrial creatures were slithering down her pant legs right now. *Honestly,* she told herself, *you'd think they'd never seen a girl wear pants before.* She was mortified.

"They are throwing Marilyn out of school for wearing trousers?" Lilli asked her neighbour. "Is that true, Miss Jeffries?" She waved her hand in the air.

Miss Jeffries, who had pretended not to hear the conversation, was trapped by Lilli's shrill words.

"Yes," she reluctantly replied. "That is it. Now, that's enough. Don't let Marilyn's misbehaviour give the rest of you any foolish ideas."

"But they can't do that. It's totally unfair." Lilli's voice was so loud that every girl in the room heard her words. "What kind of crazy rule is that?" she asked again.

While Marilyn made her way toward the door, Lilli continued

questioning her classmates. "But boys wear pants all the time. It's cold today. It makes no sense," she complained.

She was still speaking to the class as Marilyn managed a slight wave and closed the door on all of them.

Chapter Fifteen

Marilyn

The alarm clock jangled. Still bleary-eyed, Marilyn reached out of bed and slammed it off. Then, jumping up, she immediately raised the venetian blinds. It was still snowing heavily. Another day of heavy snow—wonderful! When she dashed downstairs and reported this to her sister, Sally, who was home from Seattle for the weekend, Sally was slightly taken aback by Marilyn's joy.

"I thought you hated snow. You do realize Dad won't be able to drive you to school today," Sally said. "He promised that I could drive him to work and take the car for the rest of the day. My boyfriend's old jalopy is on the fritz again."

"I know, I know, I know," Marilyn replied as she gobbled down the French toast her mother had left for her. It was usually her favourite breakfast, but today she had more important things on her mind.

"I don't get it," her suspicious sister replied.

"You'll see," Marilyn said, staring down at her trousers. Today she'd chosen a pair that matched her sweater. They were grey with a small glen-check pattern. Undoubtedly they, too, would be considered offensive.

"How come you're wearing pants—weren't you ordered home from school for wearing pants yesterday?" Sally asked.

"Mmm-hmm."

"I don't get it."

"Easy. Mom was so annoyed about them sending me home from school that she wrote a note stating specifically that I had her permission to wear pants in school if the weather was severe. I believe 'inclement' was Mom's exact term."

"So Mom's on the warpath again. Nothing new about that. It just means you'll be in even more hot water today."

"Aha! But today things will be different. I won't be the only girl in school wearing trousers!"

Sally looked blankly at her but Marilyn rushed off—she had no time for explanations.

When Marilyn got to school and reached the lockers, Barbara was already slouched against them. Barbara wore a cream shirt, a brown cardigan sweater and chocolate-coloured wool slacks. Marion arrived a few minutes later. After shaking the snowflakes out of her straight auburn hair, she hurriedly discarded her navy raincoat so her friends could view her brand-new navy stride pants, which had wide, draped legs pulled tight at the ankles, the latest rage. A few seconds later, Lois arrived with two friends who also sported slacks. The girls remained at their lockers waiting anxiously for the leader of their grand plan.

And suddenly Lilli appeared, puffing as she dropped her load of books. Marilyn still found the whole situation quite incredible. Who would have imagined that Lilli, the outsider, could have persuaded these girls from their sewing class to wear pants to school?

"I am stunned," Barbara gushed, looking down on all of them

from her superior height. "Lilli is amazing. No sooner did you leave class, Marilyn, than she started a whispering campaign."

"You forgot to mention how it all began," Lois reminded her.

"Oh, yeah. After you left, Mr. James sent round a notice to every classroom. It said that girls were forbidden to wear slacks in school."

"He specifically stated that girls could not wear pants, no matter what the weather was like," Lois continued, brushing an invisible speck off her charcoal-grey flannels.

Barbara broke into the conversation. "During recess, Lilli insisted that his demands were unfair. Then she asked what we were going to do about it. As I explained on the phone last night, at first we simply gawked at her. We thought she had flipped. Then we got talking on the way home after school and agreed that she was correct and—and—that you shouldn't be alone in this situation."

"Besides, it might be fun." Lois gave a vigorous nod of her head.

"Naturally, if the weather had improved we wouldn't have gone ahead with the plan," Barbara added.

Lilli interrupted. "I really hate people telling me what I must do when it's only good for them." The girls stared at the deep greens and blacks of Lilli's Black Watch tartan pants. Marilyn thought Lilli's pants looked rather festive given their present circumstances.

While depositing her books in a locker, Lilli continued to talk. "What right have they—Miss Jeffries, Mr. James and the school authorities—to make us freeze our bottoms when the boys are allowed to keep warm? How dare they bounce Marilyn from class just because of the way she dresses? Treat her like she's done something disgusting like wearing—oh—"

"Revealing clothing?" Barbara suggested.

"Yeah, when actually she's more covered up than before. This is a free country, isn't it?"

"Yes, you're right," Marion agreed. "And the school furnaces are on the blink again today. It's a hardship wearing skirts when it's this cold inside."

"I agree," said Lois's wispy little friend Janine, as she attempted to pump up their courage. "We don't want to let pneumonia in here, do we?" She made pneumonia sound like somebody's unwelcome guest.

"I have a note from my mother giving me permission to wear trousers." Marilyn waved her envelope in the air.

"My mother's letter is two pages long," Barbara said. "Boy, was she browned off when she heard what happened to you."

When the first bell rang they stopped talking and looked at one another nervously. Marilyn decided it was only normal to feel apprehensive when you were defying authority. Were they making idiots of themselves in front of the entire school? Maybe they were only fooling themselves, thinking that they could force a change in the rules. She glanced back at Lilli; she was the only one who didn't appear the slightest bit anxious. The other girls were fussing with their lockers or leafing idly through their textbooks as though they'd discovered unfamiliar treasures. But finally there were no more excuses for dawdling and they were forced to shuffle down the hall toward their classrooms.

"Come on, girls," Lilli urged. "We can do it. Believe me, there are a lot more frightening things in this world than wearing slacks to class."

"You're right." Marilyn nodded, picking up her pace.

Everyone gawked at Lilli and Marilyn when they entered their homeroom. Mr. Peabody stared at them silently. Although a few boys whispered feeble jokes under their breath—suggesting that the girls were attempting to steal their pants—everyone else remained silent.

There were no more disruptions, and minutes later, strolling down the corridor to their next classes, the two girls congratulated themselves on their reception.

As Marilyn settled into her seat in her final class of the morning, someone whispered that a few additional girls had defied the authorities by wearing slacks—not just grade nine girls, either, but girls from grades seven and eight. Later, on her way to lunch, Marilyn passed this rumour on to Lilli.

Lilli's face lit up when she heard this information. "Great," she said. "I told my friend Sylvie to pass around the word, so perhaps she did."

Just when Marilyn had started to relax, assuming that they were no longer at risk, there was an announcement over the public-address system.

"All girls wearing slacks in class this morning must go immediately to the office," the disembodied voice boomed.

Marilyn, Lily, Barbara, Marion, Lois and Janine all arrived at the office as the noon buzzer sounded. They were joined by a handful of girls from the lower grades. The only one Marilyn knew by name was Lilli's friend Sylvie. There were eleven of them altogether. They clustered in the outer office until a secretary directed them to a large room with a long, dark walnut table and high-backed chairs lined up like soldiers on either side of it.

Poor kids, Marilyn thought as she studied the younger students. *They're probably quaking inside, just like me.*

Mr. James kept them waiting another five minutes. "Girls," he said when he entered, scowling down on them. "You know why you are here. You heard yesterday's announcement. We have definite and absolute rules about wearing slacks in class. Slacks are forbidden. You have not complied with Totem Point rules."

Marilyn squirmed inwardly as his eyes settled on her. He looked so solemn that she wished she could melt into the seat of the hard chair. Instead, she sat up abruptly, her voice cracking with anxiety when she spoke. "But our mothers sent notes giving us permission to dress like this." The other girls murmured their agreement.

Mr. James raised his hand, open palm turned outward, demanding silence. "Young ladies, Marilyn Becker had fair warning yesterday and failed to obey my orders to change into a skirt today. You have all been given notice and I am saddened by your unspeakable behaviour. You are suspended from school until I am satisfied that you, and your families, have understood my message and are prepared to conform to school board rules."

Everyone avoided looking directly at Mr. James. Only Lilli met Marilyn's anxious glance. She didn't appear the least bit intimidated by the principal's anger. Marilyn willed herself to concentrate on Mr. James's shiny bald head, hoping he would change his mind—*willing* him to change his mind.

"Girls, you are dismissed."

He snapped his fingers, then swivelled abruptly and left the room.

"Now what?" Marilyn asked as soon as the door closed behind him.

"We go home and wait," Barbara replied.

"I think we made our point," Lilli said as they trooped out of the office. "Loud and clear."

The three office secretaries shot the girls sly glances when they marched past the front desk. Several students lined the corridor to their lockers. Not a single one spoke to them. Marilyn and the others moved closer together, almost forming a pack.

"They're treating us like criminals," Barbara muttered. She walked in a stooped position, as if to minimize her height. Nobody replied.

"Way to go, grade nine," somebody whispered hesitantly as they passed by the auditorium.

"Good for you, girls." Another, slightly louder voice.

By the time they'd reached their lockers they were feeling less sheepish and slightly more courageous.

"Thanks, Lilli. Thanks for all your support," Marilyn said as they buttoned their coats and fiddled with their boots. "Hey, give me your telephone number so I can call you after I speak to my mother," she continued as Lilli headed for the door. "I'm not sure where we go from here."

Lilli turned back now, grinning, and scribbled down her number on a scrap of paper.

"What a weird sensation, leaving school at noon on a Friday," Marion exclaimed once she and Marilyn were outside, on their way home. "I mean, it's not as if we are deliberately playing hooky or anything like that. This is certainly not your normal everyday detention. This is serious business," she continued as they crunched through the thick snow.

The following morning when Marilyn arrived downstairs for breakfast, her parents and Sally were already seated in the nook waiting for her. Her mother waved the Vancouver *Province* in Marilyn's face. Marilyn studied the headline.

Totem Point School Bans Slacks

Eleven girls were sent home from Totem Point Junior High School Friday because they wore slacks in class.

Principal F. E. James told them to go home and put on dresses after they ignored a warning that their attire was against the rules. Some later returned in skirts.

A student spokesman said both students and their parents were "incensed" by this action.

School board chairman Mrs. Jean George said she was "inclined to agree with the girls," but that it was up to individual principals to decide such matters and take what action they saw fit to enforce their rules. School Superintendent V. C. McTaggert said policy on this question was up to the individual principals.

"In the past, during cold spells, rules might have been relaxed somewhat."

Several mothers supported their daughters' refusal to wear skirts. "I don't believe girls should wear slacks all year round but slacks are the most intelligent thing they can wear in this kind of weather," one mother said.

"Oh dear, who could imagine that a pair of slacks would cause so much trouble," Mrs. Becker told Marilyn as they studied the newspaper together. Then both of them smiled.

Later that morning, Mrs. Becker announced that a reporter from the Vancouver *Sun* was coming to interview their family. "He may bring a photographer, so we will all wear our slacks today."

"Wow," Marilyn said. Then she had an idea. "I must ask Lilli to join us. It was her idea to involve the other girls. But I get the feeling they keep her pretty busy at her new place."

"Oh, really," Mrs. Becker replied. "If that's the case, maybe I should call her foster home myself?" She nodded. "Yes, I think it will be more helpful coming from me."

When Mrs. Becker told Marilyn to leave the room while she placed the call, Marilyn realized that getting permission for Lilli to visit their home was not going to be an easy task. Forced to eavesdrop, Marilyn overheard her mom coaxing a lady called Mrs. Davidson. It sounded as though Mrs. Davidson was annoyed at letting Lilli out for an hour on a Saturday.

"Of course I understand how difficult it is to change a standing hair appointment on a Saturday morning," Mrs. Becker said soothingly. "It must be very hard, but . . ."

Marilyn secretly bet on her mom prevailing in the standoff. Although she was never sure how her mother quite did it, Mrs. Becker had a special skill for persuading others to bend to her will.

"Only for a half hour," Marilyn heard her mom tell Mrs. David-son. "I promise to drive her back immediately after the interview. Yes, that's what he said. There may be a photo shoot, in which case her picture will appear in the newspaper. No, I don't know whether they'll mention her foster home in the article but I will certainly tell them about you if she comes for the interview."

After overhearing that conversation, Marilyn's admiration for her mother increased enormously. She couldn't help thinking how difficult it must be for kids who didn't have their own spokesper-son—a mother like Mrs. Becker, who would always go to bat for her kids. She'd hate being dependent on the goodwill of outsiders for everything.

Mrs. Becker's powers of persuasion worked as usual; Mrs. David-son relented and allowed Lilli to join the Beckers. She even drove Lilli there herself.

The reporter from the Vancouver *Sun* arrived with his own pho-tographer and asked them loads of questions.

"Of course, I support the girls' decision to wear pants to school. I was the one who insisted that Marilyn wear them in the first place," Mrs. Becker told him.

"Why should boys be allowed to keep warm and girls suffer frost-bite in cold weather?" Lilli replied when the reporter asked her opin-ion. "It should be the same for everyone—girls and boys alike—when it comes to their . . . their . . . well-being."

"Absolutely," Mrs. Becker and Marilyn agreed in unison.

"There are times when everyone should feel free to wear pants," Marilyn insisted.

The reporter scribbled down every remark they made. Although Mrs. Becker didn't particularly favour the year-round wearing of slacks to school, she said, "Girls should be allowed the freedom of choice during cold weather."

Pointing to Marilyn's grey slacks, the reporter asked her mother, "Do you think Marilyn's slacks are too sensational or distracting to rate acceptance by the school board? One of the trustees suggested that yesterday."

Pushing back her tumble of greying curls, Mrs. Becker smiled. "I hardly think so. Now if she had been wearing my loud pants it might have been different." She looked down at her striped trousers.

Then the photographer positioned the group for his picture. He had a huge camera with an attached flash. The following morning the article appeared in the *Sunday Sun* newspaper. The newspaper featured a huge photo of the group and an article.

Slack-Clad Girls "Bounced" From Classes at Totem Point

A secondary headline read:

Is this Garb Improper for School?
Principal Won't Talk

The caption under the picture said:

All the Beckers support Marilyn's wearing of slacks to school these chilly days even though the principal of Totem Point Junior High School would have none of it. The whole family wears them anyway.

The photo captured Marilyn with her foot raised in the air as though she were about to boot some invisible object. Marilyn thought the picture looked rather goofy and staged but had no doubt about its ability to capture a reader's attention. Her mom's hands were jammed into the pockets of her striped trousers in a nonchalant manner. Lilli was beaming as she stared down at Marilyn's out-stretched leg. Sally remained rigid as an ironing board in her pullover sweater and beige cords.

The article said:

Typical of the "rebels" was pretty 14-year-old Marilyn Becker who was "bounced" from school when she turned up in draped glen-check slacks, a fawn sweater with a Peter Pan collar and brown bebop shoes.

Her school friend Lilli Blankstein, who is a newcomer to Canada, was also sent home from school.

The article quoted Mr. James as saying, "I don't know where this will end."

Mrs. Becker grinned as she passed along the morning paper. "How do you like this?" she asked her husband.

"I'm really proud of my girls, but who is this Lilli person?"

Marilyn told her father that he'd find out soon enough "because Mom has invited Lilli to join us for dinner tomorrow." After some hemming and hawing, Mrs. Davidson had agreed to let her attend. Marilyn had been slightly taken aback to discover how restricted Lilli's life appeared to be. As the youngest child in her own family, Marilyn had always taken her freedom for granted. And there certainly hadn't been any little ones for her to babysit.

When she arrived for dinner, Lilli was almost bashful. Marilyn's mom immediately gave her a hug, as though she'd known Lilli forever—and thanked her for participating in the interview. Lilli watched Marilyn for a moment as she carried plates and cutlery to the table, and then asked Mrs. Becker if she could help too.

During dinner Mr. Becker asked Lilli where her family came from and whether she had any living relatives.

Lilli looked up from her plate with a puzzled expression on her face. "My family?" she said.

Uh-oh, Marilyn thought. Now, for sure, there would be trouble. Pops had really put his foot into it. Didn't he realize that they were not supposed to talk about Lilli's past? That any mention of the subject was off limits?

There was only a slight pause as Lilli swallowed whatever she was chewing. Then, speaking very faintly, she answered. "Why, yes, I have an older sister who now lives in Palestine. Unfortunately they wouldn't allow her into Canada because she turned eighteen before her papers came through."

"The people on your sister's boat were lucky to sneak past the British blockade into Palestine," Mr. Becker pointed out. "So many of the survivors who tried to enter the country were caught and immediately returned to the camps in Europe—places where they'd been persecuted. The fighting there seems far from over."

"A terrible situation," Marilyn's mother added. "Who could imagine that all those war refugees, who nobody else wanted, would be turned back when they attempted to land in Palestine in their leaky boats?"

Everyone had read about the current situation in the daily newspapers. The British forces were finally leaving Palestine but they still refused the immigrants entrance to that country. Meanwhile, the 600,000 Jewish citizens who were already living in Palestine— some whose families had been there for centuries—demanded the right to establish an independent nation within that country. The British had promised them their own state, within Palestine, near the end of World War I.

"I can certainly understand why you wouldn't want to live in another war-torn country," Marilyn's mom said.

"Have you any other surviving relatives?" Mr. Becker asked Lilli while Marilyn served helpings of her mom's pineapple cheesecake.

"Nobody," she said quietly. "I . . . I had two older half-brothers who were taken away many years ago, and my own little sister, but she is also dead."

Marilyn was startled to hear about Lilli's family. She had stupidly assumed that Lilli was an only child. *Why, that's almost like our family,* she thought, *except we have four girls.*

After taking a load of dirty dishes to the kitchen, Lilli suddenly announced, "I must get back to the Davidsons' house."

"We hate to see you leave us so soon, Lilli. I'll drive you home as soon as I finish my tea," Marilyn replied.

"No thanks, Mr. Becker. I can take the bus. I must go immediately. They—they need me to babysit their two children. I promised."

"Certainly." Marilyn's father didn't ask any more questions, but insisted on driving Lilli home. He got up from the dinner table without finishing his tea. Marilyn said she'd come along for the ride.

As Marilyn's mom followed them to the front door, she insisted, "You must consider yourself welcome at our home at any time, Lilli. Please believe me when I say this. We will always have a place for you at our table."

Sally piped up, "Mom always cooks too much food."

"No doubt about it," Mr. Becker added as he helped Lilli into her coat.

"Well, thanks for everything, Mrs. Becker," Lilli replied, "but I'm not allowed out after school most days because Mrs. Davidson needs me to babysit. "

"Yes, my dear. I understand," Marilyn's mom replied. "Do tell Mrs. Davidson that I tried to get their family name into the article, but you know how independent those reporters are."

Then her mother gave Marilyn one of her piercing "what is wrong with you?" looks from behind Lilli's back. Marilyn immediately figured out what was expected of her.

"Oh, hey, yes. We'd love to have you come over here whenever you're free. I can't thank you enough, Lilli, for helping me when this whole thing blew up." Marilyn followed Lilli outside to the car.

Lilli remained silent during the drive to the Davidson house. When her father parked in front of their bungalow, Marilyn felt she must say something to comfort Lilli, to make up for the dismal conclusion of their evening. It had started out so well but the positive mood had fizzled, and now Marilyn found the silence awkward.

"Hey, Lilli," she began. "It's good to have a new friend."

She punched Lilli in the shoulder as the newcomer stepped out of the car. Lilli simply turned and responded with an even harder punch.

"See you in school on Monday—that's if they don't throw us out permanently," Marilyn said.

Giving Mr. Becker a shy wave, Lilli closed the car door and hurried up the front steps without looking back.

Chapter Sixteen

Lilli

Lilli was in deep trouble Monday morning. Mrs. Davidson insisted she was "not amused" by the articles in the Vancouver weekend newspapers. Lilli wasn't quite sure what in particular had offended Mrs. Davidson, since nobody had said anything bad about Lilli.

"You didn't like the photograph in the *Sunday Sun*?" Lilli asked, looking up from under the kitchen table. She was down there on her hands and knees because that was where Little Markie had just tossed his entire bowl of oatmeal. He'd chucked it from his high-chair tray. Fortunately for Lilli, the bowl was plastic and therefore it hadn't smashed into a thousand pieces. There were only thick, mucky gobs of cereal to be scraped off the linoleum floor.

Markie was giggling so hard that he began to hiccup. He took special delight in seeing Lilli down there. Perhaps she reminded him of a pet dog. He was obviously waiting for her to place another bowl on his tray so he could pitch the hot cereal at her a second time and hope for an equally dramatic reaction. His older sister, Carol, aged three and a half, smiled as she nibbled cautiously on a slice of toast.

"Please fetch him another bowl, Lilli," Mrs. Davidson said when Lilli had finally regained her feet. She clutched a dustpan full of the mess. "There's more oatmeal in the double boiler on the back burner."

Obedience, Lilli reminded herself, *is the better part of valor or something like that.* After wiping the residue from the bowl, she filled it once again. Mr. Davidson had already left for work. He couldn't tolerate Little Markie's morning ritual of transforming breakfast into a mud-slinging event. Mrs. Davidson stood several feet from the table so her new grey suit and matching silk blouse would not be spattered.

Lilli was concerned about being late for school but, given Mrs. Davidson's mood, she was not prepared to tempt fate. The smell of oatmeal always reminded Lilli of her first day in Auschwitz. There had been a vast pot—actually more like a huge garbage can—of farina, or watered-down oatmeal, that the Hungarian guard brought to their barracks for their meal. Of course that was before Feyla and Lilli had learned how Auschwitz operated.

"Eat fast," the guard had told them as she poured the slop into their tin bowls.

"A spoon?" Lilli had asked.

The stout woman choked with laughter. "Look at her. She is demanding a spoon and it's only her first day here. Who do you think you are, girl?"

"Lilli—Lilli, are you daydreaming again?" Mrs. Davidson said.

"Sorry. Here, sweetie," Lilli told Markie. "Let's see if we can find the lion on the bottom of the bowl." She filled the silver baby spoon with hot cereal. He grinned back at her, his single upper tooth gleaming as he opened his mouth. Oh, no, she'd seen that look before.

"Here's the airplane zooming in for a landing," she warbled while directing the spoon toward his open mouth.

"*Pffft.*" He spat the mouthful in Lilli's face. Then he gleefully pounded the table with his spoon while his chubby legs kept time against the wooden legs of the high chair.

"Bad boy, you are a very bad boy, Markie," Lilli said while attempting to scrape the specks of cereal off her freshly ironed white cotton blouse.

His mother objected. "He is not a bad boy. My precious little Markie. Did yousums get hurt feelings, my poor baby?"

Again Lilli tried to direct Mrs. Davidson's attention to the time. She had only twenty minutes to tidy herself, change her shirt and make it to school. "I'm sorry, ma'am, but I must leave for school now."

"School? That's a joke. What do you care about school, Lilli? You deliberately chose to be thrown out of school on Friday. All you seem to care about is directing attention to yourself. They warned me that you're a—a rebel. I should have known better than to take you in."

"I'm sorry, ma'am. It seemed like the right thing to do." Lilli applied a thick coating of peanut butter and jam to another smidgeon of toast for Carol. Carol grabbed it out of Lilli's hand.

Mrs. Davidson tapped the morning paper. "Look at this. The school board is declaring itself neutral on the subject of girls wearing slacks to school in cold weather. What does that mean?"

Beneath this article was a smaller item, which she pointed to with her finger. It was a poll. She read it aloud.

"'Housewife Mrs. Virginia Pugh says, "Slacks seem practical for the girls in this type of weather but I don't know how the boys will like it. I don't think slacks are immoral as long as the wearing of slacks is not carried to a ridiculous extreme." Businessman Bernard Barton says, "Being a skier myself, I can appreciate the added comfort and warmth the girls get wearing ski clothes during the snow season. As long as it is nothing outrageous and they go back to normal clothing after the weather breaks."'"

"Well, ma'am, I agree with him," Lilli said. "If boys are allowed to protect themselves in cold weather, why shouldn't girls do the same? We are all wearing skirts to school today because there is no more snow." Lilli willed Mrs. Davidson to take the hint. She had to leave for school.

Mrs. Davidson continued to study the newspaper while Lilli cleaned the sticky jam from Carol's fingers. The telephone rang.

Lilli waited for Mrs. Davidson to finish her phone conversation but once again the woman had lost track of the time. Lilli didn't believe that Mrs. Davidson did this deliberately. She was often late for her own appointments. For some reason she appeared unable to keep to a schedule.

"Please, ma'am, I'll need a late slip."

Mrs. Davidson looked up from her call. "Oh dear, I didn't realize the time. It's disappeared again. Ha! Hold on, Martha, I'm talking to her right now. One moment. I'll give you a note tomorrow, Lilli. My friends can't believe you're in that photograph and it doesn't even mention where you live."

"Please, ma'am?" Lilli passed a piece of toast to little Markie, who stuffed the entire piece into his mouth. As she gathered up her books, Carol threw her a kiss. "Babysit Caro after school, Lilli? Play peek-a-boo?"

"Certainly, Carol."

It was obviously too late for her to do anything more than hide the stains under a cardigan.

Mrs. Davidson covered the mouth of the receiver with her hand as Lilli headed toward the door. "Right after school, Lilli. I have an important doctor's appointment. I do not want to see you getting into any more trouble. You will promise to behave? No backsliding."

"Yes, Mrs. Davidson."

Lilli was confused about the meaning of that backsliding remark. Obviously, Mrs. Davidson was displeased with her. Although she'd been living with the Davidsons for only a short time, the children seemed to like her. If only Mrs. Davidson wouldn't insist on running Lilli's life all the time. She kept asking where Lilli was going each time Lilli left the house.

"Out," Lilli always told her. "I'm going out."

"Out where?" she'd reply.

Did Mrs. Davidson expect a blow-by-blow description of every single minute Lilli spent with her friends? There was no likelihood of Lilli confiding in Mrs. Davidson. None at all.

"I'm going out with my friends."

"My, my, but that's a vague answer," she'd say. "When will you return?"

"Soon."

"Hmm."

Over and over again, she'd attempted to control every little thing in Lilli's life as though she were Lilli's mother. Didn't she realize that Lilli had no parents, that nobody had supervised her—unless it was a guard—since Lilli was ten years old? On the other hand, Lilli certainly didn't want to face another Mrs. Chandler–type situation. At least there was no dog in the Davidson house.

Lilli mulled the problem over in her mind until she almost crashed into Sylvie halfway to school.

"How come you're late again? You're making me late, too. We don't want to get in trouble at school. Not after Friday's episode." Then, observing Lilli's disgruntled expression, she said, "Not again! She didn't hold you back again."

Lilli nodded.

"It almost seems like she wants you to be late often enough so . . ."

"So I'll have to quit school. But frankly, I don't think she does it on purpose. She simply forgets that I'm not a full-time maid. Perhaps taking care of two little kids makes her . . . forgetful."

Sylvie shook her head, then immediately changed the subject.

"Fantastic photo in the paper. I'm so proud of you. All of us are. I spoke to Kurt and Danny and Max. Even Sophie seemed pleased for you. I clipped out the article. I'm going to send it east to Pearla and Yossel."

Then Sylvie inquired about "those girls from grade nine" and asked whether they were treating Lilli better now. Lilli had to admit that they weren't so bad, that a few of them were quite friendly. "Marilyn was the one who phoned me for the interview. She didn't have to do that. Then her parents invited me for dinner last night. That's why I missed our usual meeting. They're good people. Not at all stuffy. Quite warm and friendly."

"Well, it's about time you met some nice people. I wonder about this Marilyn Becker, though. I see her with some of the others at Sunday school at that synagogue and I think they're all snobs. By the way, I don't suppose you can come over tonight, can you? Everyone else will be there."

"Not likely. They usually take in a double feature on Monday night," Lilli said, shaking her head as they separated for their morning classes.

Marilyn gave Lilli a huge smile as she entered the classroom. Nobody said anything about slacks for the entire day, but several girls whom she'd never met nodded or smiled shyly at her when they passed in the halls. The previous week, none of them had been aware of her existence.

During the noon break, the girls sat together, including Lilli. Marion wondered whether they should do anything further about the school rule against pants.

"Well, it's rather difficult to demand our rights unless there's more snow," Lois said.

They all agreed that was true.

"What about asking whether they'd consider making changes?" Lilli said.

The girls felt that Mr. James wouldn't allow such a thing in his school.

"Yeah, without any additional snow, he doesn't have to face any more challenges to his rule," Lilli said.

Marilyn suggested: "Nobody wants to keep this dispute going. But next year, when we're in high school, we could prepare in advance and make our point more effectively. What do you think of that?" She had a mischievous smile on her face as she made the suggestion. As they separated for afternoon classes they all agreed they would postpone the battle.

By the time Mrs. Davidson returned from her doctor's appointment that evening, Lilli had almost finished feeding both kids their dinner. Mrs. Davidson appeared extremely quiet and distracted. After kissing the children, she moved to the kitchen desk, where she flipped through her address book.

Lilli had deliberately chosen pears for dessert knowing they were Markie's favourite, so, hopefully, there wouldn't be another spitting scene. For once she felt in control of the situation. Lilli much preferred those occasions when Mrs. Davidson barely noticed her to those when she couldn't seem to do anything right. She appeared to have no talent for anticipating Mrs. Davidson's moods.

After dinner Mrs. Davidson suggested that Lilli could go out if she wanted—as soon as she had folded the laundered diapers and completed her homework. Lilli was startled but pleased. After finishing her chores and making a quick phone call, she took a bus to the Elmans' home.

When she got there, she was pleased to see Danny, who was often still at work late into the evening. He immediately asked whether the girls were facing any additional suspensions from school. They all viewed the episode of the trousers as a joke.

"No. Everything was fine today. Mrs. Davidson actually encouraged me to go out this evening. But Marilyn's parents—the Beckers—they are *menchen*, good people."

"Yeah, I'd imagine she'd have great parents," Danny said.

Lilli was about to ask what that was supposed to mean when Kurt interrupted.

"Boy, you really made the newspapers," he said. "And that picture. You looked mighty good. The next thing you know, we'll read about you in *Real Heroes* comic books."

Mrs. Elman brought in a tray with hot chocolate and peanut butter cookies, which were delicious. Danny pulled out a letter from Yossel, who was now living in Toronto at a boarding house with two fellows from work.

"That's great," Kurt said. "It was only a month ago that he wrote that he was lonesome for his old friends. Life must be looking up for him."

"I bet he has a girlfriend," Kurt insisted.

Max interrupted. "Maybe he just didn't want to be with the other survivors all the time."

When Kurt asked what he was getting at, Max insisted, "It's tough having people point at you all the time like you come from . . . you know where."

When his friends disputed his words, Max covered his ears. He refused to listen as they all continued to argue.

Lilli was puzzled by Max's behaviour. He'd been doing so well at the Meltzers. He rarely complained the way the rest of the gang did from time to time.

"Something wrong, Max?" Lilli asked.

"No, no, everything is hunky-dory," he replied.

"Hunky-dory, is it?" Kurt said. They all shouted the phrase aloud.

"No, no, my paper route gets larger every week, and I think my customers like me. But please don't correct me when I speak. Okay? The kids in school do that and I really hate it."

An awkward silence fell over the group, but Max broke the tension by suddenly standing up and digging into his pocket. A grin spread across his face as he pulled out a thick, creamy envelope.

"I nearly forgot to show you," he said. "The Meltzers have invited me to a bar mitzvah. For a nephew of theirs. This is just for *mishpocheh*, for family. See, I received my own private invitation." He pointed to the address on the envelope, handwritten in a curly script.

Everyone agreed that he was fortunate to receive such an invitation. Kurt, who had already attended a bar mitzvah with his host family, explained the entire ritual to Max. Of course neither Kurt nor Danny had had a bar mitzvah, having turned thirteen while in the concentration camps, but Danny had vivid memories of the celebrations for his older brothers.

"Believe me, they were simple affairs compared to the way they celebrate a boy's becoming a man in this country."

Kurt said, "Yeah, I remember when my cousins had their bar mitzvahs but it was really nothing. A little honey cake and some wine. "

Kurt started to explain that his relatives had lived in a small village, so bar mitzvahs were held in private homes. Then he shut down abruptly, as though he'd stumbled onto a forbidden subject.

"Drink up the hot chocolate while it's still hot," Sylvie urged them, trying to be cheerful.

The others stared at Kurt, but he didn't glance back at any of them. He wiped a hand over his eyes as if he wanted to blot them out—or perhaps his memories, Lilli thought. Kurt was usually so talkative, but he had never mentioned his family before this.

Lilli felt that each of them was thinking of private events and long-lost people. Those were bittersweet memories. She wished she had the guts to ask somebody, *How do you manage to hold on to these memories without drowning in the pain that surrounds them?* Probably nobody in the group had the answer. They silently sipped their hot chocolate until it was time to leave.

One thing was certain, Lilli knew—they had no choice in deciding which memories to keep and which to destroy. For better or for worse, all their memories would continue to zoom in and out of their heads without their consent, but sometimes it was hard keeping these memories to themselves.

Chapter Seventeen

Danny

Danny worked through a long row of figures, comparing them to a list of receipts from the cash register, late on a Saturday afternoon. The two columns refused to balance. It had been a particularly long day. He rubbed his eyes and tried to get rid of the crick in his neck while studying the figures. This was the start of the Victoria Day holiday weekend for most people, but not for him.

April had been cold and May was humid and wet. He could hear his boss, in the office at the back of the store, listening to the radio. Mr. Block kept the radio on all day, with the volume turned up so he could hear it whenever he was in the shop. He said he picked up the habit during the war, and now he was permanently hooked on newscasts.

When Danny had started work, the Stanley Cup finals were playing. He discovered that his employer was a big hockey fan, and the Toronto Maple Leafs were Mr. Block's favourite team. Danny had been totally ignorant about hockey, but by the time the Leafs had won the championship over the Detroit Red Wings in a 7–2 final game, he knew a little bit about all the players, including Harry Watson, who'd scored the winning goal.

These days, Mr. Block's greatest interest was the ongoing war in Palestine. Two weeks ago, Danny had been pinch-hitting as a salesman and had just sold his first sofa to a young couple—they'd even paid cash—when Mr. Block came running into the showroom, tears streaming down his cheeks.

"What's wrong, sir? Something bad at home?"

"No." Mr. Block grinned through his tears. "The leader of the Jews in Palestine, David Ben-Gurion, has just proclaimed the establishment of a Jewish state. They'll call it Israel."

"That's wonderful." Danny felt tears welling up in his eyes. The news meant that many of his friends who remained trapped in Europe—those refugee kids who still languished in the camps without homes or states—would eventually be allowed to leave the Old World and settle permanently in Israel. According to Mr. Block, Mr. Ben-Gurion had made this proclamation based on a United Nations resolution and the historical right of the Jewish people.

In Vancouver the announcement was followed by a community-wide celebration. Lilli, and several other orphans who had relatives already living in Palestine, were thrilled. Unfortunately the proclamation hadn't resulted in peace. Israel was surrounded by unfriendly Arab nations, which had refused to recognize Israel and had instantly attacked the fledgling nation.

Peacekeeping troops from the United Nations had arrived in the divided country and were attempting to enforce a ceasefire.

On this particular Saturday, local news dominated the broadcast. That was probably why his employer was taking so long to close down the business for the holiday weekend. Danny wished his boss would stop puttering around. Mr. Block could listen to the news on his car radio. Surely the man wanted to get home?

Ah! He heard his boss slide the receiving door back into place, lock it, then shove furniture back into position. Probably Mr. Block was making a last-minute inventory check before closing down Empire Furniture. Danny was the only member of the staff who remained. He planned on attending a movie that evening with Kurt and a few guys from Kurt's school. No girls.

Again there was silence from the office. What was holding up Mr. Block now? Then the radio blared forth again. Mr. Block had obviously been disturbed enough to increase the volume. Danny could hear the radio announcer clearly.

"Across the province the rivers are still rising because of the rapidly melting snow. A Dominion Water and Power Bureau engineer warns that conditions in the interior and Fraser Valley have reached the danger point. Catastrophic flooding is possible if the dikes along the banks of the Fraser River do not hold. The Fraser is nearing the top of the Agassiz dike and this town will be evacuated if the floodwaters go any higher. The Skeena, if it overflows, will cut the CNR line to Prince Rupert. Other floods are already hitting the Kootenays."

"We are living in terrible times," Mr. Block told Danny as he walked to the front of the store after switching off the radio. "Nothing but bad news. I wonder why they never report happy events?"

"What about Vancouver?" Danny asked. "Will the rivers here also overflow their banks?"

"Vancouver will hold," Mr. Block said. "We are at least thirty-five miles from the danger area."

Danny felt his shoulders relax as he reached for his jacket. He was both thankful that there'd be no danger to Vancouver and pleased that he was finally free to leave.

When the telephone started to ring, Mr. Block told Danny, "Forget about it. It's probably my wife wondering why I'm so late again. We have guests visiting us this weekend."

Danny nodded and zipped up his windbreaker. He was anxious to leave, despite the rain pounding on the roof of the building. The phone stopped. Danny waited reluctantly while Mr. Block threw a pile of papers into a briefcase. Then, as Mr. Block directed Danny toward the back exit, the phone rang once again.

"Well, perhaps we should answer it. What do you think? Maybe there's something wrong at home, or it's an important customer with a problem. Why does this always happen right before closing time on Saturday?"

While Mr. Block wrestled with his conscience, the ringing continued. Danny managed an impatient shrug and a weak smile. He knew enough to keep his mouth shut. "Yes," he heard Mr. Block say when he finally picked up. "Empire Furniture for the Future.

"I beg your pardon. Say that again. Who? Ah, Danny Goffman, you're looking for Danny." He held up the receiver and looked questioningly at Danny.

Danny was surprised that anyone would call him at work. He had warned the other newcomers never to telephone him there. Mr. Block was strict when it came to personal calls. Employees, except in the case of emergencies, were urged to use the public pay phone situated just around the corner and leave the business line free for paying customers.

"Kurt? Kurt, why are you calling me here? Are you going to be late? Something holding you up?" Danny whispered in Yiddish, embarrassed at taking a personal call, especially with Mr. Block breathing over his shoulder. Kurt talked so fast that Danny couldn't understand what he was saying.

"Slow down, Kurt, slow down."

"Oh, Danny, Danny, it's a disaster. We must do something immediately. Get yourself over here on the double."

"Over where, Kurt? What's wrong?"

"It's Max. He's disappeared. We've got to help find him before—"

"Hold on, Kurt. Where are you?"

"At the Meltzers' home. Do you know their address? Please get over here right away. Everyone's here with me—Lilli, Sylvie and Sophie—but you know Max better than anybody. The fastest route would be the number eight Granville streetcar—"

"I'll find the place. Be there soon," Danny said as he returned the receiver to the cradle. "Sorry, Mr. Block, I must leave right away."

"A problem, Danny boy?"

Danny explained briefly and, to his surprise, Mr. Block insisted on driving him to the Meltzer house.

"I can't ask you to do that, Mr. Block. I'm sure Mrs. Block and your guests—"

"So it's a bit out of my way, that's okay. Mrs. Block and her relatives won't disappear if I'm a little later. The Granville streetcar and then a bus transfer—that will take forever this time of day."

At the house, Danny found Kurt, Lilli, Sophie and Sylvie in the living room, along with the Meltzers and their assorted relatives. Mr. Meltzer explained once again that at some point following the bar mitzvah service for their nephew, Alan Fox, Max had disappeared.

"Right after the service we crossed the hall to the social room for lunch."

"He ate lunch?" Danny asked.

Mrs. Meltzer, who was twisting a hanky round and round her wrist, nodded. "Yes, I remember, quite distinctly, because he came up to me, all smiles, saying the chopped herring tasted like something he'd once eaten as a young child. You don't forget a thing like that."

"Alice, Alice, will you stop with the chopped liver nonsense? This is not helping us. What has chopped liver got to do with a missing boy?"

"Herring, not liver. But that's what I remember," she replied, giving her husband a scornful look. Since both Meltzers were Lilliputian in size, she had no difficulty gazing directly into his eyes.

Danny and Kurt tried to guide the Meltzers, step by step, through the luncheon, but nobody seemed able to place where Max had been when all the guests were seated. "When it was time to go home, we searched everywhere for Max—upstairs and downstairs—but he obviously had left the building. Gone. We thought he probably left to join you. No? Then maybe you could tell us where he might go." She stared anxiously at Kurt and Danny.

"Where he'd hang around?" Danny asked.

"Yes."

"Max wasn't a hanging around kind of person," Kurt said.

A lanky red-headed boy approached the Meltzers. Danny decided the kid must be the bar mitzvah boy, since no one else would be wearing a suit with a prayer shawl and a skullcap at seven in the evening.

"At first we figured he'd gone off someplace with his gang," the boy said. "My friends checked the entire building."

"No," Mrs. Meltzer replied. "He goes nowhere without telling us. He is a very good boy."

"Nobody is arguing with you, Aunt Alice, believe me. We're just trying to help," a young woman, with a similar head of red hair, replied.

Kurt whispered to Danny that she was Ellen Fox, Alan's mother.

"Then we hurried home. Maybe he had a headache? Didn't feel good?" Mr. Meltzer said.

"The house was empty," Mrs. Meltzer concluded, shaking her head.

The assembled family members kept going over and over the events of the morning. Max had appeared exceptionally happy when they'd arrived at the synagogue; he had seemed at ease during the service. According to the guests, Max had been thrilled with everything about the occasion until the moment he disappeared—whenever that happened to be.

"Have you called everyone who knows him?" Danny asked Kurt.

"Everyone," Lilli replied.

"That's right," Sophie added. "And all the kids from the latest group of refugees, too."

"Did you call the police?" Danny asked.

"No, we didn't want to call the police unless . . . unless . . ." Mr. Meltzer paused.

"Max can sometimes become very . . . disheartened," Danny said haltingly. "He had a particularly difficult time in the camps. At least, that's what we all assume."

Mr. Meltzer nodded. "It makes no sense. He was more excited than I've ever seen him. We know he has problems. Who wouldn't have problems, given his past? But he wasn't listless or mournful or anything like that. He liked the service, he devoured the food, and he loved all the relatives. What could go wrong? The last time I saw him was just before the picture-taking."

An hour later the group had expanded to include Mrs. Karr, their social worker, and several additional refugee children who had arrived in late February. Most of these newcomers had been living in Germany at a children's centre in Aglasterhausen. They, too, had immediately rallied when word of Max's disappearance reached them.

The doorbell rang again, and Mrs. Meltzer ushered in two policemen. Danny automatically stepped back into the shadowy alcove behind the family piano. What were they doing here? Who had phoned them?

"Thank you for answering my call so quickly. We are terribly worried about this young man," Mrs. Karr told the men as one of them took out a pad of paper. "Given Max's sensitivity, I have no idea what he might do if he is very upset. You must believe me, I am not overstating the case."

The senior policeman spoke aloud while the younger one wrote down the information. "Max Katz. Foreign refugee boy. New to Canada. Concentration camp survivor. May be unbalanced," the officer continued.

Unbalanced—didn't that mean crazy? Were they suggesting that Max was crazy? In his past life, Danny had struggled too long against the power of military police to anticipate any sympathy from this source. He had diligently avoided any and all contact with people in uniform. But now he wanted to speak up, to explain that this was an unfair profile of their friend—that Max was quiet, clever and thoughtful. Sure, Max might appear despondent at times, but he was certainly harmless.

Lilli came over and whispered in Danny's ear. "At least these policemen didn't bring along their dogs."

"He'd never neglect his paper route. It was like a religion with him," Mrs. Meltzer told the police officer. "No matter what upset him, for sure he'll return before morning to deliver the newspapers. If something hasn't . . ."

But nobody had any answers for those *ifs*. The police decided that Max had "probably gone off on his own. A lark. Don't worry. He'll return soon because it's going to be a real wet one tonight with all this rain. You'll see."

When Danny returned to the Halpern house that evening, he had difficulty falling asleep; then his nightmare, which hadn't troubled him in weeks, returned full force. In the morning, not only were his sheets damp with perspiration but his brain felt like a squishy sponge. The rain was still pelting down. Danny called the others, but there was no information whatsoever regarding Max's whereabouts. Not knowing what else to do, they decided to return to the Meltzers' house.

Mr. Meltzer, who had just finished delivering all the newspapers on Max's paper route himself, welcomed the five orphans. Mrs. Karr was already there, and so was a new police detective, who had more questions for the family.

"Max would lose his paper route if I didn't attend to it and he'd never forgive himself," Mr. Meltzer told the detective.

"Did he spend much time down in east Vancouver?" the detective asked the children. "Hang around with folks down there?"

"No, Max wasn't exactly an explorer type. Quite shy with strangers."

"What about Stanley Park? Our people checked sections of Stanley Park last night, but you know how huge it is. A thousand acres of forest. Perhaps he had a favourite place in the park? Like Lumberman's Arch or the zoo?"

The kids shook their heads again. Of course they were all familiar with Stanley Park. It was always the very first sightseeing stop for tourists. Hundreds of paths wound through the forest area, and there was also several beaches there.

"We took pictures there when we first arrived. Right beside the totem pole? Once, when Lost Lagoon froze over, we went skating, but Max didn't come with us that time," Danny said.

"He didn't own any skates and he was afraid of falling down, since he'd never tried it before. No, he'd never go there," Kurt assured the detective.

"We've got to believe that he's fine," Mrs. Meltzer said. "Maybe a little frightened about something, but he'll be back. He's a good boy and we think so highly of . . ." She broke down and reached for her husband's hand.

The police searched Max's room for any possible clues; Danny waited until they were finished and then he and Kurt ransacked it. He had no idea what he was looking for but he hoped for some overlooked item that might lead them to Max. The boys went through all the drawers, shelves and closet and even lifted the mattress and poked their heads under the bed. Nothing. No unusual letters. No report cards saying Max was having problems in school. No complaints from teachers, no secret diaries. There was nothing to suggest a specific reason for his departure. Like most of his refugee friends, Max didn't possess a picture of his parents, so the only photograph in the room was a snapshot of Max standing between the Meltzers.

Danny studied the group photo. In the picture Max had a wide grin that showed the gap between his two upper front teeth. He leaned against the handlebars of his bike while both Meltzers had their arms wrapped possessively around his bent shoulders.

Danny held the photo for a moment, and then, making a sharp clicking sound with his tongue, he dropped the photo on the dresser and dashed downstairs. What a lamebrain he was. Why hadn't this idea occurred to him before now?

Once again the house was crowded with relatives, including the bar mitzvah family. They were clustered around Mrs. Meltzer, who was making sandwiches; Mr. Meltzer spoke on the telephone.

"His bike. Is his bike missing?" Danny asked.

Mr. Meltzer dropped the receiver on the cradle, whirled around and hustled outside to check the garage. When he came back he said, "It's gone. Now why didn't I think of that?" He smacked his forehead with his fist. "What a dunce I am."

"So, he probably took a streetcar home and then went off somewhere on his bike? Sounds crazy, because—"

Kurt interrupted. "Because it is ridiculous. Why would he leave the bar mitzvah? For weeks he wouldn't talk about anything else. Explain that, Danny."

"Maybe something happened there that upset him." Lilli raised herself from a plump armchair in the living room. She glared at the others. "Did anybody say something to upset Max? Make fun of him or tease him or anything like that?" she demanded.

Mrs. Meltzer shook her head. "Why would anyone want to antagonize Max? He's such a gentle boy."

Danny snapped his fingers. "Hey, didn't you say something about taking pictures, Mr. Meltzer? Does anyone remember how Max looked during the photo session? Like was he moping around or gloomy looking or fidgeting or anything unusual like that?"

"How should we remember his behaviour? He wasn't in the pictures," Alan Fox muttered as he reached for an egg sandwich.

"He wasn't? Not in any of them? No? How come?" Lilli demanded, crossing the room in three gigantic paces.

"Because it was just family and he's not family," Mrs. Fox replied.

"Oh," Lilli whispered as she stood leaning over Alan. "I don't understand."

But of course she understood perfectly. Danny frowned at Lilli. He wanted her to remain calm so he could continue to question Alan and his mother without upsetting them. Inside, he was seething. He already had a sense of foreboding.

"How many people posed for those pictures?"

"Oh, that's hard to say," Mrs. Fox replied. "I guess with all the *mishpocheh* we were about thirty-five."

"Did somebody actually tell Max to keep out of the picture?"

Total silence.

Mrs. Meltzer gasped. "Oh my, do you really think . . . ? Oh dear."

"Poor Max," Lilli said softly.

"What are you people getting at?" Alan said.

"We are trying to figure out why Max left home," Danny replied. "It now seems quite obvious why he ran away."

"Obvious?" Mr. Meltzer asked. "Explain, please. I don't understand it myself."

Mrs. Fox, who was carrying a tray of cups and saucers, carefully placed them on the dining room buffet. "It was a simple family picture and Max was certainly not family."

"Oh dear," Mrs. Meltzer said. "It must have happened when I left the room to freshen up my makeup. I warned you about how sensitive Max is. It took weeks before he felt secure enough with us to sleep in his bed and not on the floor. He still sleepwalks when he is disturbed about something, poor child, and you—"

"I'm afraid the children are right." They had all forgotten the social worker, Mrs. Karr. "I really think this information could be the missing piece of the puzzle. It may sound strange to you, but Max probably ran away because nobody wanted him in the family picture. He realized that he wasn't family, that he was still considered an outsider, and he was ashamed when somebody made it obvious. Surely you can understand that?" Mrs. Karr spoke softly. "That poor, disappointed child. Rejected again."

"Come on. You can't be serious. Nobody's going to vanish just because he wasn't asked to 'say cheese' in a lousy family picture. That's plain stupid," Alan said.

"Yeah, maybe for you," Lilli replied. "But people like you can't begin to understand the feelings of people like us."

"Don't waste your breath, Lilli," Kurt told her. "To them we're a bunch of freaky foreigners. Greenies."

"Hey, I really don't get how you refugees feel," Alan said. "You're so touchy and you carry gigantic chips—"

"Please, please, children," Mrs. Meltzer scolded them. She kept dabbing at her eyes as she spoke.

"Sorry, Mrs. Meltzer, but your relatives don't seem to understand how . . ." Danny paused. Impossible to get through to these people.

Mrs. Karr rushed after Lilli as Lilli stomped toward the front door. Sylvie followed at her heels. The social worker moved in front of them, blocking Lilli's path before she could open the door. "I understand how you feel," she said. "You're furious. But let's keep in mind that we have more important things to consider—like finding Max. Everything else can remain—"

"On hold," suggested Danny. "Isn't that how they say it here? I agree with you, Mrs. Karr, so listen up, guys." Danny joined the others at the door. "Now that we understand why he left, we've got to figure out where he went. And try to find him immediately. What's our next step?"

Chapter Eighteen

Lilli

"So what do you suggest we do now? Tell me," Lilli demanded of Danny. "Where do we go from here?"

And then she looked at Mrs. Karr, who was still guarding the door. "Do *you* have any suggestions?' She'd deliberately turned her back on Alan Fox; she was too angry with him to spare him even a glance. "Well?" she asked again, placing her hands on her hips.

The Meltzers' phone rang, and Alan Fox picked up the receiver. After speaking briefly to the caller he held out the phone to Lilli. "It's for you," he said.

"For me?" Lilli sputtered. "Don't be ridiculous. Nobody would call me here."

"Aren't you Lilli Blankstein?" Alan said.

"So what?"

"Someone insists on talking to you and only you."

Lilli reluctantly reached for the receiver. Who would call her here? And at such a terrible time. "Who is this?" she demanded.

"It's me, Lilli. Marilyn."

Lilli remained silent. Why was Marilyn calling here?

"So sorry, so very sorry about Max. I didn't hear until this morning because I slept over at Lois Fraser's last night—a pyjama party for her birthday—and when I arrived home Pops told me. Oh sorry, I'm rambling. Who cares about a birthday party at a time like this?"

Everyone in the room seemed to be staring at her so Lilli finally replied. "Uh, uh, thank you for calling, Marilyn, but there's nothing new to report."

"My dad was looking outside because our Sunday newspaper hadn't arrived and he saw Mr. Meltzer making the deliveries, and of course he asked what had happened to Max. Max is such a sweet little guy. So shy and sad for a boy his age, but so likeable," Marilyn continued. "Sorry for disturbing you at the Meltzers' but Mrs. Davidson said I'd find you here."

"Yes, we're all here, Marilyn," Lilli finally replied.

"I know you're friends and I'm really sorry."

"Thanks for calling, Marilyn, but I have to go now. We're trying to figure out where he may have gone. "

"There must be some really good explanation for his behaviour. My parents want to know if there is anything we can do to help."

Lilli was startled to learn how much Marilyn cared. "I appreciate your calling but I've really got to go now."

"Don't hang up, please, don't hang up yet. Sorry I didn't make myself clear but when you care about somebody you do something, right? My parents, and me, we'd like to help. My dad drives a car. What I mean is that my dad will drive you anywhere you'd like to look. Would that help?"

Lilli was almost too astonished by this offer to reply. "Well, I don't know." She had never anticipated such kindness from outsiders. She covered the receiver with her hand while she turned to discuss Marilyn's offer with her friends.

"Come on, Lilli. I'm sure you could use some help. My dad is offering his car," Marilyn insisted.

Lilli uncovered the phone. "This may seem a strange question," she said, "but Danny wants to know whether your father has a truck or a van."

"A van?" Marilyn repeated the words aloud.

"Something we could load bikes into?"

"Oh, one moment. Pops is right here beside me." Lilli listened as Marilyn repeated the question to her father.

"Of course, one of our delivery vans." Mr. Becker had taken the phone himself. "Where do you want to go?"

Lilli passed the phone to Danny. "We'd like to explore the Marine Drive area near the university, but it's an awfully long distance to bike in this lousy weather," said Danny. "Although the police seem to be making a huge sweep, we believe Max may be afraid to show himself to strangers—especially people in uniform. However, if he were to hear familiar voices—"

"I understand," Mr. Becker said. "A great idea. We'll pick you up in half an hour. You have your bikes with you? Okay?"

"Absolutely," Danny said.

When Mr. Becker and Marilyn arrived at the Meltzer house, Lilli and Danny were standing in the doorway. They shouted for Kurt and Sylvie, and then, with a little assistance from Mr. Becker, all four loaded their bikes into the back of the van.

"I can't thank you enough for offering your help," Lilli said to Marilyn after introducing Danny, Sylvie and Kurt to Marilyn's father.

"Yeah, thanks, Mr. Becker," Danny added as they pulled away from the curb. "I'm not sure we're going to find him ourselves—it's a huge city—but we're the only ones who have a chance."

Marilyn dug into a bag and handed Lilli and Sylvie rain slickers. "Didn't know whether you had any. Sorry, Mom couldn't find anything for you guys. No boys in our house."

Again, this thoughtfulness took Lilli by surprise.

"It's worth a try," Kurt told Mr. Becker, "don't you agree? He can't last much longer in this rain."

Mr. Becker spoke to them in English laced with some Yiddish, although Marilyn insisted that the newcomers' English had improved dramatically since their arrival. He also tried to explain himself using hand gestures, until Marilyn nudged him with her elbow. "Pops, please concentrate on the road."

They wound their way down Marine Drive toward the University of British Columbia. As they headed for Point Grey Peninsula, they travelled through dense parkland.

"These endowment lands are almost twice the size of Stanley Park," Mr. Becker said. "How do you expect to find him in such a wilderness?"

"The police have searched most of the city. It's our last chance, the only place left that occurs to me," Danny replied. "One Sunday when it wasn't raining, Max and I rode our bikes out this way. It felt like a real adventure. Max was excited when we discovered a path leading down to the ocean. He was really impressed with the wilderness—I think he liked being far from everything, the remoteness of the place."

They were silent as the rain continued to pelt down on the roof of the car. Lilli, who couldn't help chipping away at the polish on her right thumb, studied all of them. Marilyn and her father were in the only two seats; Lilli and the others were sitting in the back of the van. Danny sat cross-legged, staring down at his shoes, while Sylvie sifted through the contents of her small patent-leather purse and Kurt stared intently over Mr. Becker's shoulder, hoping he might spot Max from the car. Only the windshield wipers cheerfully chitter-chattered as they bumped along the winding road.

Mr. Becker switched on a newscast in case there was some word about Max. It occurred to Lilli that perhaps he, too, found the silence thick and depressing. Unfortunately the broadcaster only had information regarding the flood alert.

"The CNR line is washed out and the Glen Valley dikes have collapsed. All of Agassiz is now under water and Lake Okanagan is still rising. A warning to vehicles: all roads to Lillooet are washed out, and the Thompson River has cut off the Kamloops airport.

"Volunteers carried sandbags throughout the night to save Lulu Island with more than five thousand people working the dikes. One observer compared the dikes to 'porridge' because they are dissolving so fast. RCAF Canso flying boats are dropping fresh supplies of sandbags."

Lilli was thankful when Mr. Becker snapped off the radio. The grim weather report only emphasized the enormity of Max's predicament. Was he cowering outdoors—all alone in some isolated location in this terrible weather?

"Max wouldn't try something heroic like volunteering for the dikes, would he?" Marilyn's dad asked nobody in particular.

Four voices said no.

Kurt added, "He doesn't even know they exist. Max doesn't listen to the news. Bad news frightens him. And the distance by bike is too great."

"I'm sure you people know him best, but this filthy weather makes a thorough search almost impossible. How long can a young boy last in this downpour? Won't he give up and return on his own?"

"Not our Max. Not if we can judge by past behaviour. This isn't— well, this actually isn't the first time he's run away," Danny said.

"I see," Mr. Becker replied.

This was the first time Lilli had heard this about Max, but she wasn't surprised. All the orphans had their secrets.

"Please don't misunderstand. He never ran away from the

Meltzers. This was something that happened before he came to Canada. It . . . well, it's hard to explain."

"We thought he might try the area near the university because he really liked this neighbourhood the time we rode our bikes down to Spanish Banks," Danny continued. "Max liked sitting near the ocean. He said it was an especially peaceful place for him."

"Worth a look," Mr. Becker replied.

Lilli guessed, from his tone of voice, that he was only trying to make everyone feel better, that he didn't have much faith in their search succeeding.

"Do you want me to circle around the university and head down toward Spanish Banks and Locarno Beach, or check out the university itself?"

There was another long pause while the four newcomers eyed one another. Lilli pointed to Danny. He was their leader in this situation. He knew Max best.

"What we'd like—if it isn't too much trouble, sir—is for you to drop us off with our bikes by the university entrance so we can check out the territory near the cliffs. You see, we're afraid that he won't reveal himself unless he hears our voices . . ."

"That's if he's even there, or . . ." Lilli said.

"That's fine with me," Marilyn's dad replied. "But I sure hope you know what you're doing."

"Maybe not," Danny said. "But what have we got to lose?"

Mr. Becker stopped by the barns at the rear of the university and they all jumped out. "I'm giving you exactly two hours. I'll stay here for one hour. If I'm not here after two hours, call me from a university pay phone and I'll return to pick you up." He gave Marilyn a handful of change.

"No taking chances or doing anything desperate. Is that clear? I'll expect to hear from you in two hours. Maximum. Promise?"

They nodded their agreement as they took their bikes out of the van. Since the black surface of the roadway was slick from the rain, they rode cautiously and braked frequently while following Kurt along the winding route. Within ten minutes, the rain had found a gap beneath the collar of Lilli's slicker and soon it drizzled down the back of her shirt. The boys were in worse shape, having no special raingear to protect them.

Each of them took turns shouting, "Max, Max," as they followed the road. The only response was a muffled echo as their voices bounced back from the masses of trees. Eerie. They stopped several times to search the dense bush. Nothing. Even the birds remained silent in the miserable weather.

As they headed downhill, past the steep cliffs of Point Grey Peninsula, they caught brief glimpses of the steely ocean screened through the curtain of trees. Danny stopped at a slight clearing. A sign pointed down to a place called Wreck Beach.

"We'll spread out here," Danny said. "We wanted to go down there that day to explore. Perhaps he wandered that way?"

"Why not wait until we get to that little snack shack near Spanish Banks?" Sylvie suggested. "You know that place . . . what was it called? The Rendezvous? Maybe he found a way to break in? It's too early in the season for it to be open. That might be a snug hiding place."

Kurt and Danny insisted they'd check the snack shack later. *How much later?* Lilli wondered. Marilyn looked over at her expectantly but remained silent.

"The rain is getting worse. I'm going to be in terrible trouble for not checking in with Mrs. Davidson," Lilli said, suddenly remembering.

"We'll ask my mother to call her as soon as we're back in the car with Pops and near a phone booth," Marilyn volunteered. "Surely she'll understand?"

"You don't know Mrs. Davidson," Lilli replied. "Oh heck, I guess it could be worse. I'm sure she'll realize our predicament." But she knew she had made a major error.

"Do you want to turn back, Lilli?" Danny asked.

"Of course not."

"Are you sure?"

Lilli nodded.

Danny dismounted his bike at the top of the steep cliff. The others followed his lead. Marilyn explained that many years ago someone had cleared the old logging tracks that led down to the ocean and transformed them into hiking trails; she pointed to the deep skid marks used to transport heavy timber down to the beach, still visible if you looked carefully through the undergrowth. They agreed to break into two separate search parties. Marilyn followed Danny and Lilli while Kurt and Sylvie chose a narrower path some distance away.

When they paused at the trailhead, Lilli took a deep breath. The rain had stopped and she was stepping into another world—a murky, emerald kingdom full of mystery. The sharply sloping track took a slight jog to the left. Then, following a few crude steps, it switched immediately to the right, plunging down what appeared to be a steep ravine. Despite the luxuriance of the trees and the extravagant undergrowth of moss and ferns, it was not a welcoming place. The grasping arms of the wet branches jostled and smacked them as they trudged ahead. It was exceedingly slippery underfoot and a dense buildup of needles from the evergreens made it even more precarious.

The giant trees formed a lacy canopy so they kept moving alternately from pools of shadow to dappled areas of light where the branches separated. From time to time they passed the corpses of fallen trees scattered as casually as pick-up sticks.

Down, down, down the sheer escarpment they slipped and slid, grappling with the thrusting branches to slow their momentum as they scrambled along the gruelling trail toward the ocean. It was silent except for their cries of "Max, Max, where are you?"

Finally they spied the rusted hull of the ship, lying on its side, that provided the name for the deserted beach.

"Max, Max, we're here to help you," Danny hollered again and again as they wandered along the beachfront. The ocean continued to slap away at the jumble of waterlogged rubbish that had washed ashore; tiny sparkly shells glistened on giant logs while seaweed nestled in the creases of ashen driftwood.

Lilli searched for footprints in the debris, until Marilyn reminded her that the rain would have washed away any traces. The remote beach seemed truly desolate and unwelcoming. The sky remained overcast with an occasional scarf of fog flitting past. Lilli found herself hoping that the others would give up their quest and return to the highway. The place gave her the willies.

The two groups converged halfway down the beach. Lilli could tell that Sylvie and Kurt were agitated about something. It turned out that they had come across a two-storey concrete tower.

"There were no weapons or searchlights, but we could tell it was definitely something from a war. Why would there be a thing like that here on this beach?" Sylvie demanded. "Nobody made war here, did they?"

"They probably built it there for protection against the Japanese forces, in case they tried to invade along our west coast," Marilyn told them.

Lilli was startled by her words; the possibility of danger in this part of the world had never occurred to her.

* * *

The group paused on a rock outcropping while Danny studied the thick undergrowth behind them. Lilli followed his gaze as he stared at a barricade of trees some twenty feet below, near the bottom of the cliff. Nothing.

They picked their way through the rubble that had washed up on the beach and slipped cautiously past the kelp-covered rocks. The wind hurtled out of the ocean and up the cliffs causing the trees to sigh as it raced past them. Nothing. After checking the length of the deserted beach, they continued their search closer to the cliffs, calling Max's name.

A rattling sound captured their attention. They eagerly scanned a ledge that jutted overhead. Lilli pointed to a trail of loose stones cascading down the cliff face. They focused on a shadowy apparition, wrapped in some sort of scaly tarpaulin. Balanced precariously above them, it swayed back and forth. Then, pushing out the sides of the glittering tarp like a pair of huge wings, the creature gave a single shriek and plummeted over the ledge toward them.

Lilli jumped back, slamming into Marilyn, who put her hands on Lilli's shoulders. Both girls stood motionless as the spectre hit the beach, rolled over and then remained still. No one moved or said a word. They remained frozen, gawking at the creature.

Only Danny had the guts to walk toward the outlandish ghoul.

"Max?" he croaked. "Is that you, Max? *Vos host gehtrochen tzu dir?* What's happened to you?"

Somehow the thing struggled to a standing position. Plunging forward, it tripped over a protruding root and collapsed at Danny's feet.

"Max! Oh, Max!" Danny shouted as he peeled back the crumbling tarp. "It really is you. We've found him. Everybody, we found our Max!"

Then, despite the mucky sand, he dropped to his knees and wrapped his arms around the weeping boy.

Chapter Nineteen

Marilyn

Marilyn handed Danny a hanky to wipe some of the grit and sand from Max's face. Max sat still for a moment, allowing Danny to push back his hair, which had fallen in matted strings across his high forehead.

Danny whispered, so Marilyn could not hear his words, even though she stood right behind the two boys. Tears oozed down Max's grimy cheeks.

"So, Max, are you okay?" Kurt said, stepping closer. "We were so worried about you. You gave us quite a scare."

"*Zayde* Rachmiel, dear *Zayde* Rachmiel, when are you coming out?" Max asked, turning away from Kurt.

Everybody looked around, expecting somebody else to step out of the bushes.

"Max, it's us, your friends." Sylvie tried to move closer but Max stretched out both of his arms blocking her way.

"Max? Max, there's nobody else here. Max, who are you calling?" Danny asked. "Answer me, Max. Now."

Max looked up momentarily, then lowered his eyes again and stared right past the group to something invisible in the bush. Marilyn stared at Max, who seemed to look right through her as if she didn't even exist. She wondered what he was looking at.

"He won't come. I kept calling but he won't come out. It's too late now."

Lilli stood above Max. "Listen to me, Max. We are the only people on this beach."

"*Zayde* Rachmiel, you waited too long. *Zayde?*"

Danny placed both hands on the younger boy's shoulders and stared intently into Max's eyes. "You no longer have a grandfather, Max. There is no *Zayde* Rachmiel. You must believe me."

Max covered his ears.

"So . . . so maybe I don't want to know?" he finally said, looking up at Danny, suddenly angry. "Why don't you go away and leave me alone?"

"So, why did you run away, *boychik?*" Kurt crouched down on his haunches beside Max. "We were so concerned about you. Max, are you listening?"

At first Max remained silent. The tears made dirty rivulets down his dust-covered face. "I am sorry, I am so sorry," he cried. "I was wrong, I did everything wrong. We should have come in after you."

"What do you mean, Max? It's going to be okay now, really it will," Lilli whispered. "See, we found you. You're okay. Right? Now we'll all go back to the city."

"No, no, it will never be all right. Don't believe them if they try to tell you that. Never," he insisted.

"Why did you run away, Max?" Sylvie asked. "The Meltzers are so worried about you."

Max gave a strange, low laugh. "You believe that? Oh, sure, oh sure."

Danny and Kurt helped Max to his feet. They were leading him over to a large log where he could sit more comfortably, supporting him as he stumbled forward, when he suddenly turned to Marilyn. She moved back a step, certain that Max was going to ask the boys, "What is this stranger doing here butting into my business?"

Instead he spoke directly to her. "Marilyn Becker, 1435 West 37th Avenue. The cream stucco house with the porte-cochére. What are you doing here?"

"We were all so anxious, wondering where you were, Max. I was too, so I—I insisted on joining the search."

It was a pretty weak statement—dismal—but it was all Marilyn could think to say. She was afraid to say anything that might upset him further, anything that might encourage him to turn on the group or set him ranting once more about those phantoms that lurked in his head. Grandfather Rachmiel? She didn't understand. What was that all about? Now it was her turn to feel like a foreigner—an alien in their midst.

"You know," he began, "when they first sorted us out here in Vancouver I hoped the people would stop thinking of me as a survivor. I didn't want to be pointed at any longer. I wanted to be like them." He aimed a finger in Marilyn's direction. "A real Canadian. I actually believed that it was finally happening. I tried so hard.

"But when it came time to take the pictures at the bar mitzvah they knew I didn't belong. To them I was still a Greenie. We're just a bunch of Greenies to them. Foreigners."

Kurt said, "We heard about the picture, but you shouldn't let a little thing like—"

"A little thing?" Max laughed. It was not a pleasant sound. "Sure, sure if that's what you want to think. They look down on me. The whole family. The *mishpocheh*. Just like the Nazis and all the others. I haven't become a Canadian after all. I may as well be back on that farm, hiding in a haystack. Alone. At any moment they'll hunt me down and set fire to the hay. Because I don't belong. Me! I'm a dangerous person, that's me. There's darkness everywhere. I can feel it. You do understand, don't you?"

"No, we don't understand, Max. We can't grasp what you're saying," Lilli said.

"Shhh," Sylvie whispered. "Can't you see how talking about the past upsets him?"

Danny disagreed. "No, no more shushing. Tell us, Max. Explain. We'll try to understand."

Max shook his head. "No."

"Listen, Max," Danny went on. "I'm still alive because the adult political prisoners in Buchenwald took care of us young kids. We weren't assigned any work when we reached Buchenwald—that was most unusual. We didn't realize the Germans planned to kill us. But those brave prisoners, from all over Europe, they understood. They'd thwart the Nazi plans by sneaking us out of our barracks, then hiding us in another one whenever the Germans planned a roundup . That's why I'm here today. After our release, when we got on the train that took us away from Buchenwald to France, we scrawled on the outside of the train in huge letters: '*Wo sind unsire elterin?* Where are our parents?' Well, we eventually learned that they were gone, gone forever. However, we are alive—very much so—and you are, too."

Then Kurt removed his jacket, although the rain was still falling. He rolled up the cuff of his right shirtsleeve until it was almost at his elbow and he stretched out his arm to show the numbered tattoo that ran down its length.

"Auschwitz. That's where they branded me. It is nothing to be ashamed of. We don't have to hide our tattoos now. We should wear them with pride. Never again should such an atrocity take place."

Max ran his fingers down Kurt's forearm, pressing them gently into the puckered flesh.

"But you still don't get it. I came down here to escape all of it. I tried to hide who I was. But if there'd been no ocean, I would have walked back home to my family. I miss them. I miss my family. Mama said, 'If we should be separated, no matter where we are, we will find our way back home and we will be a family again.'"

"Max, there is nobody left back there. You've got to believe that once and for all," Danny said.

There were gasps and whispers behind him. "Please leave him alone," Sylvie said. "It's not fair."

"And we *do* understand," Danny shot back. "It's just that some of us don't have any tears left. They dried up a long time ago."

"So, tell us, Max, tell us," Marilyn said.

He raised his face up toward the cooling rain. "I don't even know the month when I was born. Can you believe that?" He looked directly at Marilyn.

"Is that such an awful thing?" she whispered.

"Yes," he said, solemnly. "Because I remember other things, lots of things that I'd rather forget, but I can't fill in the space where they ask for my date of birth, when I was born—not really. Isn't that terrible?"

"No, Max, no. There are worse things," Danny said.

Max said, "Yes, there are. We lived in Kovno, Lithuania. When the German forces herded us from our houses in the ghetto—where we had been sealed off—to the square for transportation to the camps, they shouted and screamed. They were annoyed because the old ones moved too slowly. '*Schnell, schnell,*' they ranted. 'Faster, faster.' They had already burned down many of our synagogues.

"While we stood shivering outside in the cold, each of us clutching a single suitcase, they started banging on the walls of the houses. Then they threw rocks at the people as they staggered out of their homes. Mama begged them, 'Please. My parents are still inside. They aren't well.'

"The leader of the *Einsatzgruppen*, their Action Force, laughed. Then he signalled for his men to set fire to the houses. The local Lithuanians even helped.

"My father tried to run back into our house but somebody hit him over the head with a shovel. They kept us standing there—didn't let our own ghetto police force do anything while our houses burned down. I never saw my grandparents again. Papa, when his friends finally got him back on his feet, could no longer speak."

"Oh, Max, how terrible," Marilyn gasped. Was it possible for a normal human being to ever blot out such a monstrous experience? She closed her eyes momentarily, squeezing down to prevent herself from crying.

"Eventually I ended up at one of the Dachau camps, near Munich. I was strong for my age so they put me to work carting bodies away for disposal. My mother was one of those dead people. Yes, I recognized her, but I kept right on pulling the cart because otherwise they'd have killed me, too. After the war, they brought me to the Jewish Children's Home in Feldafing. They actually took my picture, holding up a name card, to help any surviving family find me. But now, how can I ever forgive myself?"

"Max, you had no choice. You were a helpless child." Lilli shook her head. "But you must learn to live with it, Max. To remember, yes, but you have to believe that our parents—our families—wanted us to stay alive. We're still here to remember them—always."

"You really think they will forgive me?"

"There is nothing to forgive."

Then Lilli crouched down beside Max and in a monotone voice—almost as though she were repeating someone else's story—she told him about her own childhood in the Lodz ghetto before her family was deported to the Auschwitz-Birkenau concentration camp.

"Me? No numbers because it was so late in the war they couldn't be bothered to tattoo us. Four years in the ghetto from 1940 to 1944. We had a hiding place in the attic. We'd pull up the stepladder and be safe. But this one week I warned my family that the Nazis planned a huge roundup in our area. You see, I was the little spy in our family—the one who listened to the rumours whispered on the street, the eleven-year-old girl that nobody noticed. Right?

"It was the summer of 1944 when they began the final liquidation of our ghetto. Of course, we didn't actually know that—they called it 'resettlement.' I warned Mama they were coming to take all the people in our block. There had been giant deportations every day that week.

"My father was sick with dysentery, coughing up blood he was so weak. Mama decided we must leave our apartment on Wolborska Street before curfew. Where could we hide? We ran through open courtyards and a maze of passages to the cemetery in Marysin. It was still quite beautiful, although they'd cut down many of the trees for fuel. Actually the Germans had ordered the Construction Department to dig trenches in the cemetery for air raids, but luckily they didn't have sufficient manpower to do all that work.

"We'd gathered some food, although even with our work vouchers there wasn't much. A bundle of potato peels, *shobekhts*, from the Balut market. Mama made soup from the potato peels, or *plackes*, pancakes, or *kleyselakh*, dumplings. That day we also had *bourakes*, beets, and some bread."

Lilli paused to catch her breath. There was total silence as she continued. "So the family headed for the cemetery. That's where we hid—we hid among the graves, and in the evening there was a little shack—and we felt ourselves lucky to be there. At least fifty or sixty people spent a few days hidden there. Surely we would be safe with the dead? While they grabbed more people each day and whisked them off to the so-called work camps, we were safe. Mama, my sisters and me. Not Papa. He was too frail and sick to walk with us so we'd hidden him at home before leaving. He was still in the attic, barely alive when we returned three days later."

"Why not take him in a car?" Marilyn asked.

Lilli laughed. "A car? Even the ambulance was horse-drawn, when you could find it. No, the only car allowed in the ghetto belonged to the fire department."

Sylvie said, "I suppose I was just lucky. When things became dangerous in Belgium, my mother left me at an orphanage run by the nuns. Once, I remember the Mother Superior waking us in the middle of the night and someone led four of us to a hiding place in the sewers; somebody had informed the Gestapo that Jewish children were concealed in the convent. The nuns, with the help of some brave people, kept moving us from one orphanage to another. I had three toys: a stuffed monkey—he eventually lost his tail—a purse and a gas mask. My widowed mother and my older brother were taken away during a labour call-up, interned in an assembly camp near Mechlin, and sent from there to Auschwitz. Neither survived. My sister Irenee was also hidden in Brussels. After the war she joined a group of immigrants whose boat reached Palestine safely, despite the blockade."

Marilyn looked from one of them to the next as she attempted to digest their horrifying stories. She wanted to say something, anything, to soothe their pain. But what comfort could she offer? She had no magic wand that she could wave to make their past disappear. She continued nodding like some mechanical windup doll, too stunned to utter a word.

Kurt brushed back his thick, wavy hair. "Max, it is not our fault that we are here, that we survived. Take me. My family hid on a farm. One day the farmer's cow wandered away. I spent the entire day looking for the stupid beast. When I finally returned with the missing cow they were all gone. Mama, Papa and my brother. I'm here because they sent me to search for a lost cow. The Germans shot them. The farmer told me I'd better disappear before the soldiers returned. 'Go to the forest,' he said. 'There are many hiding there.' That's why I'm alive. Eventually they rounded us up in wagons and hauled us off to the railway station and then to the camps, but that cow saved my life."

Max nodded but continued to stare down at his feet until Danny spoke.

"I think it is important for us to mourn not only with tears and words, but also with deeds. Do you follow me, Max?"

Max looked up at Danny, a half-smile touching his narrow lips. "I never thought about it that way. It—it helps."

Marilyn brushed away a tear trickling down her cheek. The rain had started again. She immediately thought of Max, who'd spent the entire night outside. Wasn't he looking rather flushed? She touched his forehead. It felt hot and clammy. "I think he's got a fever. He really needs a doctor." Then she looked at her watch. "Hey, guys, we've been here over an hour. Pops will be worried. I think it's time to bring Max to my dad."

Kurt said, "Max, we have to move on."

"Come on," Lilli urged, springing to her feet, "Mr. Becker will know what to do. We must get Max up that hill before it's too slippery to climb."

Kurt nodded. "Of course, Marilyn is right. Can you walk, Max?'

Max was weak, so the boys eventually made a fireman's chair of their arms. As they neared the top of the rise Max suddenly pulled away from the boys. "Here, I left it near here. See the spot that I marked with my tie? See?"

Kurt tried to grab Max as he headed off the trail into some bushes. For a moment, Marilyn worried that Max was sinking back into a confused state.

"Aha," Max said as he darted under a clump of dead shrubs. "It's still here."

And so it was. He dragged his bike from the cunning hiding spot.

They were far too exhausted to do anything more than propel the bike up the remaining portion of the hill. Marilyn wondered aloud what they'd do when they reached the road. It would be such a long trek back to the university, and they were all too tired to even think of riding back there, especially Max. And they'd probably have another wait after they called her dad.

"Hitchhike, maybe?" Lilli said.

And then they saw the van perched at the entrance to the path. Pops. She had never been so thrilled to see her father or his van.

"Pops, Pops!" she shouted as she ran to him. "We found Max." She threw her arms around him and hugged him tightly. And as her father's muscular arms encircled her, she felt a flash of guilt—she was the only one present who had parents to hug. Reluctantly, she pulled away.

He explained: "I got edgy and started searching a bit on my own. Then I spotted your bicycles."

He introduced himself to Max and, to Marilyn's surprise and delight, he gave the boy a gigantic bear hug. He took Max's bicycle and loaded it into the van with all the others.

Once they'd settled inside, he bustled around searching for a thermos. Marilyn's mother, who believed in advance planning, had filled one thermos with hot coffee and another with ice water. Pops insisted that Max sip some of the coffee and apologized to the others for not having enough for everybody. Finally, he gently wrapped a plaid blanket around Max. Then they were once again on the road.

Marilyn noticed that everyone relaxed a bit; for the moment, they were safe. No, Marilyn chided herself, probably not completely safe. How could these newcomers ever feel safe again after everything that had happened to them?

"The Meltzers. Will they want me back after this?" Max asked nervously as he took another sip of coffee.

"Of course they want you back," Mr. Becker called from the front seat. "They're anxious to see you."

Marilyn turned round to see Kurt and Danny making faces behind Max's back, as if to say that Max might be right . . . that he might not be welcomed back given that he was a runaway.

Marilyn gave a warning shake of her head. "Listen to what my dad is telling you, Max. The Meltzers are really upset. They care so much."

Lilli turned a sorrowful face toward Marilyn. "You see, Marilyn, we're a bunch of misfits. Now you know."

"Stop that," Marilyn said. "Stop that right now or—"

Pops interrupted. "Max, we're here." He pulled the van to a stop.

Mr. Becker stepped out of the van and opened the rear door. He lifted Max down and led him up the driveway, with the plaid blanket still draped across his shoulders. Max appeared hesitant, almost dragging his feet as they reached the front stairs. Everyone else stood beside the van, holding their breath as they waited to see what would happen next.

Just as Mr. Becker lifted the heavy brass knocker, the Meltzers' cream door swung open. Both Meltzers practically knocked Mr. Becker over as they rushed past him and threw their arms around Max.

"Max, Max! Thank goodness you're back," Mr. Meltzer said. "What happened?"

Mrs. Meltzer could hardly speak as she gently patted Max's cheek. "Oh, Max, we've missed you so."

Max didn't speak, but Marilyn could see him beaming as he allowed the Meltzers to guide him into the house.

Chapter Twenty

Lilli

Lilli had to admit that she'd misjudged the Meltzers. Not only were they delighted to see Max, they forgave him for running away. Despite his little bit of craziness, they were definitely keeping him. She also heard, via the grapevine, that Mr. and Mrs. Meltzer had insisted that the relatives apologize for pushing Max out of the family picture.

Lilli found the whole episode most confusing. Of course she was happy for Max, but she believed the entire incident should never have occurred in the first place. Would those people ever understand how hurtful their behaviour was?

Was Kurt right when he said that Lilli didn't have enough faith in people? Maybe, maybe not. Danny had also hinted that she should start thinking more positive thoughts, but, given her situation, that was easier said than done. She still regretted sharing her memories at Wreck Beach the previous week, especially in front of Marilyn. It was safer to keep past experiences private. Although she had no complaints about the way Marilyn acted toward her in school—Marilyn was "all smiles and chuckles' as they phrased it in Canada—she was concerned that Marilyn might tell her friends about the events of that Sunday on the beach. About Lilli's own story. Lilli didn't know Marilyn well enough to trust her 100 percent.

Although the boys made jokes about Lilli's so-called "thin skin" she had genuine reasons for not trusting anyone. The past week had been horrendous. It had started when Lilli returned home so late from Wreck Beach on Sunday. Mrs. Davidson had been fuming.

"What is it with you, Lilli? Have you invented another wild excuse for disappearing for the entire day without so much as a phone call?"

Of course, Lilli had explained that it was impossible to make a telephone call from a deserted beach, but Mrs. Davidson wasn't buying her explanation. Although Mr. Becker had also explained, in great detail, how the kids had saved Max, his statement obviously hadn't satisfied Mrs. Davidson as well.

Lilli eventually learned the true reason for Mrs. Davidson's animosity. It hurt, even thinking about it. It was obvious that Mrs. Davidson had been searching for any excuse to get rid of Lilli and, stupidly, Lilli had provided her with a humdinger. The following morning, while Lilli fed the kids their breakfast, Mrs. Davidson had pounced on her. She'd announced that Lilli was no longer welcome in her home, that she wanted Lilli to leave. Soon. Very soon.

Her announcement caught Lilli off guard, although, when Lilli thought back to earlier events, she might have seen it coming. She suddenly remembered that night when Mrs. Davidson had deliberately shooed her out of the house. Had she already been plotting, figuring out how she'd get rid of her? Lilli never should have let down her guard. How could she have been so blind and stupid?

"Excuse me, Mrs. Davidson. I think I didn't hear right. You're sending me away?"

Mrs. Davidson nodded. "Let's say that things, generally, are not working out as I had anticipated when you first arrived here."

"I'm sorry if I failed you as a babysitter. You're sending me away because I didn't take the time to warn you on Sunday that I was going to search for my missing friend?"

Lilli was shocked and sick but continued to feed the kids their breakfast, just as though it were an ordinary morning. Only her hand trembled slightly as she wiped some drops of cereal from Markie's chin. She actually wanted to throw up but she refused to give Mrs. Davidson the satisfaction of knowing how miserable she felt.

"You're sending me away? I thought I was doing quite well with the kids. They seem to like and trust me."

Mrs. Davidson shot Lilli a dirty look and leaned forward as though she was going to grab the baby spoon right out of Lilli's hand. Then she changed her mind; at least she resisted doing anything violent. Instead she heaved a sigh.

"You really are not a reliable person, Lilli. I know my children have grown fond of you but I have to think of my family. Our needs come first."

"Of course, Mrs. Davidson."

Lilli swallowed the temptation to beg Mrs. Davidson for a second chance; somehow she couldn't find the proper words. She was too confused to argue, numb, as if her insides were iced up. Mrs. Davidson looked so . . . so above it all, so detached. She obviously wasn't going to give Lilli the slightest opportunity to say anything in her own defence.

"I see," Lilli eventually murmured.

"No, you really don't," Mrs. Davidson snapped. "You have tunnel vision. You only see a narrow world—everything from your own perspective."

Lilli wanted to shout back at her: "How else could I see the world if not from my viewpoint?" Instead she said nothing.

"Don't stare at me like I was throwing you out on the street. You brought this situation onto yourself. You are responsible for your present predicament." Mrs. Davidson paused to let that statement sink in. When Lilli failed to argue, Mrs. Davidson seemed to think her remarks needed further justification.

"But I also require your bedroom. I am expecting another child. There is not enough space for both you and a new baby in the house. Do you understand that?"

"Oh, congratulations."

Lilli wanted to suggest that having her as a helper—as a sitter—might be even more sensible with a third child on the way, but when she looked up at Mrs. Davidson, with her tightly pursed lips and that huge frown splitting her face, she thought better of it.

"When do you want me to leave? I'll have to get in touch with my social worker."

"I've already spoken to her. The end of this week would be best."

"That soon?"

"I've suggested to Mrs. Karr that perhaps the Vancouver Vocational School might be the best place for you. It's a trade school where you'd receive practical training so you could earn your own living."

"I see. And . . . and does she agree with you that I shouldn't be placed in another home?" At that point Lilli was seething. How dare this woman go over her head and make major suggestions that would affect Lilli's life forever?

"She actually said she'd discuss that with you privately. Another group of orphans from Europe is about to arrive, and squeezing them in—finding foster families for all of them on such short notice—could be a problem. Even some of those children might be temporarily placed as boarders."

"Oh. May I leave for school now?"

Mrs. Davidson nodded. Lilli grabbed her books and dashed out the door before she made a fool of herself by bursting into tears.

It was Monday morning—another full week of school ahead of her. Lilli still couldn't get her head around the whole mess.

When she contacted the social worker after school, Mrs. Karr apologized.

"I am so sorry, Lilli. Sometimes these domestic situations change abruptly. There is one place where you could move to immediately but—but it would mean giving up school, at least for the time being."

She paused, waiting for Lilli's reaction.

"Give up school?"

"There's an older man—a very nice man—from the community, whose family requires someone to take care of him in his home in New Westminster. He's in a wheelchair now. Just out of the hospital. What do you think? Should I arrange an interview?"

Lilli was too crushed to protest. Reading between the lines, she realized that she was probably considered a major pain in the neck. Any orphan girl who had been asked to leave two homes in such a short period of time must be considered unmanageable. Nobody wanted to deal with that type of person. She was—how did they phrase it? An "obligation"—an unpleasant obligation.

"Could I think about it?"

Mrs. Karr said, "Certainly, Lilli, give it some thought, but get back to me in the next couple of days. Meanwhile, I'll search for other alternatives."

Lilli continued to attend school for the next few days. That phrase, "other alternatives," kept her from going out of her mind. Did it mean there were no more available foster homes? Was it two failures and you're out? What a dilemma! Even a new home would probably require transferring to a different school, just when she was finally getting accustomed to Totem Point. Was it possible to assist the sick man during the evenings and still remain in school? Since it was already the middle of June, and school was almost over, maybe they'd let her finish grade nine? Probably not. If they pulled her out of regular school, would they allow her to train for some . . . some vocation? Maybe they'd insist that she immediately find a job, as a cleaner or a seamstress. Then she'd never learn to speak proper English. Had coming to Canada been a terrible mistake? Maybe she should write and ask her sister about Israel. No, it was too late for that now.

At the moment the situation seemed hopeless. Somehow she couldn't tell Sylvie or the others about her problem. Frankly, it hurt too darned much to talk about it. She refused to face the inevitable. Perhaps she should take the suggested job so she could save enough money to eventually rent a single room and—and attend night school in the fall? She really didn't want to take care of a sick person right now. She wanted to go to school and become somebody. She felt hurt at being chased away like some badly behaved mongrel dog. Everyone would think she was jinxed—why else would people keep rejecting her? Worse still, they'd decide she was a total screwball.

Later that week Marilyn invited Lilli for a Friday night dinner at their house. She asked all the kids involved in Max's rescue. Max wasn't attending because he was still feeling rather shaky. He wanted to stay close to the Meltzer home—except for delivering his newspapers, of course.

During recess Marilyn suggested that her mother would be happy to call Mrs. Davidson if there was a problem about Lilli's being able to come.

"No, thanks. Don't bother. I'll tell Mrs. Davidson myself. This time I'm not asking her permission," Lilli replied. Once again, she avoided mentioning her predicament. "I will be there. For sure."

Marilyn looked startled and Lilli realized that she had been rather vague.

"Sorry. I'll explain—sometime." Oh dear, she had probably insulted yet another person.

Marilyn opened her mouth, then immediately shut it as she grasped what Lilli was saying. "Don't worry, Lilli. You don't owe me any explanations. See you Friday." She turned away but not before smiling back at Lilli.

Marilyn's blind acceptance of her words made Lilli feel even worse. Why had she snapped at Marilyn? She was messing up everything.

That Friday evening Lilli refused a ride from Mr. Elman; she was afraid Mrs. Davidson might blab something to him when he came to pick her up. She didn't want to spoil the evening.

The weather was too warm for the black wool dress. Since she didn't own another dress, she chose her favourite red skirt with a white, eyelet, peasant-style blouse that Mrs. Davidson had discarded. It fit quite well once Lilli took in the side seams. Mrs. Davidson hadn't asked Lilli to return the blouse, so she supposed it now belonged to her, despite everything else that had happened.

Danny, Kurt, Sylvie and Lilli all arrived at the Becker home around the same time. Mrs. Becker rushed from the kitchen to greet them, asking how they were. She cocked her head to one side like a bird and listened carefully to their replies, even though her daughters shouted that something was about to boil over in the kitchen. Two of Marilyn's older sisters—Sally and Helen—were also present. They were quite friendly, although Helen never stopped talking about Toronto. Apparently she was moving there permanently the following month.

Mrs. Becker had prepared a wonderful dinner. The embroidered tablecloth was burnished with a delicate set of gold-and-cream china, while a centrepiece of fresh flowers, in a cobalt-blue bowl, was the crowning touch. Gleaming cut-glass goblets and matching wineglasses were perched at every place. Marilyn placed a braided challah bread on a silver plate in front of her father.

"You'd think they were expecting important guests like Prime Minister Mackenzie King, or King George and Queen Elizabeth," Sylvie whispered to Lilli.

Kurt looked quite snappy. His fair hair shone with Brylcreem and a white handkerchief peeked out of his breast pocket. Danny had managed to slick back his wild mop. He wore a pinstriped suit that didn't fit him very well. Although he claimed the suit was brand new, it looked as though he'd borrowed it from a much larger person. Sylvie had chosen a flowered blouse for the occasion, while Marilyn looked cool in a checked dress of crisp cotton with a wide belt.

"Hey, everybody looks really sharp," Marilyn said when they were seated at the table.

After Mrs. Becker lit the Shabbat candles and Mr. Becker made the prayer over the wine, everyone started to eat. The food was delicious, but Lilli had difficulty concentrating on the conversation. She knew she'd soon be living in another part of the city, too far away to maintain contact with these people. If she nursed the elderly man, she'd be living really far away and she'd probably be on duty full-time—even at night. Not that choosing a regular job would be much of an improvement. In that case, she'd attend night school and still have limited opportunities to see her friends. On the other hand, living alone promised her the luxury of total independence, not having any bosses after work. Maybe. Then, as she started feeling soppy, she reminded herself that there were far worse crises in the world. Look at Danny. He worked full-time and managed to keep up with the rest of the gang on weekends.

"Lilli, Lilli, what's wrong with you?" Kurt finally said during dessert. "Has the cat got your tongue? You're so silent tonight. Anything the matter?"

She dropped her fork and almost knocked over the goblet of water beside her plate. "Oh, sorry, sorry. I guess I was daydreaming."

"Come on, Lilli, you never daydream. Not you." Sylvie shook her finger at Lilli.

"Is something troubling you, Lilli?" Marilyn asked from the seat beside her. Marilyn had lowered her voice to a whisper.

"Nah," Lilli replied, digging her dessert fork into the lemon pie. She'd been toying with the mucky stuff, tossing it over and over on her plate, hoping it might melt or disappear.

Mrs. Becker asked whether the newcomers knew that another group of orphans was arriving shortly. "And we're thinking about applying for a boy again," she continued.

Mr. Becker nodded while the others wondered aloud how many children would be arriving this time.

"Marilyn asked whether we would join her family for a picnic and a swim at Horseshoe Bay next Sunday," Danny said. "That would be great because that's my day off. What do you think, Lilli?"

Suddenly they were all very quiet. "Would you care for something different, Lilli? I know lots of people don't like lemon meringue pie. There's some marble cake in the kitchen if you'd rather," Mrs. Becker said.

"No, no thank you, Mrs. Becker. I'm not particularly hungry tonight. It's wonderful but . . ."

She was at a loss for suitable words, and leaving the table would only emphasize her mortification.

"Lilli, you will join us at the beach next week, won't you?" Mr. Becker said softly.

It was all too much. She dropped her fork. It made a huge clatter as it hit the plate. She could no longer keep her secret.

"I won't be going to a beach next week because—because I'll be moving."

A whole chorus of voices shouted, "Moving?"

"What are you talking about?" Sylvie demanded.

"Exactly what I'm telling you." Lilli took a big gulp of water from the heavy goblet. How could she admit that she'd been kicked out of another home and she didn't know where she was going? It was pitiful.

"Okay, you really want to know? I don't have the slightest idea where I will be living one week from today, but it probably won't be anyplace near here. I'll most likely be nursing a sick man in New Westminster." Then she helped herself to Marilyn's glass of water because her own appeared to be empty. She downed it in two gulps.

"Lilli, Lilli, why didn't you tell us about this earlier?" Kurt demanded.

"Leave her alone, Kurt," Danny said. "Take it easy, Lilli. We'll help you figure out something."

"Like what? Is she going to move in with you, Danny?" Sylvie shouted back.

"Of course you'll have a place to live," Marilyn's sister Helen said. "That's simply ridiculous. Everyone has a home."

"I don't," Lilli said flatly.

"Oh, do shut up, Helen. Sometimes you say the most impossible things. You're a nitwit," Marilyn told her sister.

Lilli stood up abruptly. "Please, Mrs. Becker, would it be okay if I go outside in the backyard for a moment or two? You wouldn't mind if I leave the table?"

"Of course not, my dear." Mrs. Becker touched her shoulder briefly, then turned to Danny and Kurt. "Boys, please escort Lilli to the garden. We'll join you there as soon as we clear the table."

"Oh, no, I'll come back in a few minutes and help clean up," Lilli replied. "You can count on me."

"I know. But it won't be necessary tonight. I have plenty of help without you and Sylvie. Another time, Lilli."

For some reason Mrs. Becker's sympathetic remarks pushed Lilli over the brink. She knew there wouldn't be another time and that realization really set off her tears. She had behaved disgracefully, spoiling the special evening, while her hostess, Mrs. Becker, had remained polite and understanding.

Suddenly she couldn't stop crying. Silly, wasn't it? She hadn't shed a tear in years . . . not under the worst of circumstances in the camps. And now she couldn't shut off the faucet. What was happening to her? She was falling apart.

Mrs. Becker guided everybody, with the exception of her own family, to the back door. She led the gang down the steps and pointed to what she called a "gazebo" at the far end of the garden. It was a small, circular structure with a pagoda-like roof. Purple wisteria covered the roof and latticework exterior; a built-in bench curved around the inside. "Why don't you sit in the gazebo and relax while we—while the girls help me clean up. We'll join you soon. All right, Lilli?"

Lilli merely nodded because her English vocabulary had vanished.

"Sorry, guys," she whispered when they entered the gazebo. Something about the sheltered place made her lower her voice. They remained in the gazebo for a long time while Sylvie and the boys discussed Lilli's next move.

"Poor Lilli," Danny said. "Don't you worry. There's got to be some other solution."

"No," Lilli replied. "There's nothing left to figure."

She reminded them of the new group of children who would be arriving from Europe. "They've got to find places for those kids.

Let's face it, I had my chance. Maybe they'll let me finish school this month, or perhaps I'll go to work for this—this sick person. Eventually, after I finish my job with him, I'll attend Vancouver Vocational School and become a . . . whatever."

"But you planned on going to high school," Sylvie objected. "Isn't that what you want?"

"We don't always get everything we want," Danny replied, brushing away some cobwebs from an overhead beam.

"He's right. I had my chance and I blew it." Although Lilli tried to speak with confidence, she was feeling so depressed that she choked out the words.

"Don't give up so easily, Lilli. You never know . . ." Kurt said, ruffling her curls.

"Oh, I know."

She looked out through the arched entrance of the gazebo. Shadows fell across the garden. It was such a lovely place, with two huge apple trees and all sorts of unfamiliar plants and flowers. For a moment another garden flashed before her. She could see it in great detail. It, too, contained a magnificent apple tree, a fancy metal bench and—and—yes, a high wooden fence surrounded the place. She was positive. How strange. And wasn't there a gate that you opened with . . . with a large metal key? How could she have forgotten it so completely? Of course, this was her grandfather's private garden, behind his apartment block. He always took Lilli outdoors to explore the garden whenever the family visited. She still heard the scissors snip snipping as her *zayde*, her grandfather, picked a special bouquet just for Lilli. She desperately willed that garden to fade away. *Not here. Not now,* she told herself.

"Hey, isn't it time we were going home?" Sylvie said.

Lilli agreed. They'd obviously wrecked the Beckers' evening, she thought. The family was probably embarrassed for her—they didn't know what to say to somebody who was . . . doomed to fail.

As they stepped out of the gazebo, Marilyn ran down the back steps. "Sorry, really, awfully sorry we took so long. Are you feeling a little better, Lilli?" She put her arm around Lilli's shoulders as they headed back toward the house.

"A family conference. You know how those things are . . ." Marilyn began. Then she covered her mouth with her hand. "Forgive me, what a stupid thing to say."

They paused on the bottom step, but Marilyn urged everyone into the house.

"We'll be heading home," Sylvie said. "I'll call Mr. Elman. He promised to pick us up."

"Certainly," Marilyn's father replied as Sylvie headed for the telephone in the den. "But hold your horses a few more minutes. We'd like to say something first, if you don't mind."

Then he led the group through the den and into the adjoining living room. It was a welcoming room. Lilli admired the white fireplace, which stretched the length of one wall. And the couches—they looked so cozy, slightly faded with cushions puffed up at odd angles. The chairs, too, were soft. There were lots of pictures on the walls and none of those simpering china figurines—those silly ladies fighting off the breezes in their period costumes. And there were no plastic covers on the lampshades.

Then Mrs. Becker, accompanied by her daughters, entered the room, tugging off her apron. Although it really was time to leave, Mr. Becker insisted the orphans take seats. *Oh dear,* Lilli thought, *I'd rather not prolong our goodbyes . . . not tonight.*

"Now, Pops, now," Marilyn told her father. "Please."

There was a moment's silence while the Becker parents nodded. Lilli wondered what on earth they wanted to say—all the Beckers looked a bit uncomfortable, even tense.

"Okay," Lilli murmured to Sylvie. "Let them get it over with already."

"Lilli," Mrs. Becker began. "Lilli, my husband and I and Marilyn would like you to move into our home."

"Me, too," Helen added.

"Live with you?" Lilli croaked.

"Yes, Lilli. How would you feel about living here with us?" Marilyn asked.

"I don't get it. You mean in this house?" Lilli mumbled. They couldn't mean that they wanted her to live here forever, this family who made her feel so—so comfortable. No, that was hoping for the impossible.

"Well, obviously not in the garage," Marilyn replied with a grin.

"That's very nice of you—it really is—inviting me to stop here temporarily until I find—until they find me a place. But there's no use—"

"Lilli?" Marilyn interrupted. "Lilli, I don't think you understand."

Lilli was determined to continue. "No, absolutely not. It's very generous of you to let me stay here until I sort things out but it's time—I've decided it's time I found a job. And a place. My own place. Someplace permanent. Like—like Mrs. Karr said. There is a position available with this sick gentleman and if I take it, I'll finally be independent. "

"Lilli, what is wrong with you?" Kurt demanded. "What's happened to your hearing?"

She was stuttering. "I–I–I can't keep moving around forever, Kurt, I really can't."

"Oh, Lilli," Danny and Sylvie groaned in unison.

"We don't want you to live here for just a short time, Lilli. Do you understand that? We want you to be a part of our family," Mrs. Becker said, leaning toward her.

"But—but, you already have so many girls. And what about that boy you were hoping for?"

"Don't you want to live with us?" Marilyn whispered.

"Me? You want me here? I'd love to live here with you, but for how long?"

"Well, hopefully for as long as you feel comfortable and happy with us," Mrs. Becker said. "Forever, or until you want to leave someday."

"Oh," Lilli said. "Oh my."

"That's why we took so long," Marilyn explained. "In this family we make group decisions. We agreed that everyone wants you to come here and be part of our family. Do you think you'd like that? You'd have Helen's old room."

"It would be a shame to leave that room vacant," Mrs. Becker said.

"And I certainly could use another daughter," Mr. Becker added. "There's a real shortage of women around here, as you can see." Mr. and Mrs. Becker both laughed and the others gradually joined in, breaking the tension.

"And I'd like to have a friend living with us," Marilyn said firmly. "Of course you'd no longer have any tiny children to care for here, but I suppose you could get used to that, too. We've got oodles of space . . . you'd be able to have all the privacy you want. "

"And hopefully lots of love to share, too," Mrs. Becker said.

Lilli still didn't believe this was actually happening to her. She wanted to pinch herself but she hated to wake up and have this amazing dream dissolve. Then again, perhaps it wasn't a dream. She searched the faces of her friends. They were all smiling.

She risked pinching the soft space between her thumb and finger and nothing changed. Nobody disappeared. All eyes seemed focused on her. They remained grouped together, like a room full of statues. Then Lilli felt a sappy grin spreading across her face. Finally, she realized, finally she could talk openly to Marilyn and her parents about her past.

"What happened to you is important to us," Marilyn said, looking affectionately back at Lilli.

Lilli nodded. She no longer had to keep all her memories bottled up inside.

"Oh, yes. Absolutely yes!"

"You're home now," Marilyn replied.

Then the Beckers stepped forward and wrapped her in a great, mushy embrace. It felt like a hundred arms were encircling her, but she didn't feel the least bit squashed. It felt warm and cozy and right.

Author's Note

I first became aware of the Canadian Jewish War Orphans Project while growing up in post-war Vancouver, but it was many years before I realized the immensity of the tragic predicament of these children. Few countries were willing to offer a permanent haven to these displaced children, survivors of the Holocaust, after the war.

The mass extermination of the Jews of Europe—the Holocaust—began with the rise to power of Adolf Hitler and the Nazi Party in Germany in January 1932. During World War II their reign of terror grew as they methodically attempted to wipe out the entire Jewish community of Europe. It did not conclude until the surrender of the German forces to the Allies at the end of the war. By then, six million Jewish men, women and children, along with millions of non-Jews, had perished under the Nazi regime. Approximately 1.5 million of the victims were Jewish children who were annihilated in the death camps, ghettos, slave labour camps or during the death marches.

Despite the systematic slaughter of the Jews by the Nazis, some managed to survive the war. In total, 250,000 displaced Jewish refugees remained in Europe, many of them uprooted children who no longer had families or homes. These children, whose lives had been shattered, were housed temporarily in Displaced Persons camps set up by the United Nations Relief and Rehabilitation Agency (UNRRA); often these shelters were former concentration camps, still surrounded by barbed wire. Later, some orphans were settled in camps, children's centres and trade schools provided by Jewish welfare organizations and the American Joint Distribution Committee.

Few countries were willing to take in these forgotten children. Canada had a highly restrictive immigration policy prior to and during World War II. However, Canada eventually became one of the few countries to gradually open its doors. In 1947 the Government of Canada issued Privy Council Order-in-Council #1647 granting permission for one thousand Jewish war orphans under eighteen years of age, "full orphans" (meaning they had no living parents) and in good health, to enter the country.

The Canadian Jewish Congress, assisted by international Jewish aid agencies and UNRRA, combed Europe to find and collect eligible children. However, by the time they had completed the screening process, many of the waiting children were too old for admission and thus children were often split from their siblings, sometimes not to meet again for several decades, if at all.

The Canadian Jewish Congress and the Canadian Jewish community agreed to assume full responsibility for the support of these orphans, including finding them foster homes and providing education and jobs. At that time Canada had a small Jewish population of forty thousand. The children were shipped to thirty-eight different communities across the country: 790 to Montreal and Toronto; 131 to Manitoba; 12 to Saskatchewan; 28 to Alberta; and 38 to British Columbia.

Between September 15, 1947, and January 1949, 1,123 Jewish orphans eventually arrived and were provided with homes in Canada. The orphans came from fifteen countries—783 were from concentration camps and 229 had been in hiding. Of that number less than one-third were girls, only 106 were under fourteen years of age and 37 were under the age of ten.

Despite their nightmare childhoods and gruesome experiences, and without the benefit of families to guide them, these surviving orphans proved to be most resilient. Although society originally predicted irreversible psychological damage in these children, as a group they have transcended their past and have become upstanding Canadian citizens in all walks of life.

This book, although fiction, attempts to tell some of their stories.

Acknowledgments and Sources

I am indebted to many individuals who assisted me during the creation of this novel. My special thanks go to the Vancouver Holocaust Education Centre, and their director, Frieda Miller, for allowing me access to their comprehensive files and their collection of scrapbooks from surviving orphans. I am equally indebted to the Jewish Historical Society of Southern Alberta and their president, Jay Joffe, for letting me study the scrapbooks of Jewish refugee children who lived in Calgary.

I am infinitely grateful to my editor, Lynne Missen, for her encouragement and advice. While several people were most helpful during my research, the characters I have portrayed exist only in fiction. Any errors or omissions are mine alone.

Among the generous people whom I interviewed were: Ruth Mehler and her sister, Rae Hirsh, Robbie Waisman, Oscar Kirshner, Mariette Doduck and several other child survivors. In addition, I extend my thanks to many others who answered my

Acknowledgments and Sources

frequent questions, including Aron Eichler, Mira Koschitsky and Ida Horwitz. Those who answered specific queries concerning life in 1948 Vancouver are too numerous to list. Thanks, again.

Books that I found helpful include *The Boys,* by Martin Gilbert; *The Children of Buchenwald,* by Judith Hemmendinger and Robert Krell; *The Chronicle of the Lodz Ghetto 1941–1944,* edited by Lucjan Dobroszycki; *Open Your Hearts: The Story of the Jewish War Orphans in Canada,* by Fraidie Martz; *None Is Too Many,* by Irving Abella and Harold Troper; *Siedlice, Libro Recordatorio, In Memoriam de los Judios Masacrados en Nuestra Ciudad Natal,* edited by Sociedad Residentes de Siedlice; and *Treblinka,* by Jean François Steiner.

Finally, a word about my family members who supported and encouraged me during my endeavour, faithfully reading—and criticizing—the various drafts as I completed them. My heartfelt thanks and love to all of you: Marina, Shep, Samara, David, Audrey, Anna, Cathy, Ron, Lorne, Raechelle, Bruce and always Maurice.